BEST BOY

VICKI THARP

JPC PUBLISHING

BEST BOY

1

———

For the first time in his life, Vincent Aldino dreaded an upcoming date.

And he had his friend Sebastian's charity auction to blame for it. That, and the fact that Vin had a difficult time telling people no.

You did tell him no. But you caved like he knew you would.

In his usual corner at Bean There, his local coffee shop, Vin sipped his coffee—straight-up black—and kept a close eye on the time.

Nerves made his stomach churn, the coffee refusing to mix with the pool of acid that had dumped into his belly.

"I guess now that you're famous, I don't have a chance with you at all."

Juan, the twenty-something barista, dropped into the seat across from Vin, devilment playing in his soft, brown eyes.

"What are you talking about?"

"Clearly, I never stood a chance." Juan waggled his thick brows. "After seeing the guy, I completely understand your crush."

"I'm still not following."

Juan dropped the local weekly alternative newspaper on the table and pushed it toward him. On the front page, in full color, was a publicity photo of Vin with Niko Stavros.

The winning bidder.

His boss.

And the man Vin had been crushed out on since the early days after Niko had pulled his skinny, scared, troublemaking, homeless ass off the streets of Los Angeles.

In the early months, when he'd first lived with Niko, Vin had considered the crush a phase. Hero worship for a man who'd taken a chance on him and changed his life for the better.

But ten years out, his feelings had only gotten stronger.

Now they'd developed well past the crush stage and bordered on stupid, unrealizable obsession.

Maybe he should take Juan up on his offer. Maybe what he needed was a hot guy with a big dick to exercise his Niko demons.

"You two have that date yet?" Juan's hushed voice all but said, *spill the beans.* "I need deets. I've never fucked a porn star before. Is he as hung as he looks in all his old videos? Or is that a trick of camera angles? Or maybe a dick double?"

"Dick double?"

"Yeah, you know, like a stunt double, but for your dick."

"You're insane, do you know that?" Without waiting for an answer, Vin continued. "The date's not for another hour. And besides, we're not having sex. We wouldn't even be going on this date if it weren't for the bachelor auction. I doubt he really even wants to go."

"Dios mio." Juan slapped a hand to his forehead. "The guy shelled out ten grand to go on a date with you."

"For a charity."

Juan reached across the table and laid his hand on Vin's forehead. "Are you sick? Did a fever melt your brain or something? A guy like Niko, who can land anyone he wants, doesn't get into a bidding war to win himself a man if he isn't interested."

"If he were interested, he could have asked me out any time over the last seven years since I turned eighteen, and it would have cost him a hell of a lot less than ten grand."

Vin's ego wouldn't let him admit to Juan that Niko had already shot him down and made it perfectly clear nothing would ever happen between them.

"Besides, Niko was bidding against Pierce Hatchett. He didn't want me having one-on-one time with his rival studio."

"Good one, dude." Juan laughed. A rich, hearty sound. Vin almost smiled with him.

Vin took a sip of his now cold coffee and grimaced. He didn't have to convince Juan. Vin knew the score. He glanced at his watch. If he wanted to make it across the valley to pick up Niko at his home at Black Stallion Studios, he needed to hit the road.

Vin grabbed his motorcycle helmet and stood. "I gotta split."

"Call me after. With details. How big. How long. How hard…"

Vin gave him a playful shove. "In your dreams, dude."

"You suck, Vin," Juan called out to his retreating back. "And not in the good way."

Vin laughed as he pushed through the door, trying not to think about what it would feel like to have his lips around Niko's thick cock and taste his saltiness when he came.

Vin headed to his bike he'd parked on a side street and adjusted himself before swinging his leg over the seat.

You've got it bad, man, when just thinking about Niko's dick gives you a hard-on.

He had to get his mind off the person he couldn't have.

As soon as he got back from his date/non-date, he'd reload Grindr on his phone and find someone attainable. Niko wasn't the only man out there, and it was way past time for Vin to get on with his life.

He shoved his helmet over his head, balanced the Kawasaki Ninja between his legs, and started the engine. He blipped the throttle and pulled in the clutch. A hand came down on his shoulder.

He glanced at the guy on his right. One of the many down-on-their-luck people that could be found on the street in that part of the San Fernando Valley. The man said something Vin didn't catch.

Having escaped life on the street himself, Vin tended to have a lot of tolerance for the people who lived on the fringe. He flipped his visor up. "What was that?"

"Vinny, Vinny. It's me, man."

Vin's veins pricked with heat, and beads of sweat formed on his brow as adrenaline dripped into his system. The long, greasy hair and the threadbare clothes made the man almost unrecognizable, but that voice...

A blast from Vin's distant past.

One that he'd rather not remember.

Back then, meals had been scarce and money nearly impossible to come by, unless you wanted to turn tricks in the parks or dark alleys behind the bars late at night.

"Stu." Somehow, Vin managed to keep the venom out of his voice. "You still owe me twenty-three bucks."

Stu threw his head back and laughed. "Does it look like I've got any money?"

"What do you want?"

"Just sayin' hi to an old friend."

"Whatever friendship we had ended when you stole the last of my money and ditched me on that train in the middle of the night."

"Hey, man." Stu held his hands out. "No hard feelings."

It had been ten years, but the betrayal hit harder than the johns that used to beat up on some of Vin's friends. Life on the streets had been grueling, trying, and scary as all fuck, and there had been a time when Vin had thought he and Stu had each other's backs.

Turns out, Vin had been wrong.

If Stu hadn't stolen your money, you wouldn't have been desperate enough to proposition men driving by the park. And if you hadn't done that, you never would have met Niko.

But the fact that Niko had saved Vin from survival prostitution—like a lot of the gay kids who'd been thrown out by their parents and found themselves homeless and fending for themselves—didn't make up for Stu's betrayal. One he still felt to that very day.

"Have a nice life." Vin flipped his visor down and stomped down on the gear shift, a car horn blaring as he swerved into traffic.

All the way across the valley, Vin drove too fast and too reckless, trying to outrun his demons. As much as he'd grown from a boy to the man he was today, his younger self had a way of popping into his life unbidden, reminding him that no matter what, he could never truly escape what he was... a worthless street kid with a dark past that refused to let him go.

That's how he'd found himself on stage the previous Saturday as the last bachelor in a live auction fundraiser for The Cory Center, the local LGBTQ youth center.

He'd been a last-minute replacement for a B-list actor that couldn't make it. At the time, his greatest fear had been that no one would bid on him.

But people had.

The ensuing bidding war had brought in a pile of cash for the Center. Which was great, but now it was time Vin gave Niko what he'd paid for.

———

Niko Stavros stamped his feet into his black boots, a pair he hadn't worn since his days in front of the cameras, back when he'd been the latest young stud in the gay porn industry.

He'd found the boots stuck in the back of his closet. They'd needed a good polish, but the time spent spiffing them up had given Niko the chance to contemplate some of his recent life choices. His conclusion? He must be having some sort of mid-life crisis.

Forty-three is hardly mid-life.

Still, how else could he explain shelling out ten grand for a date with a kid almost twenty years his junior.

He's not a kid. He's a twenty-five-year-old man.

A date with a *man* who Niko had long ago put at the top of his *No-date, No-how* list.

A date you'd insisted on even when Vin had given you an out.

Not to mention, said date totally negated the recent vow Niko made to himself to start dating men closer to his own age.

Which brought Niko right back to reconsidering his life choices.

With the whole studio leaving for the Bahamas in a few days for a series of shoots, he'd shut down the studio for the weekend and had the luxury of having his property to himself. The security panel in his bedroom beeped, notifying him that someone had used their code at the front gate.

Vin.

That familiar twist in his gut that he used to get back when he'd first started dating returned. He hadn't felt that flutter, the awkward combination of nerves, anticipation, lust, and fear in a long time.

Maybe it wasn't too late to cancel.

But Niko couldn't bail. Not after he'd canceled on Vin the night before.

He plucked his wallet off his dresser and left his keys behind. Vin had insisted that he would drive.

Coming down the stairs, his footfalls echoed on the Italian marble floors. He pulled open his front door before Vin had a chance to ring the bell, only to find his nephew on his porch, his hand raised to knock.

Niko drew up short. "Sebastian. What are you doing here?"

Sebastian stepped forward as if he were coming in, but Niko didn't budge.

"What? You're not going to invite me in?"

From his front door, Niko couldn't see the imposing gate that shielded Black Stallion Studios from all the looky-loos who streamed into the San Fernando Valley on any given weekend.

Niko glanced down the long driveway. He'd really prefer Sebastian not be there as a witness when Vin pulled up. "I was just leaving."

Sebastian stepped back and gave him the once over. "Hot date?"

"Hardly." Though the semi Niko had been sporting since he'd woken that morning called him a liar. He really should have jacked off while he'd had the chance. "It's just a... thing."

A grin spread across Sebastian's face, and he crossed his arms over his chest, rocking back on his heels. "A *thing*?"

Knowing Sebastian, he wouldn't let it drop until Niko confessed. If it would get Sebastian out of there any faster, he'd tell him.

Niko huffed out a breath. "I'm waiting for Vin. For our date."

"I thought that was last night."

"Had to reschedule."

Sebastian's eyes narrowed, and that protective streak flashed in his eyes. Sebastian had youth on his side. Niko had size and muscle on his. But he wouldn't put it past his nephew to take a swipe at him to protect Vin. "Why?"

"I didn't blow him off for a hookup if that's what you're thinking."

The animosity dropped from Sebastian's face. "Maybe this date isn't such a good idea. Vin's into you. Like *into* you, into you. Don't toy with his emotions. I don't want to see him get hurt."

"I'm not going to hurt him. We're going to spend a few hours together, and then we'll go back to the way things are supposed to be, me directing and him behind the camera." Niko crossed his arms over his chest. "We're done discussing my private life. Why are you on my doorstep so early on your day off? Did Grant kick you out of the house already?"

And yeah, that might have been a shitty thing to say, but Sebastian was rubbing Niko all kinds of raw.

That's what happens when someone hits too close to the truth.

"Just the opposite."

And damn if Sebastian couldn't keep the smile off his face. The smile his boyfriend, Grant Hardy, had put there ever since he'd come out of the closet and asked Sebastian to move in with him.

And since Grant could put that smile on his nephew's face, it was worth all the money he'd lose not having Grant as one of his performers anymore.

"How so?"

"Grant wants me to come work for him at The Cory Center as their fundraising chair."

"How do you expect to do that and keep up with our production schedule, we—" Niko cut himself off when Sebastian couldn't look him in the eye. "You're quitting."

It wasn't a question. As soon as the thought popped into Niko's head, he knew it was the truth. "What the actual fuck, Bass?"

"I know it's kind of sudden. But it's what I'm meant to do. For

Grant and me, for the Center, and for the LGBTQ kids the Center serves."

"If this is about your salary—"

"You've always paid me well. It's not about that. This is just something I have to do. As the guy who took Vin in as a teen, I figured you of all people would understand."

"Fucking hell." Having his production manager quit on him didn't make Niko's life any easier, even if he did understand.

"I'm not going to leave you in the lurch. I'll stick around until you can find someone to replace me." Sebastian lost color in his complexion. "There's just one tiny hiccup."

This ought to be good. Niko made a get-on-with-it motion with his hands. Maybe it wouldn't be as bad as he feared.

"I won't be able to make it to the Bahamas."

Meaning the big Bahama shoot Black Stallion had been planning for months and months. The shoot with the highest cost, the tightest schedule, and the most significant monetary risk to the studio.

Niko ran his hand across the scruff on his jaw and over his mouth, keeping all the cussing inside his head. The heavy sigh he couldn't restrain said the *are you fucking kidding me* for him.

"I wouldn't stay behind if it wasn't important. Child services had to bump the date for the home inspection and interview back, and since I've been included on the paperwork for fostering Tavi, I have to be there."

Tavi. The stray teen Grant had taken in, much like Niko had taken Vin in all those years ago. Though back then, they'd never had anything official to set Niko up as a guardian. But Grant was the kind of guy who played by the rules, at least when it came to the Center and the kids.

Just because Niko could relate, didn't mean he had to like it. "What am I supposed to do?"

Sebastian turned pasty white—all evidence of their Greek

heritage lost. Niko almost stopped him from what he was about to say next.

"Betty Hardy said she could help."

"Betty Hardy? Grant's hundred-year-old grandmother? Is this a joke?"

"She's only eighty. And keen and smart and the queen of organization. She makes Marie Kondo look inadequate. Plus, she kicked ass on the last-minute preparations for the Center's fundraiser when Grant was hospitalized. She can do this. I've got everything planned already anyways. All she has to do is follow my notes, and everything will go as planned."

"These things never go as planned. You know that. I know that."

"Look. Just talk to her. If you don't like what she has to say, I'll try to figure something else out."

Jesus fucking Christ. Niko would regret the next words coming out of his mouth. "Fine. Have her come in first thing Monday morning. But you better be looking for an alternative."

Sebastian's color returned. "I will. Promise. I would be there if this wasn't so important. You know that, right?"

"Yeah. Yeah. I get it."

The roar of a motorcycle engine caught their attention, and they both turned to see Vin riding up on his orange and black Ninja.

Niko closed his eyes and swallowed the groan. What had he gotten himself into?

Sebastian clapped Niko on the shoulder, and Niko opened his eyes to see his nephew smiling like a loon. Then the smile slipped, and Sebastian leaned in. "He's a good man. Don't break his heart."

———

VIN STOPPED IN THE CIRCULAR DRIVE AT BLACK STALLION STUDIOS to find Niko and Sebastian already outside. He killed the engine, pulled off his helmet, and raked his hands through his sweat-dampened hair.

If this had been any other kind of date, he would have driven his car, but with what he had planned for Niko, having a bad hair day would be the least of their worries.

"Hey, Vin." Sebastian waved as he backed away and headed toward his car.

"You don't have to run off." Though if he and Niko were going to get to the airfield on time, they couldn't hang around for long.

Though Vin would gladly make an exception on their departure time if Niko invited him in for a quickie. Or even a handjob. For that, Vin would say to hell with his reservations and the huge favor he'd called in. But sex with Niko was never going to happen, so Vin tried to put it out of his head.

"We're done here." Niko gestured toward Sebastian. "He was just leaving anyway."

Niko gave Vin a once over, the corners of his mouth going down a fraction, and those dark brows over his deep brown eyes creased.

"What?"

Jesus. Vin should have made reservations for dinner or bought tickets to a movie or planned on dinner and a couple of drinks at The Trojan Horse, one of the local gay bars. Niko wasn't going to like what Vin had planned.

"You expect me to get on that?"

"When you rescheduled, you told me the day was up to me and to surprise you." Vin managed a very Vanna White wave of his hand across his bike. "Surprise."

Niko still didn't say anything. Though a man like Niko didn't have to say anything to be seven kinds of hot. Between the stubble, the black boots and matching jeans, the *Tom of Finland* T-shirt with the boot print stretching across his chest, he kept Vin's attention. "You scared?"

"Terrified." A hint of a smile made a welcome appearance.

Vin reached down and unclipped his spare helmet from the clip beside the back seat and tossed it to him. "You ain't seen nothing yet."

Shrugging out of his backpack, Vin unstrapped a borrowed motorcycle jacket from the rear seat. "Put this on. Helps to keep you from getting road rash if you come off."

Niko blanched when he glanced at the tiny seat behind Vin. "Am I coming off?"

Vin grinned. "Not if you hold on tight."

A small, diabolical part of Vin liked the idea of Niko's legs bracketing his thighs and having those strong arms wrapped solidly around his waist.

Small part?

Okay, not so small, but if Niko wouldn't touch Vin of his own volition, he only felt marginally bad that he'd engineered the close contact for the cheap thrill.

That's not all you engineered.

When Niko had given Vin free rein to plan the date, and knowing he had Niko as a captive audience for the day, Vin took full advantage of the situation.

Maybe if he shoved Niko out of his comfort zone and brought him into Vin's world, Niko would see him in a new light, and not as some skinny-ass street urchin that needed rescuing.

Niko shrugged into the jacket and pulled the backpack's straps over his shoulders. Vin kicked down the footpegs for the passenger seat and balanced the bike between his legs.

"Hop on."

"You sure about this?"

For the first time since Vin had made the plans, he seriously reconsidered what they were about to do.

Vin leashed his disappointment, trying to keep it out of his voice. "Look, if you don't want to do this, we can—"

Niko raised a hand to shut him up. "No. It's fine."

Though Niko's misgivings etched deep into his expression, he put on the helmet, snapped the strap under his chin, and threw a leg over the seat.

When Niko settled behind him, Vin flipped his visor up, and Niko did the same. "The button for the helmet-to-helmet intercom is on the left side. It's voice-activated after that."

It took a minute to make sure the comms system worked, then Vin flipped his visor down and started the engine. Pulling in the clutch, he downshifted to first.

"Scoot up and wrap your arms around my waist."

When Niko did, Vin said, "Tighter."

And no, that wasn't just because he wanted to feel Niko's arms around him, he also had a feeling Niko had no idea of the raw power between their legs, and he didn't want Niko sliding off the back the first time they accelerated.

"If I die," Niko said, though Vin heard the humor in his words, "I'm going to come back and haunt you."

"Fair enough." Which meant nothing would change, considering Niko had haunted Vin's dreams for years now.

They rounded the circular drive and headed for the front gate. "You ever been on the back of a bike before?"

"Never."

He didn't want to scare Niko, but he did want to give him a bit of a thrill. "All you really need to do is lean with me into the curves and hold on. I'll do the rest."

"Trust me, you'll have to pry my arms off of you."

Vin chuckled, enjoying having Niko's chest pressed against his back much more than he should.

2

———

Niko leaned into the hairpin turn, on their way into the San Gabriel Mountains, the grip he had around Vin's waist so tight he was bound to leave an imprint when they got off. *If* they ever got off.

His ass was starting to hurt—the passenger seat on the back of the Ninja was little more than an afterthought. But holy hell, leaning into the curves, with the bike, Vin, and Niko all working as one, made his heart race and his nerves jangle. But in the best way.

Or maybe Vin was responsible for all those feelings because more than his heart and nerves were involved.

They came out of the turn, and Niko readjusted himself on the seat, his erection pressing neatly into the small of Vin's back.

Vin reached back and patted Niko's thigh. "You good back there?"

"My ass may never be the same again, but yeah, I'm good." And because he couldn't contain his curiosity any longer, he added, "Where are we going?"

"We're almost there."

Which didn't answer the question, but if Vin wanted to keep it a secret until the last minute, he didn't want to spoil the fun.

A few minutes later, Vin slowed and turned onto a narrow private road. Scrub trees and rocks everywhere. They topped a rise, and the land flattened out onto a plateau. Vin pulled up in front of a tall, wide metal building, the huge double doors open wide, revealing what looked like single-engine Cessna inside the hanger.

Niko released his hold on Vin as they came to a stop, the rear tire skidding a couple feet on the loose gravel. Niko hopped off and unzipped his jacket. Vin lowered the kickstand and did the same.

"Well?" Vin asked when they'd both pulled their helmets off. "What did you think?"

Because of the excitement in Vin's eyes and the massive grin on his face, Niko would have said he'd loved it even if it had been a lie. He didn't ever want to be the guy who dimmed Vin's genuine light.

"Actually, I loved it. Though my heart is still pounding after that last turn. Feel it."

For reasons Niko couldn't quite articulate, he took Vin's hand and pressed it to the center of his chest. He held it there for a beat too long before releasing it.

Don't break his heart.

Niko kicked Sebastian out of his head and focused on the way Vin took a half-step closer, not breaking the eye contact. "Nothing like that adrenaline kick to let you know you're alive. Am I right?"

"It was definitely a rush."

A man came out of the hangar with a scowl on his face, and Niko took a step away from Vin. Niko had no issue with being gay, but the rest of the world hadn't fallen into step. Even in a progressive state like California, Niko conducted his personal life with caution while in public.

"You sure we're in the right place?"

"Positive." Vin hooked his helmet on the handlebar and met the man as he approached.

"Hey, Vinny." The guy skipped Vin's outstretched hand and pulled him into a hug, engulfing Vin with his arms. "Long time, no see."

"Sorry," Vin said as the man leaned in and kissed his cheek. "Work's been busy."

The big man tucked Vin against his side, a possessive arm slung over Vin's shoulder.

Niko cocked his head. Who was this guy?

Not that it was any of Niko's business. Vin was a grown man, entitled to his own private life. But that didn't mean Niko liked what he saw.

You can't be jealous of a man you can't ever have. Back the fuck off, and be nice.

Vin and the other man stopped in front of Niko. "Niko, this is my good friend Joss Kincaid. Joss, this is—"

"This him?"

And from Joss's tone, that didn't sound like a good thing.

"Stop," Vin admonished, the color rising in his cheeks, and Niko had to wonder what Vin had said about him in the past. "This is my boss, Niko Stavros."

The words seemed loaded, but Niko wasn't sure why.

Joss had to unwrap his arm from around Vin to shake Niko's hand, which was just as well as far as Niko was concerned.

You don't own Vin. In fact, you do everything in your power to stay away. Don't be a jealous prick. This could be his boyfriend for all you know.

Joss pulled a grease-stained rag from the back pocket of his work coveralls and wiped his hands before sticking one out.

"Nice to meet you." Niko called on his years of acting to infuse his voice with sincerity.

"Likewise," Joss said, without the same sincerity.

Then Joss turned to Vin and said, "He has no idea why he's here, does he?"

"I'd thought I'd surprise him."

Joss raised a brow at Vin but didn't voice his apparent misgivings.

"What *are* we doing?" Niko feared the answer.

"Maybe I should show him." Vin took off his motorcycle jacket and turned to Niko. "You can leave the gear here, but hand me that backpack. It needs refrigerating."

Niko shucked the jacket and left the helmet on the seat, giving the backpack to Vin to shoulder. Vin gestured for Niko to precede them, and the three of them walked into the hangar where Vin stuffed the whole backpack into the refrigerator.

Maybe Vin planned on taking him up for a spin around the valley to see the sights.

In a tin can.

Niko's stomach revolted, but he swallowed back down the bile. It was fine. He'd been in a small plane before. He'd survived then. He'd survive it again.

In the hangar, laid out on a long table, was a bunch of gear. Vin stopped in front of it and turned to Niko. "I realized that we spend many hours together every day, but we don't talk much about our lives outside the studio. I wanted you to see a part of my world. Something I've found that I love, that I never would have found if I'd never gotten off the streets."

Vin's voice got thick at the end, and Niko had to clear his own throat when he asked, "So what's all this?"

That churn in Niko's gut told him that he probably already knew, though he didn't want to jump to any false conclusions.

"A tandem parachute. For us."

Damn.

Niko didn't know if his face blanched, but his heart fluttered, and all that blood didn't seem to know where to go. Good news... he didn't have an inappropriate boner anymore.

Joss crossed his arms over his colossal chest, his biceps straining his shirtsleeves. He looked like the kind of guy who pulled Sequoias up by the roots and used them for toothpicks. A grin... no, it was more of a self-satisfied smirk, toyed with one corner of his mouth.

"Told you this was a bad idea," Joss said to Vin.

For some stupid, irrational reason, Niko wanted to prove Joss wrong, and Vin right about him, he said, "I think it's a fabulous idea."

"You do?" Vin and Joss sputtered at the same time. Joss frowned, but Vin's grin made his cheeks hurt.

"Sure. Why not?" Then Niko hitched his thumb over his shoulder at the plane in the hangar with the engine shroud up and what looked like a couple of vital components in pieces on the ground. "But, please tell me we're not going up in that thing."

That got a genuine chuckle out of Joss. "Naw, man. Come see my new bird."

They walked out the open bay doors at the rear of the hangar. Sitting on the private tarmac was a twin-engine plane, its side jump door wide open.

In the sun, the white skin of the plane gleamed.

"Wow." Vin walked over to the plane, wanting to skim his hands over the plane's skin, but he didn't want to leave fingerprints. "A Twin Otter. She's beautiful."

Joss had wanted a new plane ever since Vin had started parachuting with him. The old Cessna in the hangar had gotten the job done but, man, now they'd be flying in style.

"Been looking for a reason to get her up in the air, I had a corporate event cancel, so I don't have any clients scheduled until next week."

Vin turned to Niko. "You ready?"

"Right this second?"

Vin noted the panic in his voice. "I meant ready for the instruction. It's a tandem jump. You'll be attached to me, but we'll need to make sure your harness is adjusted properly and instruct you on how this is going to go."

"And you're qualified to do this? Do they just let anyone jump out of a plane or is there some sort of certification or—"

Vin stopped Niko before he spun out of control. "Relax. I'm instructor certified. I've been taking people up with Joss on my days off for a couple of years now."

Niko cocked his head and looked at Vin in a way he'd never looked at him before. "How did I not know this?"

"You never asked."

Vin kept any recrimination out of his tone. It wasn't Niko's fault he didn't know about the more intimate parts of Vin's life. He'd held that part to himself for the longest time, wanting something that was all his, something he hadn't gotten through Niko.

They spent the next thirty minutes preparing Niko for the jump, explaining body position, landing, the equipment. When Vin was satisfied Niko knew what was expected from him and what would happen on the dive, they zipped up their jumpsuits and strapped into their harnesses.

"I'll go get Joss."

"I'll wait here."

Vin walked over to the workbench, where Joss had some

airplane parts stripped down to all their basic components. Nuts, bolts, screws, springs, lever arms, and housings.

"You guys ready?" Joss asked.

"Yeah."

With Niko waiting at the rear of the hangar, Joss took the opportunity to turn his back to Niko, effectively blocking Vin's view. He leaned in and said, "I'm not getting what you see in him."

Vin fought back the eye roll. He never should have told Joss about his feelings for Niko. Someone, please remind him to never drink Jägerbombs around Joss again.

"People said the same thing to me about you at one time." Most people who didn't take the time to get to know Joss only saw what was on the outside, not the big heart and the bigger brain on the inside.

"That dick though." Joss bumped Vin's shoulder with his own, a sly grin on his face. "I've seen Niko's work. If I can get past the rest of him, I'm sure there's something under there I'd like."

"*Jesus Christ.* Get your head out of the gutter and go fly that plane."

Having a private airfield behind Joss's house had its advantages. As soon as Joss finished his pre-flight checklist, the three of them were airborne.

Vin and Niko each wore a helmet, and Joss raised one ear of his headset so he could hear them in the back. The plane climbed higher and higher, and Niko lost a shade of color with every thousand feet they climbed. His knee started to bounce, and Vin put a hand on Niko's thigh to still the motion.

"We don't have to do this if you don't want to."

"We'd think you were a wuss," Joss hollered from the cockpit, the smile evident in his voice. "But you don't have to do it."

"It's fine," Niko said, though it sounded like a lie.

"Really, I don't want you doing anything you don't want to."

"Look at it this way—" Joss started.

"Dude, shut the fuck up already. Let me handle this."

Vin glanced up at the cockpit and caught Joss flipping him the bird.

"What are you worried about?" Vin instinctively lowered his voice.

"Dying."

A low rumble of laughter came from the front. Either they hadn't been as quiet as they'd thought, or Joss had exceptional hearing. Joss cleared his throat. "Sorry."

"We're not going to die," Vin said. But because there was the slightest chance things would go to shit, and they would, he added, "Most likely."

This time, Niko laughed, though Vin wasn't trying to be funny.

"What if the parachute doesn't open?"

"It will."

"How do you know?"

"Because Joss packed it. And if it doesn't open, there is a reserve parachute that Joss packed as well."

"And if *that* doesn't open?"

"Then, I'll be glad I got to spend my last jump with you."

———

THEN I'LL BE GLAD I GOT TO SPEND MY LAST JUMP WITH YOU.

Those words shouldn't have given Niko any comfort, not when he'd wanted assurances that he *wouldn't* splat back to earth in a pile of blood and bone and broken bodies, but for some reason, they did.

"Five minutes," came Joss's warning from the cockpit.

Vin stood and had Niko stand as well. With the mild turbulence, Niko braced one of his hands on the side of the plane. Vin rechecked Niko's harness, making sure all the straps were tight over his torso and groin, before attaching Niko to Vin's harness.

You really going to do this?

He really shouldn't have canceled on Vin the night before. They could have gone to that stellar sushi place in Burbank, maybe gotten a little buzzed on saké, and called it a night.

Nothing dangerous and death-defying.

But that's why you'd canceled in the first place, wasn't it? Because contemplating a relationship with Vin was, in its own way, so very perilous?

Perilous? Perhaps that word was a tad dramatic.

Risky then. Either way, you shouldn't be thinking about Vin like that. It isn't right.

"One minute," Joss said.

Niko swallowed down the rising dread.

Because Vin must have sensed the second thoughts swirling in Niko's mind, Vin put a hand on Niko's shoulder. "People parachute all the time and live to tell about it. It's going to be fine. *We're* going to be fine. You trust me?"

The funny thing was, Niko had asked the same thing when Vin had flagged his car down all those years ago while Vin had been looking for his first john. Niko had offered a meal instead. All Vin had to do was get in the car.

It had been a leap of faith on Vin's part.

One that had changed both of their lives.

Niko liked to think for the better. Now Vin asked for that same trust to be bestowed on him.

Niko straightened as much as he could, considering he was attached to Vin. "I trust you."

Niko craned his neck to look back at Vin. Damn that grin. So wide and bright. Niko's chest tightened, and his heart galloped when the full wattage of that smile landed on him.

"Come with me."

Not that Niko had much choice considering he was strapped to Vin's chest. Vin rolled up the plane's side door. Cold air buffeted them, and Niko instinctively grabbed the handhold overhead.

With the door secure, Vin rechecked their connection.

"Twenty seconds."

"Copy," Vin called up to Joss.

"I've got the handhold," Vin said, his voice raised over the engine noise and wind. "Let go and cross your arms over your chest."

Niko let go. One of the hardest things he'd ever done in his life. He stared down at the ground, more than thirteen thousand feet below.

"Last chance to chicken out," Vin said.

Oh, hell, no. Niko's pride wouldn't allow it. Especially knowing he'd have to face Joss's judgment if he didn't go through with it. It shouldn't have mattered, but stupidly, it did.

"I'm ready."

"Three... two..." Vin counted in his ear. Calm. Confident. Niko blew out the breath he held. "One."

Vin let go, and they jumped.

Out of a fucking plane.

What the ever-loving hell was wrong with him? Holy-fuuuuuuck.

Vin's whoop and laughter echoed in Niko's ear, even above the whoosh of blood and rushing wind that assaulted his eardrums. His heart kicked against his sternum, a brutal, erratic rhythm that seemed incompatible with sustaining life.

But Niko didn't die.

And he didn't pass out.

The wind slung Niko's lower legs between Vin's as they fell, fell, fell.

Niko checked the altimeter on his wrist, the way Vin had told him.

Vin must have pulled the cord because it felt like he'd been jerked to a stop, the straps cutting into his groin. Vin whooped again and started steering them in long, slow, sweeping circles as they continued their descent.

That high up, all Niko could hear was Vin breathing in his ear, the rush of the wind, and the slamming beat of his own heart.

As they floated, he stopped focusing on the fall and took in the view. The San Gabrielle Mountains were vast and green below. All the nooks, crannies, creeks, and streams. In the distance, the San Fernando Valley and the Pacific Ocean.

He'd seen the valley and the mountains from the air many times before, but those experiences could never compare to this one.

Not when they soared like the eagles.

The trees and the roads got bigger and bigger as they spiraled down. As much as he hadn't wanted to jump out of a plane, he didn't want to land. He could see why Vin loved skydiving so much.

As they came in for a landing, Vin pulled on the steering lines directing them to Joss's landing zone. Joss had already landed and jumped into a UTV and started driving toward them.

"Feet up," Vin reminded him as the ground rushed up at them.

They landed, Vin skid on his feet and slid on his ass. A gust of wind caught the parachute and jerked them.

They rolled to their sides, Vin's laugh warm in Niko's ear.

Then Niko felt the give of his harness, and they were no longer tethered together. Niko rolled onto his stomach and braced himself on his arms.

Vin clapped him on the back. "Told you, you wouldn't die."

Niko laughed. "That was incredible. I don't think my adrenal glands have ever had that kind of workout."

Sitting up, Niko held out his arm and watched his handshake.

Vin held his out in comparison. Completely still, not a quake or a shake or a shiver. Which was part of what made Vin such a top-rated cameraman.

"It's the adrenaline burning off," Vin said. "You'll get used to it."

Which assumed that Niko would do it again.

"You made it." Joss's long strides ate up the grass in the meadow.

Joss had directed the comment at Niko. There might have been a hint of disappointment in his voice.

Niko didn't know what the guy had against him, or what Vin had told Joss, but he let the comment slide. He wasn't going to get into a pissing match with one of Vin's friends.

3

THEY SPENT THE NEXT HOUR REPLACING THE GEAR BACK IN THE hangar and helping Joss refuel the plane so it would be ready to go for his next flight. But as quickly as Vin could, he retrieved the backpack out of the fridge, and they said their goodbyes.

Vin didn't know what the hell was wrong with Joss, but he had a giant stick up his ass about Niko, and Vin didn't want to stick around any longer and let Joss ruin the day for them.

They zipped up their motorcycle jackets, and Niko shouldered into the backpack. "What the hell do you have in here anyway? I can barely lift it."

"Lunch."

At that, Niko's stomach grumbled, and Vin chuckled. "Hop on. I know the perfect place. It's a bit of a ride, but—"

Niko made a face and rubbed his ass.

"It will be totally worth the numb ass. Promise."

Niko seemed skeptical, but he put his helmet on and buckled it under his chin. A good sport, if nothing else.

The ride to their destination took them down the mountain and across the valley to the ocean and to a narrow trail that led down to a private beach north of Malibu that Vin had discovered years before.

They dropped down to the flat sand-covered concrete by the beach, and Vin stopped before he got his bike stuck in the deeper sand. He killed the engine and waited until Niko climbed off before he put his kickstand down and dismounted.

The early afternoon sun shone bright, but the cool breeze off the ocean felt good on his sweat-dampened hair. He brushed the hair back from his face and glanced up at Niko and the way his boss rocked his own sweaty helmet head.

"What is this place?" Niko asked as he laid his jacket on the seat of the bike and balanced his helmet on top of it.

Vin did the same with his gear and picked up the backpack Niko had laid on the ground. "It's a private beach."

Niko's eyes narrowed. "Whose private beach?"

Vin gave a slight shrug and started walking toward the water before Niko could stop him. "No idea."

Niko caught his arm and brought Vin to a stop. "You're not going to get us arrested, are you?"

"Relax. I come here all the time, and never once have I run into anybody. Besides, with the way the trail drops down from the road, no one driving by can see that we're here."

Niko glanced up at the steep incline of the trail that had led down to the secluded cove and back at Vin. "I'll have to take your word for it."

"This way." Vin inclined his head toward a large flat rock along the shoreline, the incoming tide licking at the base.

Niko didn't immediately follow. Vin glanced back, catching Niko rubbing his ass. *I can help with that sore ass* was the first thing that came to Vin's mind. But that would be juvenile and wouldn't help Niko see that Vin wasn't a kid anymore.

He kept his thoughts to himself, as well as the ideas of other things he could do to that ass if only Niko would let him.

Think all you want. You know it's not ever going to happen. This will never be anything other than another lascivious scenario to fill up your spank bank for later.

In the dry sand, Vin ditched his boots and socks, rolled up his pant legs, and waited while Niko did the same. As they moved closer to a flat boulder, the cool, damp sand squished between his toes as the surf pounded against the natural rock jetties at the edges of the cove, the angry water frothy, white, and turbulent.

Water and slick slime coated the lower half of the boulder. Vin climbed to the dry area at the top and reached a hand back to help Niko.

When Niko clasped his hand, Niko's firm grip gave Vin all kinds of stupid ideas of where else that grip would serve Vin well.

Jesus. Maybe Niko's been right all these years. You are definitely too immature for him if you can't keep your dirty mind in check for more than three seconds at a time.

Standing on top of the rock, they stopped to take in the view. Nothing marred the far horizon as the cloudless sky met the blue ocean. Not a tanker, or sailboat, or fisherman, or jet ski in sight. Their secluded spot seemed impervious even to the road noise up above.

Two to three-foot rollers came into shore, a consistent rush and rhythm that always left Vin feeling settled and grounded. This spot was where he'd always come to figure out his shit. And bringing Niko here somehow felt... revealing. As if everything Vin had told the world had been captured by the cove and reflected back on Niko.

That somehow, by Niko knowing this place, he'd know Vin as well.

Absurd.

But there it was.

"What do you think?" Vin almost feared the answer. This cove meant so much to him that a blithe, 'it's nice' would gut him.

Niko turned his focus from the incoming waves to Vin, his expression inscrutable as his eyes dropped to Vin's lips before meeting Vin's gaze again. "The view is stunning."

Was Niko talking about the ocean or Vin?

"Um…"

Vin swallowed hard. Jumping out of the plane didn't faze Vin, but that one look, that quick flick of Niko's gaze down to Vin's lips, had his heart thumping and what felt like a whole bevy of bees buzzing in his belly.

He let the backpack slip from his shoulders and caught it in his hand. "You hungry?"

That heavy gaze of Niko's flicked down again, and a shadow of a smile flashed at the corners of Niko's lips. "Always."

The crashing surf almost obliterated the deep, quiet timbre of Niko's voice. A more massive wave hit, the spray sprinkling them with cold salty water.

Luckily, Niko wiped the moisture from his face before Vin decided it would be a good idea to lick every inch of Niko dry.

They sat on the rock, and Vin unpacked their lunch. Sandwiches, bottles of water, cheese, crackers, and homemade fudge brownies for dessert. He even had some wipes to clean their hands. "Sorry, I don't have a towel or blanket, but I ran out of room."

"It's fine." Niko brushed away a few strands of dried seaweed and clumps of sand. "I'm impressed enough as it is that you were able to get all of this in your backpack."

As Vin started laying out their meal and taking lids off the plastic containers, he said, "Can you get the knife and condiments out of the front pocket?"

Niko grabbed the near-empty backpack and unzipped the

smaller pouch as the realization came to Vin of what else he carried in that part of his backpack.

Vin's hand shot out and held onto the pack. "Never mind, I'll get it."

The surf betrayed Vin by not covering the panic in his words. Niko held tight.

That smile that had ghosted around Niko's lips before looked like it was there to stay.

One of the things Vin loved about Niko was his intelligence. Right now, one of the things Vin hated about Niko... was his intelligence.

"What do you have in here?"

NIKO KEPT A GRIP ON THE BACKPACK AS VIN TURNED THREE different shades of red in as many seconds. Definitely, something in the bag that Vin didn't want him to see.

"Let go." Niko kept his voice low, not so much demanding as cajoling. With the near terror on Vin's face, Niko wasn't going to be a dick and look without his permission, but still, it intrigued him.

"*Fuck*," Vin muttered as he let go of the backpack. "In my defense, I totally forgot that stuff was in there."

Vin tucked his legs in, his elbows on his knees, as he peeked through the gaps in his fingers.

This ought to be good.

Niko pulled out tiny containers of mayo, mustard, relish, a kitchen knife, a handful of napkins in a Ziploc baggie...

All far from mortifying.

He dug around the bottom of the pocket and came up with several sachets of lube, a strip of condoms, and... his hand went around a velvet bag, the contents of which had a healthy weight.

Niko knew what it was as soon as his hand went around it. He could have spared Vin the embarrassment, but a small part of him, that same small part of him that refused to agree that this date had been a bad idea, that bidding on Vin in the first place had been a terrible decision, wanted to see Vin's reaction when he opened the bag.

Niko pulled out the purple Crown Royal bag. No bottle of whiskey inside that baby. Something much more enticing.

He pulled apart the scrunched-up top, reached in, and pulled out the most glorious stainless-steel butt plug he'd seen in a long while. He judged the weight of it with his hand, taking in the sheer size of the flared bulb.

"I admire your dedication to quality and your... ambition."

"Okay, okay, okay."

Vin couldn't have been redder if he'd been basted with butter and set out to bake under the summer sun. For a guy who had videoed hours and hours of some pretty kinky porn, Niko found it endearing that Vin could be embarrassed by a sex toy.

"You've had your fun," Vin said. "Now, you can put it back."

"Oh, no. I think we should put it right here."

Niko put the empty velvet bag on the highest part of the rock with the butt plug on top. It wasn't that much higher than the flat area where they sat, maybe a foot or so, but high enough to catch the sun, their reflections distorted in the curve of the gleaming metal.

Niko had spent a lot of time trying *not* to think about the particulars of Vin's sex life, and now, having it glint back at him, he couldn't quite think about anything else.

Vin laughed at last. Shaking his head, he reached for one of the sandwiches and handed it over. They didn't say much as they layered the condiments and took their first bites.

Niko sunk his teeth into the roast beef sandwich on ciabatta bread, complete with lettuce and tomato that had fared well, considering they had spent the day in a backpack with Freez Paks.

Niko swallowed then washed the food down with water. "Where did you get these sandwiches? You should give the number to Sebastian. We could use them to cater some of our lunches."

"I didn't buy them. I made them."

"No, shit?"

Though the question seemed rhetorical, Vin said, "No shit."

Niko set his sandwich on a napkin and reached for the cheese, cutting off a few slices for him and Vin. "Let me guess, you milked the cow and grew the cultures for the cheese as well."

Vin topped a cracker with one of the cheese slices and took a bite, tucking it into his cheek. "And grew the wheat, and made the dough, and baked the crackers. The hardest part was scalloping the edges, but hey, whenever a guy pays ten grand to go on a date with me, I pull out all the stops."

The lick of humor slid off Vin's face, and the question remained in his hazel eyes. The one that asked, *Why did you do it?*

But the question remained unasked, and because Niko didn't have an answer for Vin, he pretended like the question hadn't been there, as plain on Vin's face as his nose or that sexy scruff of stubble on his jaw.

Vin glanced from Niko to the butt plug and back again. When he reached to put it away, Niko said, "Leave it."

"You're kidding me, right?"

"No fine meal is complete without a centerpiece."

"A centerpiece?" Vin's eyes narrowed. He knew Niko well enough to know he had more on his mind than meal decor.

"You know, a conversation starter at dinner time."

Vin took another bite and shifted, resting his weight on one hand. "Go ahead then. Start conversing." Vin's words came out as a dare. For a man who'd been embarrassed when Niko had pulled the toy out, he now seemed more curious about what Niko would say next.

Niko should have changed the subject. He should have put the fucking butt plug away and slowly backed out of the conversation. But instead, that stupid part of him, the one that bid on Vin and kept raising his bid until he'd won, asked, "Joss use that on you?"

Vin choked on a cracker, and Niko thought he'd have to slap him on the back to get him breathing again.

Note to self, brush up on the Heimlich maneuver.

"You okay?"

Vin swallowed down half of his water, the flush on his face from all the coughing subsided. "I didn't expect you to go there is all."

"Does that mean the subject of Joss is off-limits?"

Getting to know Vin better doesn't mean you have to get personal, you get that, right?

But now that the question hung in the air, a sick, masochistic part of Niko needed to know the answer. Because that protective streak Joss had shown back at the hangar hadn't all been in Niko's head.

What was Vin to Joss?

More importantly, what was Joss to Vin?

"Not off-limits."

He detected a hint of caution in Vin's tone. Niko didn't push. Instead, he took another bite of the incredible sandwich that Vin had made for him and looked out over the ocean. The waves rolled in and crashed against the rocks in the surf zone, sending salt spray into the air. He waited for Vin to collect his thoughts. If he wanted Niko to know more, he'd tell him.

"We were together for a while," Vin allowed, "but that was

before…" Vin bobbed a chin toward the butt plug, indicating he hadn't had the sex toy then.

Niko filed that information away for later. Right now, he wanted to know more about Joss. "Did you love him?"

Vin laughed, sitting up straighter. "You go straight for the meat of it, don't you? Kinda personal, no? Did you love Peter?"

He should have expected that question in return. "No. And after ten years of friendship, you don't think that's a question I have the right to ask?"

"Friendship? Is that what we have?"

"Is it not?" Niko answered the question with a question and shrugged, not because he was indifferent, but sometimes people talked to fill a silence, and he didn't want the focus to be on his self-serving motivations for asking.

Maybe Vin had a better definition of their relationship.

While Niko had had nothing but platonic feelings for Vin when he first came to live with him, what he felt and thought when he looked at the man before him now couldn't be described as platonic in any way. It confused and terrified Niko at the same time.

And after Sebastian had lost his temper a few weeks back, letting it slip that Vin had been crushed out on Niko for a long time, Niko needed to know how Vin viewed their relationship.

Vin never denied what Sebastian had blurted out. Did that make it true? Or did it mean that Vin hadn't wanted to debate Sebastian when it was clear Sebastian wasn't in a mood to see reason?

"Joss and I… we saw each other for a while." It wasn't lost on Niko that Vin hadn't defined his and Vin's relationship, but Niko would let that slide in exchange for the scoop on Joss. "We were pretty close."

"What happened?" Niko polished off his sandwich and started in on the cheese and crackers with focused intent. Part hunger, mostly nerves, if the lightness in his belly meant anything.

"Nothing *happened*. No explosive event blew us apart. We dated. It got hot and heavy for a time and then..." It was Vin's turn to shrug. "Then, it ended."

"Had to be a reason."

The glare Vin shot him said it wasn't any of Niko's business, but at the same time, Vin said, "We both wanted different things."

"He's kind of old for you, don't you think?"

Vin threw his head back and laughed. A sweet, pure sound that made Niko laugh with him.

"Jesus Christ," Vin said, "he's only a couple years older than you."

"You have a type, then? Older men?" That unwise part of Niko wanted it to be true.

But as soon as those words escaped Niko's mouth, he'd wanted them back, having seen his mistake.

Niko braced for the response.

4

PRICELESS.

Vin had a type?

This from the man who Vin hadn't known to ever hook up with anyone close to his own age.

Niko had a long parade of immature boy toys that only wanted him for what he brought to the table, and Vin wasn't just talking about the dick. It was the money and the prestige and, yeah, some of the notoriety of being the guy on the arm of one of the most popular porn stars back in the day.

Hell, if Niko would get back in front of the camera, Vin had no doubt he'd hit the top of the list of performers in record time. He was hot, and built, and sophisticated, and intelligent, and compassionate, and kind, and...

What does Niko's intelligence and compassion have to do with porn? No one watching Niko in front of the camera cares what he's like off of it.

"I could say the same about you having a type," Vin said.

"Do tell." Niko seemed more amused than annoyed and damn if that coy, confident grin didn't make Vin's heart trip and stumble.

"Needy. Vapid. Gold digging. Hung."

Niko laughed but didn't deny any of it.

"That last bit, I'm assuming because otherwise, I don't understand what you saw in them."

"They filled a void." And before Vin could vamp on the double entendre, Niko sent him a quelling look.

"Which begs the question…" Did Vin dare ask it? He'd almost asked earlier, and now that part of his brain dialed into self-preservation seemed to have disappeared.

Why hadn't he brought the whiskey instead of the butt plug? He could use a fortifying sip.

Vin took a long slug of water. Maybe he was dehydrated, and the inhibitory part of his brain would reboot and keep him from asking what he shouldn't. But the rehydration did nothing.

Taking in a deep breath, Vin asked, "Why did you bid on me?"

Niko stretched out, his bare feet dangling over the edge of the rock, his head on his upturned hand. "You know why."

No, he didn't. That's why he'd asked. He knew what he'd hoped, though. "And don't say it was for the kids. You could have sent Grant the money at any time if that's what you really wanted to do."

"I don't know why."

"Okay. Fine. Suit yourself. You don't have to tell me." Clearly, Niko thought Vin was avoiding answering him when instead, he didn't have a clue why Niko had bid on him.

Probably better this way. The truth doesn't always set you free, as Vin had learned the hard way when he'd come out to his parents at fifteen.

Sometimes the truth gutted you.

Vin started cleaning up the leftovers and their trash, stuffing it all back into the backpack, butt plug included. He left the brownies out because he figured after this conversation, he'd need a chocolate induced sugar rush to fortify himself.

Niko reached out, placing a stilling hand on Vin's arm. "I'm not being willfully obtuse."

Vin shook him off and kept packing. Niko grabbed the backpack and set it out of Vin's reach. "Would you listen to me for a second?"

Vin closed his eyes and took in a calming breath, settling back on the rock with his arms around his upturned knees, not even caring that it looked like what it was, his body subconsciously protecting himself from what Niko was about to say.

"I don't know why I bid on you. I had no number. I only went to the auction to support Grant and Sebastian. I had every intention of making a direct donation."

"And then?"

Niko's laugh came out rueful. "And then..." Niko's voice dropped, and that low register he hit made goosebumps race along Vin's skin, and his dick take notice. At least with his legs up, Niko wouldn't be able to tell the effect his voice alone had on Vin.

"And then I saw you."

Vin swallowed, his saliva thick as if he hadn't had any liquids in a year.

"Only I didn't know it was you. I saw you from behind when I was backstage. I noticed the confidence in your stance..."

Niko reached up and dusted a fingertip across the tattoo on Vin's left forearm—an intricate grid map and compass. "And the tattoos. And that ass."

Vin couldn't help the laugh that escaped. It felt good, having that release—and the thought that Niko liked his ass, that Niko found him attractive, made his chest tight with an emotion Vin couldn't quite describe.

Some silly combination of hope and lust.

But Niko didn't laugh. In fact, he didn't look amused at all. The lines around his eyes tightened. "I was curious, especially when Hatchett started bidding, so I returned to the ballroom."

"And then you saw it was me."

"I did." A frown tugged at the corners of Niko's lips, and Vin decided he didn't want to hear the rest.

"You know, maybe—"

Niko caught his arm again. "Stop. You asked. Let me answer."

One of these days, Vin would learn to leave well enough alone. When Joss had dumped him, he'd kept after Joss until he'd finally caved and told him why—that Joss couldn't love a man who was in love with someone else.

Vin hadn't known he'd been that transparent.

He hadn't liked what that had said about himself. That he'd been willing to settle for a man he knew he couldn't love with all his heart.

Joss hadn't been his first choice, and Joss had been right to break it off. A good man like him deserved to be someone's first choice.

But that reality hadn't made the breakup any easier on either one of them.

"When I realized it was you, I must admit, I saw you differently. But it felt wrong—no, it *is* wrong."

Vin didn't agree, but he wasn't going to stop Niko to argue the point. Not yet, anyway. "You still bid."

"Hatchett had upped his bid and—"

"So, the only reason you bid on me was because of some twisted competition between you and Hatchett to see which one of you had the bigger dick?"

"Fuck, Vin, it wasn't like that."

At the *oh come on* look Vin shot him, Niko raised a hand. "Okay, it was a little like that. You know I lose my mind a bit whenever that bastard is involved. But that wasn't the only reason."

Niko fell silent and, after a while, Vin made a rolling motion with his hand, encouraging Niko to continue.

"After Sebastian outed you about your crush on me, a part of me was curious about you and me. I know it's improper, but..." He waved a hand between the two of them. "I wanted to see how a night—or a day—would go. And the auction seemed like a logical way to do that without anyone questioning it."

"You're kidding me, right?"

"What?"

"I'm not sure if I'm flattered or insulted."

———

WHEN NIKO TRIED TO DEFEND HIMSELF, VIN CUT HIM OFF. "Basically, what you're saying is you were afraid what people would think if we went out."

"Yes. No. I mean..." Jesus Christ, he was fucking this up. He regretted making Vin finish this conversation. "You're right. We should go."

"Nuh, uh. Unless you plan on walking your ass back to the valley. I want to know what your issue is with being seen out with me."

"I've been out with you many times."

"Work lunches and dinners don't count. I mean a date."

"I'm old enough to be your father."

"But you're not, and that never stopped you from fucking guys younger than me. Try again."

Niko didn't know the last time he'd felt so cornered and vulnerable. He wasn't used to someone else having the upper hand, and it made him feel unbalanced and off-kilter, especially when he hadn't been able to come to terms with the truth himself. And he found it much more difficult articulating it to someone else.

Someone who had been a big part of his life for a decade.

"In my mind, you've always been off-limits. It's hard to flip that mental switch."

"Because you took me in as a kid. Because you helped me, mentored me."

Niko nodded. "Exactly. It's wrong. It's—"

"Did you want to fuck me? That night on the street corner when I approached your car."

"*What?* No. Of course not. You were just a kid—"

"I wasn't a kid. I was fifteen. What about during those couple of years I lived with you before I turned eighteen and moved out?"

"No." *This* answer, *this* truth, was easy.

Vin nodded as if they were finally getting somewhere. "When you saw me on the street that night, what did you see?"

"I saw a kid about to make a life-altering mistake, and I wanted to help you. Protect you. I'd met enough men who'd grown up on the streets and know too well how harsh that life can be."

"I get what you're saying. And I appreciate it." Vin's eyes softened, and that shy smile returned, the one that did all kinds of things to Niko's erotic imagination. Which showed exactly why starting anything with Vin was a bad idea. "I don't tell you that enough, how much it meant and still means to me that you were there for me when no one else was."

Which brought up reason number six-thousand and seven why *this* was a bad idea. Vin's crush? Nothing more than hero worship. Niko had been accused of being a bastard on more than one occasion, but it took a special kind of asshole to take advantage of a dynamic like that.

"I've got news for you, Niko." Vin leaned in as if what he had to say was a secret, that they weren't alone on a private beach with no one else around to hear their confessions. "I'm an adult. It's not up to you to protect me anymore. I'm free to make my own mistakes, and I'm mature enough to deal with the consequences. *Are you?*"

Niko didn't say anything, because he didn't have the answer.

A rogue wave slammed into the rock, hitting higher and harder than all the rest, splashing them with salt and sea spray, the frigid water drenching Niko's feet and ankles. Niko glanced around. The tide had come so far in, they'd have to wade in shin-deep water to make it back to dry land.

When Niko glanced back, Vin had shifted closer, his gaze darting to Niko's lips. Niko knew what was coming and should have told Vin to stop, or he should have at least put up a blocking hand, but he did neither.

The brush of Vin's lips on his had the blood roaring in Niko's ears, drowning out the surf. Though ill-advised, he rolled onto his back and welcomed it when Vin followed, taking the kiss deeper.

Vin tasted of roast beef and expensive cheese, and Niko couldn't get enough. He wrapped a hand around the back of Vin's neck and pulled him tighter into the kiss, their tongues fighting for dominance.

A fight Niko might lose.

Damn, that boy could kiss.

Boy.

Fuck.

Vin pulled back, and Niko took in the faint lines at the corners of Vin's eyes, at the growth of beard that definitely didn't belong to a boy. "Where did you go?"

"I'm here," Niko said as he pulled Vin back into the kiss. He'd allow himself this. This taste. But nothing more.

Vin's roaming hand found the exposed skin at the waistband

of Niko's jeans, where his shirt had ridden up. Vin wasn't tentative. His fingers skimmed along Niko's abdomen. Vin groaned, seeming to love the way Niko's muscles quivered at the touch.

And for the second time that day, as Niko grew hard behind his fly, he regretted not rubbing one out before Vin had picked him up. One of the drawbacks of having a big dick was how nearly impossible it was to hide when he was aroused.

Stop. Niko had to stop, but the fist of hair in his hand only encouraged Vin.

Vin settled on the rock on his side, kissing and nipping his way along Niko's jawline and down his neck to the pulse point that pounded harder than the surf.

A sharp edge of the rock dug into Niko's back, but he didn't care about that. All he cared about were Vin's lips on him and the slow descent of Vin's fingers toward the waistband of his jeans.

With minimal fumbling, Vin popped the fastener on Niko's pants and slid the zipper down. He loved the way Vin took charge, so much different than the other men he'd dated where Niko had been the more dominant one. In bed and otherwise. Something about letting Vin drive tripped Niko's erotic gears and made his dick ache for freedom.

Vin tossed a leg over Niko's, pinning him in place. Vin's cold feet made his warm fingers even more enticing.

Then Vin's hand landed over the triangle of Niko's exposed briefs and closed around the length of him. Vin swallowed Niko's groan, the chuckle a low reverberation in the back of Vin's throat as he seemed to enjoy every second of the sweet agony he was putting Niko through.

Niko thrust up into Vin's hand, his underwear already damp with pre-cum. Niko lifted his head, loving the sight of Vin's hand on him.

Vin nipped his chin and caught Niko's eye.

"You like watching my hand on your cock?"

Niko grinned. Vin liked a little dirty talk? Good to know. "Fuck yeah," Niko managed, his words coming out mangled and strangled.

Then Vin slipped his hands beneath the cotton fabric. Having that warm hand on his swollen dick made Niko's head fall back, and his eyes drift closed. Niko spread his legs wider, allowing as much access as the confines of his clothing allowed.

"*Christ*," Vin muttered as he stroked Niko from root to tip. "I'm glad I'm the kind of guy that likes a beefy butt plug. Otherwise, this might be a challenge."

Niko found skin beneath the hem of Vin's shirt. The thought of Vin stripping Niko's pants to his knees and sliding down on his dick under the open sky in a cove where anyone who took the path down could watch made Niko that much harder.

Then Vin took hold of the waistband of Niko's jeans and hauled them down to his knees, his cock springing free and pointing at the sky.

Which would have been a perfect place to stop Vin before things got entirely out of hand. Niko had been down for the kiss, but he hadn't seen this coming.

Seriously? Who are you trying to kid? He has a crush *on you, and you didn't see this coming? Had no clue that things would escalate? And—*

"Fucking hell." Niko sucked in a ragged breath as Vin went down on him. All firm lips and teasing tongue, driving Niko mad.

He rose on his elbows and stared down at the sight of Vin bobbing up and down on his cock, like Niko's personal porno reel, only this one wasn't in his imagination.

His hand went to the back of Vin's head, holding him there even as his balls drew up, and the base of his spine tingled.

Vin had just started, and Niko wasn't going to last.

You'd think he'd never been sucked off before.

Other men had been more skilled, some more practiced, but none as enthusiastic as Vin.

Vin pulled off, his hand taking over where his mouth left off. "Christ, I love your cock."

Vin set a punishing rhythm with his hand. Niko's eyes crossed, and all coherent thought ceased. All Niko could do was go with it, his hips pumping, the groans scraping up the back of his throat.

Then Vin dove back in, taking Niko deep, deep, deep to the back of his throat.

"I'm going to come." Niko tried to pull him off.

Instead of turning Niko loose, Vin doubled down on his efforts, and Niko was taken away by the sight and the sounds of his dick in Vin's mouth combined with the roar of the sea and the cry of the gulls overhead.

He'd never be able to listen to one of those nighttime nature apps again without getting hard.

Vin cupped Niko's balls, and he lost his load as the orgasm hit, Vin sucking and slurping and swallowing him down.

Holy fuck.

Niko was pretty sure he saw a white light as his soul left his body for a fraction of a second. Vin released him, nipping and tasting the tender skin around Niko's groin, a soft laugh escaping him when he saw how hard Niko panted.

Vin worked his way up Niko's body, hand over hand, until he was on all fours over Niko, his legs straddling Niko's hips, his hands by Niko's head.

Vin went in for another kiss, and Niko tasted the saltiness of himself on Vin's tongue. He didn't want Vin to stop. Ever.

What had Vin done to him?

Breaking the kiss, Vin traced the shell of Niko's ear with his tongue, his breath warm on Niko's skin when he said, "Ever since that first night when you pulled your car over and you offered a hot meal instead of accepting a blowjob, I've wanted to fuck you. You would have been my first but—"

Niko shoved Vin away.

This is wrong, this is wrong.

"What the fuck?" Vin's brows drew together, and the red rushing up Vin's face Niko read as anger, not embarrassment.

"You need to take me home. This was a mistake. We'll forget this happened, yeah? Monday morning at work, we'll go about our lives like we had before. No harm, no foul."

Vin stood, and the fact that he had to adjust himself wasn't lost on Niko. Vin didn't say a word, he just packed up the last of the stuff, jumped off the rock into the now knee-deep water, and trudged up the shoreline toward his boots and socks.

"Look, Vin..."

But Vin didn't look. He put his boots on, shouldered into his motorcycle jacket and strapped on his helmet. He started the bike, and Niko scrambled into his gear, half afraid Vin would leave him there if he didn't hurry.

"Would you say something?" Niko said into the comms as he threw his leg over the bike.

"There's a strap on the back of the seat. I suggest you hang on to that."

Niko only had one hand on the strap when Vin popped the clutch, and the bike lurched forward.

"Fucking hell." Niko clutched at anything he could to keep himself from coming off the back.

Niko thought he heard an evil chuckle, but that was probably just his imagination.

The ride back to the studio proved hair raising and eye-opening. Niko didn't think he'd ever seen Vin that pissed. And there was no other way to describe the emotion, with the way

Vin cut through traffic, shifting and braking and dodging cars as anything but a bad temper.

This disaster was his fault. He should have stopped Vin before their lips even touched. What the hell had he been thinking?

That you wanted to get laid?

Fuck.

And shoving him off you like he was radioactive? Smooth move.

On the ride back, Niko almost shouted out several times, but he refused to give Vin the satisfaction of knowing he'd scared him. The harrowing drive home turned out to be more death-defying than jumping out of Joss's plane.

Vin skid to a stop in Niko's drive, not bothering to kill the engine. Niko hopped off, his knees wobbly and weak.

He removed his helmet and slipped out of the motorcycle jacket. "Can we talk about this?"

Vin flipped up his visor. "I'm not going to beg. Some guys might be into the humiliation thing, but that's not my kink."

For a nanosecond, that idiotic part of Niko's brain wondered what Vin's kinks were. He shook his head and rattled that thought loose.

"Look, I'm sorry. It's just..." Niko motioned between him and Vin. "This can't work."

Vin nodded. "Yeah. I got that. Hard for it to work when I'm good enough to blow you but not good enough to date."

"That's not—"

Vin flipped down his visor and blipped his engine, effectively cutting off communication. He left Niko standing in his driveway with nothing but the borrowed gear and a building, blinding headache.

5

———

Early Monday morning, Vin stood in the studio and checked one of his cameras for the upcoming shoot. The sound of approaching footsteps made the knot in his stomach twist tighter until it felt like the coffee he'd drunk that morning tossed and rolled. If Christopher Columbus had encountered seas that turbulent, he would have turned around.

Christopher Columbus.

Vin figured having Christopher Columbus on the brain was what happened when you downloaded the thickest biography you could find to keep your mind off having to face the boss you'd blown two days before.

Besides a few fun facts about ol' Chris, like that his father was a wool weaver and Chris and crew brought back syphilis to the old world, the only thing the biography had done for him was make him tired. He certainly hadn't gotten any sleep, and he damn well hadn't forgotten that he had to face Niko bright and early this morning.

Fuck, this is going to suck.

You're the Einstein who said you were an adult. Pull your big boy jockstrap up and fucking act like the man you proclaimed to be right before you started sucking off your boss.

A hand clapped Vin on the shoulder, and he jumped, already so far up in his head he'd forgotten he'd heard someone coming.

"So," Sebastian said, his smile wide and his eyes lit with benevolent mischief. "How was the date?"

Vin tossed the tiny screwdriver back on the worktable. "It sucked."

A strangled chuckle, then a cough, came from the hall. Vin glanced up, expecting to see Niko, but only heard retreating footsteps.

"Nooo." Sebastian dropped down into Niko's director's chair. "What happened?"

"Nothing."

"Yeah. Wanna try that again? Maybe with a little more conviction and a lot less woe, and I'll believe you this time. Promise."

"There's not much to say. I picked him up. We went skydiving. We survived. I brought him home. What did you expect? Wedding bells and Niko's declaration of undying love?"

Sebastian's face fell, and he looked like he almost felt as disappointed as Vin did. "I just thought—"

"Yeah, well..." Vin shrugged, wanting to change the subject. He hadn't lied to Niko when he said he wouldn't beg. He'd spent enough time working on himself, on building up his self-esteem, to know better than give Niko the power to shred it.

"What was the name of that dating app you used to use?" Vin asked.

"*HotDix.* It's between Grindr and Recon on the kink scale." Sebastian's grin returned. "It's awesome."

Sebastian pulled out his phone and paged over to the app,

clicked on the icon, and started flipping through the profiles to introduce Vin to the app.

"What's that mean?" Vin pointed at the red heart on multiple pages that Sebastian swiped through.

"That means you've 'favorited' them. You know, like you wanna hook up."

"Wait." Vin took the phone out of Sebastian's hand and looked closer. "You favorited this guy yesterday. This one, too."

"So?"

"You just moved in with Grant, and—"

Sebastian leaned in, though they were alone. "We're trying to set up a threesome. You know, for kicks."

Here Vin couldn't even find *one* guy. And Sebastian had one of the best guys, and they were looking for another. "Of course you are."

And damn, if his tone didn't sound as dejected and jealous as Vin felt.

Sebastian bumped Vin with his shoulder. "I'm sorry it didn't work out for you two."

Vin considered cracking a joke or acting as if it were no big deal, but he couldn't muster up the effort to do it. Along with Cat, Black Stallion's makeup artist, Sebastian, was one of his best friends. If Vin couldn't be real with Sebastian, who could he be real with? "Yeah, me too."

"What about Joss? You had to have seen him when—"

"Tell you what." Vin did his best to keep the bitterness out of his voice. "You worry about you and Grant and your lucky third, and let me worry about me, cool?"

"Yeah, sure, I didn't mean—"

"Where the hell is everybody?" Niko came into the studio on a tear, the frenetic energy wafting off him would be enough to disrupt satellite signals for three counties.

"Up in the residence," Sebastian said. "I sent them up to—"

"Well, get them down here. We should have been shooting ten minutes ago."

This is going to be such *a fun day.*

Sebastian stepped in front of Niko, making him draw up short. Niko hadn't even glanced Vin's way yet. "What kind of dick thing did you do to Vin?"

Niko glanced over Sebastian's shoulder at Vin, the *what did you tell him?* clear on his face.

Vin hadn't wanted to get into it with Sebastian, so he certainly didn't want to get into it with Sebastian and Niko. Besides, he'd told Niko he didn't need protecting.

Vin grabbed Sebastian's upper arm. "Bass, leave it."

Sebastian glanced between Vin and Niko and swallowed whatever he'd been prepared to say. Then he shook his head as if he'd thought better of it and met Niko's gaze head-on. "If you ask me, you're passing up a good thing."

"Bass," Niko and Vin said at the same time. At least they agreed on one thing. They both wanted Sebastian to shut up.

———

On a break between the first and second shoot, Niko sat in his director's chair and flipped through some notes and tried not to feel like the total douche bag he'd been to Vin on Saturday.

He needed to get Vin alone and clear the air. The tension in the studio put everyone on edge, and it was Niko's fault for being the cause of that uneasy environment. Talent flocked to Black Stallion because of the fun they had before and after shoots and how well they treated their people.

This... This shit show? No one had signed up for that.

Niko stood and caught Vin's arm as he walked by. "Hey."

Vin stared down at Niko's hand. Vin didn't shake him off, but the inclination to do so was clear. "You have a few minutes to meet me in my office at the end of the day?"

"I've got plans... with a friend."

"It will only take a minute. Besides, I need to get the helmet and jacket back to you."

"You could have brought them to the studio."

"I could have." But they both knew that making Vin go to the office to get them would give Niko the opportunity to get Vin alone.

"Yeah. Sure. Whatever." Vin started backing away. "You're the boss, right?"

He was, but this had nothing to do with work, and Vin damn well knew it.

Congratulations, Stavros. You really know how to fuck up a good thing.

Which was exactly what he'd been trying to avoid. Even considering all the other valid reasons why he shouldn't date Vin, being his boss and still having to work with him day in and day out if things went sideways, wasn't something he'd wanted to risk. Vin was the best cameraman Black Stallion had ever had. He didn't want to fuck that up.

Too bad you already have.

"Niko."

Niko turned to see Sebastian walking his way with a little old lady. He glanced around, making sure all the talent had their robes on. The set of a gay porn studio wasn't exactly the kind of place you brought your grandmother to. Except this wasn't Sebastian's grandmother.

This was Grant's.

How had he forgotten that Sebastian was trying to force her on him so that she could take Sebastian's place for the Bahama shoot?

It wouldn't work. And he needed to come right out and tell

Sebastian that before things got out of control.

Sebastian held the woman's hand in the crook of his arm. "Niko, you remember Grant's grandmother, Betty."

Niko shook the frail hand. How was this woman going to replace Sebastian? She would probably need a nap or a place to sit and rest before they got through the next scene. "Nice to see you again. I have to say, Ms. Hardy, I have reservations—"

She patted the hand she still held in her own. "I know you do, dear. That's why Sebastian invited me here for the day. I can get my feet wet and show you I can do this. I may be an old lady, but I'm not in the grave yet."

"No, ma'am, you certainly aren't." Niko admired her spunk.

"And don't ma'am me. Call me Betty or Nana B."

"Yes, ma'am." When Betty gave him the side-eye, he amended, "I mean, Betty."

She patted his hand again and let go.

Then Chet, one of the newer talents—a Southern-fried, stocky cowboy—approached in a skin-tight pair of white pants with a giant rip in the crotch. "We have a problem."

He pointed to his crotch, which wasn't necessary, since his bright-red, jock-covered bulge lay exposed through the tear, making the problem self-evident.

"First, my girlfriend decided she didn't want to move in with me," Chet said, "and now this. Nothing is going right today."

Tell him about it. Niko hadn't wanted his first interaction with Vin to be so fraught either. Looked like they were both off to a shitty start.

"We'll have to find him something else in wardrobe," Niko said. "Get with Cat and—"

"There's nothing else in wardrobe that's going to fit him," Sebastian said. "With his short inseam, we had to have those pants custom made just for him."

"Then get Cat to sew them back together. We'll do the other scene first."

Cat, his makeup artist who also served as his wardrobe manager, walked in. "Someone talking about me?"

One of the advantages of the high ceilings and partial walls was that voices traveled through the studio. Cat got a good look at Chet's crotch and laughed. "Yeah. I can't fix that. We could put him in athletic shorts."

Niko could see the day going to hell already. "He's supposed to be a stripper. Shorts aren't going to cut it."

"I can fix it." Betty wedged her way to the front and got eyeball-to-crotch with the problem. "It may take me a few minutes, but it shouldn't be a problem."

She reached into a purse that was half her size and dug around until she came up with a wallet-sized sewing kit.

"You have a sewing kit in your purse?" Cat's grin widened, and the piercing in her left brow went up. "You are the bomb, Nana B."

"Off with them," Betty said. "Unless you want me to fix them with you still in them."

Chet slapped a protective hand over his crotch. "No. I'll take them off." He hitched his thumb over his shoulder. "I'll go change and—"

"No one has time for that, dear." Betty clapped her hands. "Chop, chop, off with them."

Chet looked from Niko to Sebastian to Cat, who looked like she was about to bust a gut from keeping the laugh contained.

Then Betty leaned in, and in a terrible stage whisper said, "Honey, you ain't got nothing I haven't seen before, and if you do, I wanna see it."

Niko couldn't hold the laugh in, and some of the tension he'd been holding onto throughout the weekend evaporated. Niko bobbed his chin at Chet. "Go on. Do what the lady says."

With a shrug and his own grin, Chet shucked his pants and handed them over. Betty took the pants, her purse, and the sewing kit to the back table where Sebastian found her a chair and a task light.

Niko turned to where Vin had been setting up the lights for the scene and directed him to the next set over. They'd get a different scene done and then go back and do Chet's after lunch.

———

AT THE END OF THE DAY, NIKO PLOPPED DOWN IN HIS CHAIR AND scrubbed his hands down his face. He needed sleep and a beer.

Not necessarily in that order.

Vin packed away his cameras for the night, and Sebastian was going over a few things with the talent concerning the scenes they were going to shoot the next day. They were a tad behind on the production schedule, and with them leaving for the Bahamas on Thursday, they had a lot to get done between now and then.

Chet sat down next to him after showering and changing back into his street clothes, a smile on his face that hadn't been there before.

"You're in a good mood." At least one of their days had improved. Niko still had the talk with Vin ahead of him, and from the way Vin had been avoiding him all day, he didn't hold out much hope that it would go well.

"My girlfriend agreed to sit down and talk to me about moving in. I thought I'd blown it, but Nana B had me—"

"Nana B?"

"Oh, man. I love that lady. I wish she were my grandmother. Wicked smart. Funny as hell. And she knew just what I needed to say to Victoria to get her to agree to talk with me."

"I hope it all works out."

"Thanks."

Sebastian and Betty came down the back hall. That woman had more fire and energy than everyone else in the studio combined, and not only had she saved the day with the wardrobe mishap, she'd sorted a catering issue while Sebastian had been out of the studio working on some last-minute things for the Bahamas, as well as helping Chet sort out his private life.

"We're calling it a day unless you had anything else for us," Sebastian said.

"No. We're good here." Niko stood and turned his attention to Betty. "Thanks for the help today. I know it's asking a lot to have you dropped into the middle of production like this, but you handled it beautifully, and if you still want to fill in for Sebastian while we're gone. I'd be grateful to have you along."

Sebastian nudged Betty with his elbow. "Told you he'd love you."

"I'm so excited to help, dear. It makes an old woman's heart happy to know that she's needed."

"If Sebastian's not careful, you may work him right out of a job before he's ready."

"*Hey*," Sebastian groused, though humor lit in his eyes. "I'm standing right here."

"I plan to be here the next couple days if that's okay with you," Betty said. "I want to learn as much as I can about my duties before we leave."

Niko leaned in and kissed her cheek. "That would be great. I really appreciate it. Now you guys go on. It's late, and tomorrow is going to come early."

They said their goodbyes, all the while Niko kept his eye on Vin, who'd busied himself by setting the lighting up for the first scene the next morning.

Niko gathered up his iPad and started heading toward his

office. He stopped at the base of the stairs and turned back to Vin. "You coming?"

Vin stopped fiddling with the Fresnel light and hung his head. Straightening, he refused to face Niko. "I'll be there. Give me a minute."

THAT MINUTE VIN WANTED, TURNED INTO A LOT MORE, SPENDING most of it in the back hallway debating whether or not he was going to comply with Niko's request, or leave and hit his favorite bar on the way home.

It wasn't like he needed to return the motorcycle jacket he'd borrowed from his friend that night. Another day or two wouldn't matter, not with his friend's bike in the shop for the foreseeable future after laying it down while coming into a corner too hot and too tight.

Frankly, his friend was lucky to be alive.

So are you.

If Niko hadn't taken you in, your life would be so much different. Most likely, unrecognizable. Are you seriously going to hold it against him that he doesn't want a romantic relationship with you? No matter Niko's reason, you being butt-hurt is fucked up.

Still didn't take away the sting of rejection. Vin had gone for it. He'd gotten shot down. Now all he wanted was some space to lick his wounds and recover.

Which was hard to do when he had to face Niko for twelve or more hours every day.

When Vin finally turned into Niko's open office, twenty minutes had passed.

"There you are." Niko stood and came around his desk and sat on its front edge. "I thought you weren't going to show."

"Almost didn't."

Vin reached for the helmet and jacket only to be stopped by a hand on his arm.

"We need to talk."

"Actually… we don't. You got your point across loud and clear." He picked up the gear only to have Niko strip it out of his hands and drop it back on the floor.

"Listen to me."

Vin stepped into Niko's personal space, tapping Niko's chest with the tip of his index finger. "Unless this is work-related, I don't answer to you anymore. Like I've said before, I'm not a kid. I'm a grown man with full autonomy. I don't have to listen to you or anyone else."

The fact that Vin sounded like a bratty kid wasn't lost on him. He would have laughed if he could find any humor in the situation. One of these days maybe, but not today.

"Jesus Christ, Vin. Would you cut me some slack? I want to apologize."

Vin took a step back. He didn't want an apology. He wanted Niko. But that wasn't going to happen so… "Great. Apology accepted. Can I go home now, *boss*?"

"Look, if things were different—"

Vin held up a hand to shut him up, knowing that if Niko finished that sentence, it would only make him hurt worse, not less. Especially when Vin knew that there was nothing he could do to change Niko's mind. Time to move on. Plenty of other men out there.

All he had to do was step into a leather bar, and he'd have all the dick he could ever want.

Except you don't want all *the dicks. You want Niko's dick.*

And God help him, having had Niko in his mouth, only made him want him more.

"You wanted us to start out today fresh. Okay." Vin held out his hand to shake. "Fresh start. All we had was a date. Nothing more. Right?"

Niko eyed Vin's hand before clasping it and giving it a shake. "Right."

Vin couldn't do anything about the skepticism in Niko's eye, all he could do was put Niko and that glorious dick out of his mind.

For good.

6

Niko had been up most of Wednesday night, packing the last of his things for the Bahamas, and had fallen asleep on the couch in his clothes.

Now he had to scramble to catch his flight.

He rounded up his belongings out of the bins after clearing TSA and hot-footed it to his gate. His phone pinged as he neared the gate.

Betty: *Everyone is here. Five minutes to boarding.*

He punched in his response: *Almost there.*

"I'm telling you, forget about him." The voice belonged to Cat, who had to be just around the corner.

Niko should have kept walking, but he leaned against the wall to eavesdrop. Not a proud moment.

"All you need to do is find another hot dick to jump on. Trust me," Cat said with a self-deprecating laugh. "Been there. Done that. Nothing like the next cock to help you forget the one you can't have."

"I don't know."

And damn if that wasn't Vin. He'd hoped Cat was talking to someone else, but Niko's luck wasn't running that way.

"I do. And this trip... you are going to have an amazing time if you let yourself. All the hot men in bathing suits oiled up and laying out on the beach and at the pool. What's not to love? You just have to put yourself out there."

"Sure."

Vin hadn't sounded that defeated since shortly after Niko had taken him in. That Niko was the cause of Vin sounding so down, made him feel like a heartless asshole. He'd never wanted to hurt Vin. In fact, that's why he'd pushed him away, to begin with. Nothing good would come of them getting together, better to not start anything, and let Vin live with that rejection than start something that would only fall apart later.

"Besides," Cat said, "have you seen the two older guys? Hayes and Greer? Holy hell. I'd bang them, and I'm not into the daddy thing either."

"They're straight."

"You sure about that? Black Stallion hasn't exactly been batting a thousand on the straight guy talent lately, and I'm getting a bi vibe from Greer."

Vin laughed as the attendant called their flight. It was good to hear Vin laugh. It was going to be okay. *Vin* was going to be okay.

"Don't worry about me, Cat. I can find my own men, but I appreciate the concern."

Niko backed away from the wall and waited half a minute before coming around the corner.

Betty ran up to him, waving a ticket in her hand.

"What's this?"

"New seating assignment." Betty looked like she could hardly control her excitement. She leaned in and lowered her voice. "I know you and Vin are having some problems, and well..."

"What?" The floor dropped out from beneath Niko's stomach. What had she done?

"I was able to get Vin upgraded to first class for no charge, and they seated both of you together. Now you can work things out between you two on the flight."

"You shouldn't have." *Really*, shouldn't have.

But maybe, if that was the only way he could have Vin to himself for half a minute, it wouldn't be so bad. As much as Vin said, things would go back to normal, they hadn't. And if a person who'd just joined Black Stallion could tell something was off between them, then no doubt everyone else knew there was a problem as well.

Betty reached up and patted his cheek. "It's really no problem, dear. Happy to do it."

They stood in line to board, Vin at the back of a line with Cat, when he should have been in the priority line with Niko.

NIKO STRODE DOWN THE JETWAY, DETERMINED THAT THIS FLIGHT would be the turning point in getting his and Vin's working relationship back on kilter. This kind of thing was exactly why Niko had a personal rule of not playing in his own sandbox where work and dating were concerned.

He stowed his briefcase above his aisle seat and settled into his business-class accommodation and waited. It wouldn't be long now before he had Vin as a captive audience, and they could settle this once and for all.

Vin and Cat came down the aisle, talking between themselves. Vin glanced at his ticket and then at the overhead numbers, and Niko watched as the realization sunk in that he'd be trapped between Niko and the window with no escape.

The smile fell from his face, and his body visibly stiffened.

The line of passengers had come to a stop one seat away from Niko, and Vin swiped the ticket out of Cat's hand and replaced it with his.

"What's that for?" Cat asked.

"First-class living for a first-class gal."

Vin's tone sounded light, but Niko had known him long enough to discern the underlying tension. Niko had really fucked up badly if Vin refused a first-class flight across the country if it meant he didn't have to sit with Niko.

"Sweet!" Cat grinned and stood up on her toes and gave Vin a peck on the cheek. When the line advanced, she scrambled over the top of Niko before he even had the chance to stand and let her in. "This is going to be amazing."

Yeah... amazing.

He glanced up at Vin, but Vin had already put his headphones in his ears and focused his attention down the aisle, shutting Niko out.

After all the passengers were seated, the safety instructions given, and they'd pushed away from the gate, Niko turned in his seat and searched the rear of the main cabin. He found Vin in an aisle seat near the back of the plane next to Greer, a burly black man, new to Black Stallion, but well known and sought after in the industry.

Greer leaned into Vin and said something that made Vin throw his head back and laugh. Vin's eyes flicked to the front of the plane as if he'd felt Niko's eyes on him, and that laugh died on his lips.

Niko turned back and faced the front.

"Dude," Cat said, her voice carrying even as the engines revved for takeoff. "I don't know what you did to Vin, but you need to unscrew that pooch."

But that was the problem, wasn't it? He didn't know how to fix things. And despite all the reasons why they shouldn't, couldn't, wouldn't be together, it hadn't stopped Niko from jacking off every night to the memory of that day on the rock and that mind-numbing blowjob.

———

Their flight landed in Nassau, and their entire trip was someone's comic version of *Planes, Trains, and Automobiles*, but with boats instead of trains since their private resort was located on a small, neighboring cay.

Between the cameras and lighting equipment, luggage, and the Black Stallion crew, they'd filled up their chartered water taxis.

As the boat pulled away from the dock, Vin settled into one of the bench seats at the back beside the hum and whine of the engine. Cat scrambled to the rear on unsteady legs, the sun highlighting the red undertones in her brunette hair as they crossed a boat wake. Vin caught her hand and scooted over to make room for her next to him.

"Thanks for your seat on the flight." She'd leaned in, but she still had to talk loudly for him to hear her over the drone of the engine. "It was fucking amazing. I've never flown first-class before."

"Trust me, you did me a favor."

"You and Greer looked like you were getting cozy."

Vin rolled his eyes. "He's a good guy..."

But he's not Niko.

The unsaid 'but' hung in the air between them.

Vin didn't voice his thought, the empathetic look Cat sent him told him he didn't need too. "The flight gave me time to think. I've been acting childish and immature. Niko doesn't want me. I may not agree with his reasons, but they're his reasons, and I have to respect that and move on."

"Sebastian chartered one of these water taxis for the week." She had to raise her voice even higher as they cleared the no-wake zone, and the captain laid on the throttle.

Between the engine and the wind noise, he didn't fear anyone would overhear. Besides, no one was paying them any attention, except Niko, and unless he'd taken up lip-reading, Vin wasn't concerned.

"We have the boat at our disposal 24/7," she said. "With Nassau only a twenty-minute boat ride away, I'm sure there is plenty of fresh dick you can get there any night of the week."

Even though he wasn't at the point of wanting any dick other than the one he'd had in his hand and his mouth at the beach, Vin had to laugh. Cat wasn't wrong. If he said that in a weak moment that he hadn't done a quick check for guys looking to hook up on Nassau on the *HotDix* app, he'd be lying.

The boat bounced through another wake, and Vin wiped the warm, salty sea spray off his face and carved out a semblance of a smile. What was that saying? Fake it till you make it?

As they pulled up to the resort's dock, Vin decided that saying would be his new mantra. And if that meant availing himself of some of the hot guys on the islands, he'd do that—or *them*—too.

———

They all stood in the lobby of the resort, their gear and luggage on carts in a corner while Betty checked in for the group and sorted through the room assignments, her head barely higher than the counter.

She turned with a smile and a stack of keycards in her hand and started passing them out.

Vin's stomach rolled over and growled. Time for dinner and a few drinks to unwind before their long week started.

Cat dropped her backpack onto the luggage cart next to Rose's suitcase and glanced around the large foyer. "What is this place, anyway?"

"Sebastian said it used to belong to some real estate mogul who lost his ass when the market crashed in '08. He'd bought the private island and had the mansion, the pool, and the chef's kitchen built to wine and dine his associates."

"So why shoot here and not somewhere in Nassau? There are plenty of resorts and beaches there."

"Niko wanted to be able to shoot outdoors and on the beach without having to deal with someone seeing what we're shooting and risk shutting us down. Out here, it's just us and the employees at the resort we have to contend with."

"So, I could sunbathe in the nude on the beach on my off time, and no one would care?" Cat asked with a gleam in her eye.

Vin held out his hands in an 'it's up to you' motion. "I won't get between you and a tan-line free body."

"Sweet," Cat said, "I always wanted to lay naked on a beach."

Vin grinned at her. "Pretty sure it's not as amazing as it sounds. All that sand in cracks and creases and crevices." He pretended to shudder. "No, thanks."

She bumped him with her shoulder and dropped her voice. "You mean to tell me if Niko had wanted to get naked with you on the beach back in California, you would have turned him down?"

She had a point, and as much as he tried to put that moment behind him, he loved how she didn't treat Vin's encounter with Niko like a death that shouldn't be spoken about, but a crazy thing he did that should be celebrated and not given more weight than it deserved.

Millions of people got shut down every night of the week. Vin was no exception. You live, you grow, you move the fuck on.

Rose came over and handed Cat the keycard she'd gotten from Betty. Rose was somewhere in her late fifties if her gray hair was any indication and was Black Stallion's resident mother and overall talent wrangler. If they had a problem, they went to her.

"Cocktails in our room in fifteen. Niko sprung for open mini bars," Rose said.

Vin stacked his own suitcase onto the cart with the cameras and lighting equipment. "Sure, I just need to find the storage locker to dump all the gear, go up and change, and I'll be over."

Cat stopped her cart by Vin. "Need help?"

Vin could use some time alone, as well as the physical exertion of packing the gear away to finish getting his mind right. Besides, he was a mother bear about his equipment. "Naw, I've got it. Thanks."

"Room 201. Don't be late, or we may run out of booze."

"I'll consider myself forewarned." Vin made his way to the front desk and had the receptionist find someone with the storage room key.

By the time he'd dropped all the gear, he'd surpassed the fifteen-minute mark, but Vin wasn't too keen on drinking the night away anyway. He had to be up early with Niko to scout locations. Facing his crush sober would be bad enough. Having to face Niko hungover, with a pounding head and rolling stomach, wasn't something Vin wanted to contemplate.

Vin took the elevator to his room on the fourth floor and touched his keycard to the key reader. When the light turned green, he turned the handle and opened the door, flicking on the overhead light as he passed.

He stopped in the middle of the room, dropping the handle on his suitcase and letting his backpack slide off his shoulders and hit the floor.

There had to be some sort of mistake.

This couldn't be his room.

He stood in some sort of master suite. Across from him lay a wall of windows that led out to a balcony and the breathtaking view of the Caribbean Sea beyond.

The waves rolled in and crashed on the beach one after the other. Even with the French doors closed, he could hear the roar of the surf.

Maybe Niko had felt so bad about the blowjob on the beach incident that he'd given—

A toilet flushed, and Vin glanced around the room, noticing for the first time a briefcase lying on the bed and the suitcase on a luggage rack in the open closet.

Shit. He was in someone else's room.

He grabbed his backpack and his suitcase and started backing toward the door as Niko came out of the bathroom in nothing but the jeans he'd worn on the plane.

Niko stopped short, his hands going to his open fly to button and zip up.

Vin held up his keycard. "Must have been a mix-up."

Niko took the sight of Vin in, one long, slow scan from head to foot. He opened his mouth, but by the expression on his face, whatever was about to come out wasn't about the screwup with the rooms, and Vin didn't have the mental bandwidth after the long travel day to go *there.*

Taking a step back, Vin said, "I'll go downstairs and get my room sorted."

"Take a load off." Niko gestured toward the sofa facing the water and reached for the phone on the table beside the king-sized bed. "I'll call Betty and let her sort it out."

"I can do it. There's no point in disturbing her." Betty had to be as tired from the trip as the rest of them. Besides, if Vin hung around waiting for Betty to show up, it would be that much longer that he had to be alone in the suite with Niko.

"Sit." Niko wasn't asking.

Vin sat, and Niko called the front desk and had them connect him to Betty's room. The conversation took mere seconds, and then Niko hung up. "She's on her way up."

Niko came around the bed and sat on the arm of the sofa opposite Vin. Vin stood and escaped to the French doors pretending to be engrossed in the view beyond.

"Look." Niko's voice came out low and intimate. Even though he was halfway across the room, goosebumps erupted on Vin's skin as if Niko had come up behind him and whispered in his ear. "We don't need to make this awkward. We're going to be seeing a lot of each other this next week. Even more than we normally do."

Yeah, Niko really didn't have to point that out, especially when that tidbit of information had kept Vin up and sleepless for the past few nights.

I'm going to be mature. Vin shoved his hands in his pockets and turned around. "It's fine. You and me... it's all good."

Saying that out loud to Niko almost made it seem real and true. Niko's frown disappeared, the furrow between his brows relaxed, and the subtle grin that slowly spread across Niko's face felt like a slap to the heart. Niko had no idea how devastating that smile was when it went all the way to his eyes. "Yeah?"

Vin was *so* fucked.

But he pushed that thought way down and held on tight to his newfound maturity. "Yeah."

Vin jumped at the knock on the door, and Niko went to answer. Betty followed him into the room, a keycard in her hand.

"I'm so sorry," Betty said as she handed a keycard to Vin. "I'm not sure where the mix up was. If you'll give me just a few minutes to repack my suitcase, I'll be out of—"

"Wait. This key for your room?" asked Vin, holding up the card.

"Well... I..." Betty's shoulders slumped, and though she put on a good front, she couldn't hide the exhaustion. "Yes, because you were supposed to room with Sebastian, so I put you in with Niko instead. But you take it, dear. There are no other rooms. I'll just call down to the front desk and have them bring a cot to Rose and Cat's room. It will be fine."

Vin glanced over at Niko. He couldn't kick an old lady out of her room. "No. You stay put. I'll bunk with Greer and—"

Niko scowled, crossing his arms over his chest. "Those other rooms are too small for three people."

What the hell was Vin supposed to do with that? He turned his attention back to Betty. At this point, he didn't care where he slept as long as he found a corner to curl up in. "We can be roomies," he said to Betty. "I promise I'm housebroken."

"You're a sweet boy," Betty said as she patted his arm. "I'd love the company."

"He stays here." Though the words came out of Niko's mouth, he didn't look pleased that they had. The furrow between his brows deepened again, and a vein ticked at his temple.

"I really don't mind," Betty said.

Niko crossed his arms over his chest. "I've got more room."

Which technically was correct if he based the statement strictly on a square footage basis, but Vin and Sebastian were supposed to share a room, so he knew the other rooms had two beds. All the suite had was a king-size bed and the couch.

"I'm sorry," Betty said again.

Niko's face softened, and he put his arm around her shoulder as he led her to the door. "None of this is your fault. Go back to your room, put your feet up, and relax. I'll see you down at dinner at seven."

"Look on the bright side, sweetie," Betty said as Niko opened the door. "Maybe this will be for the best."

"Perhaps," was all Niko managed before he closed the door behind Betty and leaned back against it, scrubbing his face with his hands. At that moment, Niko looked more than his years.

"Fucking Sebastian," Niko muttered as he walked back into the room.

"It's not his fault."

Niko sent Vin a look that said, *seriously?* Okay. Technically it *was* Sebastian's fault.

"Sebastian had a lot on his mind, Niko. I think with everything going on between the fundraiser, planning this shoot from four thousand miles away, and working on becoming a foster parent, he had a lot on his plate. If all we are is short one bed, I think we can call the shoot a success."

Unconvinced, Niko whipped out his phone and scrolled through his contact list and hit the call button, putting the phone to his ear.

"Who are you calling?" Like Vin didn't know the answer to that.

Before Niko could respond, Vin swiped the phone from his hand.

"Hello? Hello?" Sebastian's voice sounded tinny and far away.

Vin answered. The look he shot Niko dared him to take the phone back. "Hey, it's Vin."

"What's wrong?" The apprehension in Sebastian's voice rang clear through the miles.

"Nothing. Niko wanted me to call and let you know we all got here safe."

"Oh. Okay. For a minute there…" Sebastian let the rest of the sentence drop. Vin knew how much Sebastian hated to disappoint his uncle. "How's Betty?"

"She's good. Hey, Bass, I'm going to let you go. We're tired and hungry, but Niko wanted to touch base."

Sebastian hesitated. Vin heard the unasked question. If Niko had wanted to touch base so badly, why hadn't *he* been the one to call?

They said their goodbyes, and Vin hung up and dropped Niko's phone on the foot of the bed.

Niko had wandered over to check out the view while Vin talked. Niko glanced back at Vin. "Why'd you do that?"

"What did you expect Sebastian to do from California? It's not like he could magically add an additional room. All that call would have done was make him worry and fret. We handled it. There's no need for that."

Niko leaned against the French doors, the animus falling away. "You're right. All we can do is make the best of it."

Vin grabbed his suitcase and rolled it over to the dresser. "Mind if I use the bottom drawer?"

"No. Take it. And whatever closet space you need."

"The drawer's fine. I don't need to hang my Speedos."

Something dark like desire flicked across Niko's eyes before he glanced away. If Niko couldn't scrub the image of Vin in a Speedo out of his head, could Vin really be faulted?

Niko removed his briefcase from the bed and placed it in the closet. "You can have the bed."

Vin straightened and glanced over his shoulder at the bed that was plenty big enough for them both. That Niko hadn't offered to share—even in a platonic sense—told Vin everything he already knew.

"That's okay. It's not like I've never slept on your couch before."

7

———

"And then I said, 'That's okay. It's not like I've never slept on your couch before.'"

Vin sat propped up against the headboard beside Cat, a sea of baby liquor bottles bobbed in the waves of wrinkles on the crumpled bedspread. Which is what happened when you said to hell with staying sober and swiped all the booze out of the minibar and trudged downstairs and barged into your friend's room.

After seeing Vin's face and the armful of booze, Rose had followed her stomach downstairs and met everyone else for dinner, while Cat and Vin had called for room service.

A knock came at the door, and Cat got up and let room service in. Vin sat cross-legged on the bed and motioned for the guy to place the tray in front of him.

Cat signed the receipt, saw the guy out, and plopped down beside Vin. "I'm fucking starving."

She pulled the silver lid off her burger and fries. "What did you get?"

Vin pulled the lids off his plates. "Conch burger, conch fritters, and a fresh conch salad."

Cat grinned. "I'm sensing a trend here."

"When in Rome."

They dug into the food, letting it sop up some of the alcohol swirling around in their bellies. He was going to regret his decision to get drunk come morning, but until then, he'd enjoy it.

"Maybe this is a good thing," Cat mumbled around a bite of ketchup-covered fries, picking up on the conversation they'd abandoned when the food had arrived.

Vin bit into a piping hot fritter and fanned his hand in front of his mouth. His tongue burned, and steam scorched his hard palate.

After he managed to swallow, he said, "It's bad. Here I am trying to make Niko see me as the adult I am and not the kid he'd rescued off the streets, and now I'm back to sleeping on his couch. That's not going to make it easy for either of us to forget."

Cat eyed him over a fistful of fries. "What did I tell you about forgetting the dick you can't have?"

"Find another dick to jump on."

Cat winked and did the shoot-the-finger-gun thing at him. "You *were* listening."

She snapped her fingers at him. "Gimme your phone."

Reluctantly, he unlocked his phone and handed it over. "What are you going to do?" He really should know better than to hand his phone over to Cat. He'd have to blame it on his buzz.

"Find the perfect dick for you."

"You know," Vin said, unable to stop the chuckle. "It's not *all* about the dick. I kinda want to be into the guy, too."

She eyed him. "If you say so. Gonna make it harder, but I'm always up for a challenge."

Patting the bed beside her, he scooted closer so he could see his screen. She found his *HotDix* app and opened it.

"At least you already have your profile in." Then she started clicking through the photos he'd uploaded.

He grabbed for the phone, but she switched hands and held it out of reach as she scrolled to the last photo.

His dick pic.

"*Jesus Christ.*" The heat rocketed up his neck and exploded on his face.

She whistled in what he took as a sign of appreciation. "Wow, dude. Nice pic."

The app *was* called *HotDix* for a reason.

"Okay, okay. Would you give me that back now?"

"Hold on." She had a hand on his chest, holding him at bay. "Have you sent Niko this pic?"

"What? No. Are you crazy?"

She laughed. "No. But, you know... This pic could be a game-changer."

She handed back the phone, and he switched off his profile to search. "Not likely."

"All I'm saying is that Niko doesn't know what he's missing."

"And he's not finding out either." He pinned her with a glare that only made her laugh harder.

"Okay. Okay. He won't see it from me."

Vin turned on the app's GPS location. One of the genius advantages of the app was that he could punch in the dates he'd be in town, and the app only showed profiles of men with overlapping stays at the same location. Which helped greatly at a place where people came and went.

"What about that guy?" Cat said.

Vin shrugged. "Too young and twinkie. He doesn't even look old enough to be on the apps. He'd probably have to sneak out of the room he was sharing with his parents to meet up."

"Fair enough. What about him."

"Too uptight. He looks like the kind of guy who has high tea with the queen."

Cat blew out a frustrated breath as if she could see a pattern developing.

Finding someone to hook up with wasn't a terribly bad idea, but if he was going to hook up with someone, they at least had to be the type of person he could see himself dating, even if it was only going to be a one and done sort of deal.

He had to have *some* standards.

Vin continued scrolling through. She grabbed the phone and went back through a couple profiles. "Ooooh, he's—"

He thumbed through the photos of a guy suspended by the ceiling with ropes, a leather hood over his face. "Definitely too kinky."

"Well, duh, for you, maybe. But not for me."

Laughing, he swiped his phone back. "Get your own damn profile."

"Fine."

Vin continued to scroll through, rejecting men for various reasons some he could defend, some he couldn't.

He'd just about given up when he stopped on a profile.

"Did you find one?" Cat stepped back into the room after putting their room service trays into the hallway.

"Maybe." It came out as more of a question. He angled the phone in her direction when she sat beside him.

Her eyes narrowed, scrutinizing the photos, then she started nodding. "I like this guy. The Goldilocks of the dating world. Not too young, not too conservative, not too kinky, and with those the flecks of gray in his chest hair, he fits within the acceptable 'daddy' range."

"I'm not into the *daddy* thing."

Cat's brows rose, the ring in her left eyebrow almost reaching her hairline. "Coulda fooled me."

"Plenty of guys are into mature men. Nothing wrong with that."

She held her hands up. "Preaching to the choir, babe. Have you seen my fuck-buddy, Truman?"

If there was anyone who loved cock more than Vin, it had to be Cat. Maybe they were twins, separated at birth. "I have."

"We're getting off-topic." Cat pointed at the phone. "Message that guy before you scrote out and don't do it."

He wasn't gonna chicken out. Most likely. "Here goes nothing," he said as he 'favorited' the guy. Now they had to see if they matched.

Cat clapped her hands and bounced on the bed, letting out this earsplitting shriek. "I'm so excited for you."

Tossing his phone on the bed, he reached for a tiny bottle of tequila. "Don't be. He may not even like me. He—"

The phone chirped when a message landed in his *HotDix* message folder, and that maddening pierced brow rose again. "You were saying?"

Vin picked up the phone, his heart skittering in his chest, a drunken, excited beat that left his head spinning and his mouth dry.

@dickful69: *Hey.*

With his thumb hovering over the reply button, he took a calming breath. You'd think he'd never been out on a date before, much less planned to hook up with a stranger.

"Go ahead," Cat said. "You won't be sorry."

———

Niko paced his room. Where the hell was Vin anyway? It was after midnight. They'd had a long travel day, and they had to get up early in the morning to scout locations for the upcoming week.

You're not his keeper.

No. But that didn't mean Vin didn't need one anyway. Something thumped against the door. The handle jiggled, but the door didn't open.

Jesus Christ. Was Vin so plastered he couldn't manage to press the keycard against the lock?

Niko didn't bother looking through the peephole, no one was on the island besides his crew and the resort staff. He yanked the door open. Vin sat slumped on the floor and, without the door for support, his torso toppled into the room, his eyes blinking rapidly as if bringing Niko into focus.

"Oh, fuck," Vin slurred. "Am I in trouble?"

Niko didn't bother answering because Vin's eyes rolled into the back of his head. He hitched his hands under Vin's arms and hauled him to the couch.

Déjà vu.

How many times had he done just that in the first few months after Vin had gotten off the streets? Too many to count.

Retrieving a pillow off his bed, Niko scooted Vin over and lifted his legs onto the couch, only going so far as to remove his shoes.

Not that he couldn't control himself if he helped Vin out of his clothes, but he also didn't see the point in torturing himself either.

Besides, if Vin had been concerned about comfort, he never would have gotten shit-faced.

Vin started to snore. A loud, raucous sound that reverberated off the walls and made the building's foundation shake.

Niko wasn't going to get any sleep tonight.

Rolling Vin onto his side, the snoring quieted to a gentle, almost soothing rhythm. With Vin on his side, if he vomited, he wouldn't choke to death in the middle of the night.

The moonlight filtered in, casting a soft glow through the blinds, catching the ridge of Vin's cheekbone, his brow, and the long line of his nose. He looked peaceful.

Something he hadn't looked in a long while.

Before Niko could question his decision to push Vin away, he turned to leave.

Vin reached out as if to grab Niko's arm, but his aim was off, and he only managed to slap at Niko's hand. "Sit."

Vin's eyelids cracked open, and he tried to shove himself back and make room. With little strength, Vin's hand slipped on the cushion, and he almost flopped onto his belly.

Niko righted him and sat one ass cheek on the couch. "What is it?" He reached to brush hair out of Vin's eyes but stopped the intimate gesture.

He's not yours. You made damn sure you didn't have a right to touch him.

Those lips formed a kissable pout, and damn if Niko didn't start to go hard. It felt wrong and forbidden and right and permissible all at the same time.

Vin hit himself in the face when he tried to scrub a hand over his eyes. When it looked as if Vin had finally managed to focus on Niko with at least one eye, Vin said, "Am I grounded?"

A dry chuckle ripped out of Niko's throat. *Fuck.* This kid.

But he's not a kid, is he?

Niko patted him on his chest. "Get some sleep."

Vin's eyelids slammed down with the finality of a last curtain call. Niko got one of the throws out of the closet and draped it over Vin and tucked it in along the edges.

He patted Vin's arm, but Vin was out colder than a drunk who'd stumbled into a free case of booze. Leaning in, he did what he'd promised himself he wouldn't do. He pressed a kiss to Vin's forehead, smelling the spirits on his breath and the dried sweat on his skin.

"Sleep well."

Vin's chest rose and fell in a slow, hypnotic rhythm that

made Niko want to curl up beside him and put his back to Vin's chest and pull Vin's arm over his side.

Instead, with the room dimly lit by moonlight, Niko made his way into the bathroom to get ready for bed.

Because the wall separating the bathroom from the rest of the suite was heavily frosted glass, Niko only flipped on the light in the commode area, leaving that door ajar so that turning on the bright lights in the bathroom wouldn't wake Vin.

Not that anything short of a Cat 5 hurricane would probably wake Vin at this point, but Niko wasn't taking any chances.

He brushed his teeth and stripped down to his boxer briefs, trying to ignore the tenting of the cotton from the semi he sported. Climbing into bed, he rolled onto his back, locking his hands behind his head, refusing to jack off to that erotic reel he had in his head of Vin going down on him.

Not that he hadn't jacked off to it before, but somehow it seemed a greater offense to do it with the subject of that memory passed out on his couch not twenty feet away.

He stared up at the ceiling, afraid he'd be awake most of the night, but the slow turn of the ceiling fan kept his skin cool and his mind occupied as he watched the wide blades turn and turn until the exhaustion crept in, his arousal waned, and sleep pulled him under.

Before his alarm went off the next morning, Niko woke to water running in the shower, and the sun rising over a sea so clear and blue, it made the sky jealous.

His morning wood begged for release, but he didn't want Vin coming out of the shower and seeing him with his dick in his hand, furiously jacking off.

Even though the frosted glass was nearly opaque, with Vin backlit by the bathroom lights, Niko could make out Vin's shadow as he lathered himself on the other side of the glass.

What would Vin do if Niko stripped naked and climbed into the shower behind him?

Don't even think about it.

Go for a run. Go for a swim. Do something, anything. Just get out of the damn room before you regret it.

But he didn't run from the room like he should have. He also couldn't lay there and let his mind wander. He clicked the switch on the wall next to the headboard. A motor whirred, and a TV rose from the footboard.

He reached for the clicker on the bedside table, and rolled onto his side, facing away from the shower to give Vin the privacy he deserved.

But instead of the TV turning on, the room got brighter. He clicked the power switch again, and the room darkened, but he didn't see an overhead light turn on and off.

Weird.

He rolled out of bed and stood, pressing the button again.

Holy hell.

He tore his eyes from the wall of frosted glass that now stood crystal clear. But his eyes didn't stay diverted for long.

It wasn't right, he knew that, but still, he didn't re-energize the smart glass. He'd seen the privacy glass advertised before but had never seen it in person.

I'm a fan.

Christ.

On the other side of the now clear glass, Vin showered. His back to Niko as water from the rain showerhead pounded his skin. Vin soaped himself up, his arms coming around his back, trying to reach that unreachable spot in the middle. Steam billowed from the showerhead, but not enough to obscure Niko's view.

Then Vin bent over, sudsing up his legs, that fine ass pointed at the sky like a virgin offering to the sex gods. All Niko wanted to do was slide behind Vin and tuck that sweet ass against his cock and bury himself to oblivion.

Then Vin's hands went to his groin, and Niko imagined what it would be like to wash Vin's cock and balls, to feel the soft skin and the weight of Vin in his hands.

On its own accord, Niko's left hand slid into his briefs, the pre-cum already leaking from his slit and spotting his underwear.

At some point, he became aware that Vin was no longer washing but pleasuring himself. Was he thinking about Niko? About Niko joining him in the shower and going down on his knees and taking him deep to the back of his throat?

Vin's head fell back, then rolled on his shoulders, his hips flexing into the grip he had on his dick. *Fuck.* That quick, Niko's spine tingled, and his balls drew up tight to his body.

He was going to cum on the white marble floor, and he didn't give two fucks about it.

Vin turned.

Their eyes locked.

Vin's hand stopped for a second before one of his brows rose in a challenge, and a smile toyed with one corner of his mouth.

Then Vin's strokes got faster, and his eyes grew heavy, but they didn't leave Niko's. Not for one second. A single-minded race to the finish.

Always a competitive guy, Niko knew he wouldn't lose, especially when he could already feel the first pulses of his orgasm at the base of his cock.

He concentrated on the head of his dick while Vin concentrated on his shaft with fast, fluid strokes. Then Vin's eyes drifted closed, and for once in Niko's life, as he watched the climax take Vin higher, as the exquisite pleasure washed over Vin's features, as the cum filled his hand and hit the glass wall, Niko didn't care that he'd lost.

––––––

As soon as Niko came—while he should have been in that post-orgasmic glow—Vin watched the shame and the regret shove aside the lust and the longing.

Vin hadn't even finished washing all the jizz off his hand before the glass turned opaque again. Some sort of fucked-up special glass. Though the view on the other side—Niko standing with a hard dick in his hand—had been exceptional.

Vin leaned his forehead against the cool glass and let the warm water pelt his skin as his breathing returned to normal. Every thumping beat of his heart made his headache pound. The orgasm had been a brief relief from the hangover, but he was paying for the exertion now.

He waited for Niko to come into the bathroom, but he never did. When Vin's fingers started to prune, he shut the water off and dried himself, his mind still too off-kilter from the hangover to process what just happened.

You had one of the most mind-blowing orgasms you've ever had, and it was from your own hand. That's *what happened—with a little assist from Niko and that nuclear gaze that seared your heart until you thought you smelled smoke.*

Vin wrapped a towel around his waist and stepped into the room. The French doors were open, and Niko stood on the balcony in a robe, the sash hanging at his sides by the loops.

Either Niko was engrossed in the view, or he was doing everything he could to avoid Vin. Which wasn't exactly going to be easy with them sharing a room on a hundred-and-fifty-acre rock for the next week.

But if Niko wanted to pretend what happened *hadn't* happened. Fine.

It was just an orgasm.

Just. Ha.

You would think a porn director would be more mature about masturbation. And here Niko thought Vin was the kid.

Vin threw on the first thing he grabbed out of the dresser—a pair of cargo shorts, which always came in handy while shooting, and a black T-shirt. In the Bahama sun, he may come to regret his choice later, but getting out of the room was his top priority.

When dressed, he stepped to the door, prepared to pretend the mutual jackoff session had been a figment of his alcohol muddled mind.

"I'm headed down to grab a big coffee and a small breakfast. I'll—"

Niko turned, his robe open in the front, his briefs unable to hide the fact he was still aroused even after coming.

But that wasn't what unsettled Vin. It was the conflict warring in Niko's eyes that almost had Vin saying *he* was sorry even though he hadn't done anything wrong.

"I apologize," Niko said, which was *such* a Niko thing to say.

They both had gotten off. In Vin's book, that meant no apologies were necessary.

Vin only had one question for him. He knew the answer, but he wanted to see if Niko would admit it. "Did you like what you saw?"

Niko ran a hand through his sleep-tussled hair, ducking his head but refusing to break eye contact. For a second, Vin thought Niko would lie to his face.

Then Niko's features softened, and his voice dropped. "You know I did."

"Alright, then." Vin gave him a nod because he didn't know what else to say to that.

Backing up, Vin turned to go, and Niko said, "You're really messing with my head."

Vin glanced over his shoulder. Perhaps more honest words than Niko had intended if Niko's scowl was any indication.

"Then we're even."

8

———

Niko and Vin sat under the overhang of the bar by the pool as afternoon thunderclouds rolled in, the way they tended to do that time of year. The breeze picked up, but the sun still shone on their corner of paradise.

While the two of them discussed the scene locations they'd scouted that morning, the rest of their crew hung out around the pool and drank, enjoying their only day of rest and relaxation before shooting started the next day.

At least he and Vin could talk business without all the awkwardness of that morning getting in the way.

Niko nursed a Kalik beer, and Vin had a Bloody Mary. A bit of the dog that bit him, Niko figured.

A wet volleyball rolled onto the pool deck, and Vin kicked it back to where the talent, Chet, Hayes, Preston, and Greer, played water volleyball.

Niko couldn't wait to start shooting. The scenes he'd shot in the past with the 'daddies' always did well for Black Stallion, and with Greer and Hayes to fill those roles, they couldn't lose.

And of course, everyone always loved a cowboy, so Chet, Black Stallion's stocky, Texan, always made the guys hard and open their wallets. Niko couldn't call Chet one of the studs of his stable yet, but Chet had the raw talent to get there.

Then there was Preston, the quintessential twinkie college kid with a sweet, fuck-me face and shaggy blond hair that always seemed to be in his eyes.

On the far side of the pool, the three ladies in their entourage relaxed in the sun. Rose sat with Betty, both of them slathered with sunscreen and wearing wide brim hats on their heads. Already thick as thieves.

A couple loungers over, Cat lay naked on her stomach without a modest bone in her curvy, tattooed body.

"Another?" Niko asked Vin as both of their drinks ran low.

"Sure."

Niko raised a hand to the waitress and made a motion indicating another round. From somewhere off to his side came the sound of shattering glass, and Niko glanced over to see Cat rolling onto her back, and one of the waiters sprawled on the ground at her feet, the tray of drinks he'd been carrying scattered across the ground.

Vin laughed. "The resort is going to start charging you hazard pay if Cat keeps sunbathing in the nude. I saw the pool guy slip down the stairs because he was so busy staring at Cat's ass as he passed by."

"She's like one of those fish that lay in the dark at the bottom of the sea with the light dangling from an appendage, luring their prey to their certain deaths."

"I'm not sure being compared to an anglerfish is a compliment."

"It'll be our secret."

Much like what happened in their room earlier that morning.

From what Niko knew, and from the conversation he'd overheard in the airport lounge area, Vin and Cat didn't have many secrets between them. He held Vin's gaze. He wasn't going to come right out and tell Vin not to say anything about what happened that morning, but discretion for a one-off would be considerate.

Because it was a one-off.

It had to be.

Vin raised a brow and sat back in his seat as the unspoken message came through. "Wow." And yeah, that sounded more like hurt in Vin's voice, not sarcasm. "You really think I'm going to say something?"

Niko glanced around, but no one paid them any attention, The guys were busy with their volleyball, Rose and Betty were in deep conversation, and Cat had slipped on her sandals and was helping a befuddled waiter clean up his mess.

"No." But even to his own ears, Niko didn't sound convincing.

"You really think I want it broadcast that I'm the only guy under thirty that you refuse to stick your precious dick in?"

The bartender appeared in front of them, drinks in hand. "Um..." She glanced from Vin to Niko and back again. "I'll just put these here."

Niko picked up his beer and took a long swallow. "That's not true or fair. We've been through this."

"Fuck it." Vin held up his hand. "You're right."

Niko's phone buzzed, and while he wanted to finish the conversation with Vin, Sebastian was on the line. "I should get this."

Vin motioned for Niko to take it. Niko moved farther away from the bar and Jimmy Buffet's *Margaritaville* piping through the speakers.

"What's up, Bass?"

"You've got a problem."

Between the shoot and Vin, he had about all the issues he

could deal with now. Sometimes it fucking sucked to be the one in charge. "What?"

"A story broke on *Queer-y* with Black Stallion at the center."

Niko almost laughed. "No one follows them anymore. Their reporting is shoddy, and they'll sensationalize everything at the detriment of anyone. Ignore it. It will go away."

"Not this." Even through all the miles and the poor connection, he heard Sebastian's concern. "They actually got it right this time."

Sweat trickled down Niko's back, and he tried to convince himself it was from the Bahamian heat and humidity. But porn studios were rarely in the news for good reasons. Black Stallion had had its fair share of detractors over the years. It wasn't anything the studio couldn't weather because the truth was, men like their porn. And Niko's healthy bank account said they like Black Stallion's porn *a lot*.

"What did they get, right?"

"That some of our 'straight' talent is gay."

Fuck.

Part of what Black Stallion brought to the table was straight actors. A lot of their viewers had a thing for straight men in gay porn, and that preference showed in Black Stallion's download numbers.

Many studios said the men in their scenes were straight when they weren't. Black Stallion was the only studio that made those men avow to that in their contract or face the financial repercussions.

Unfortunately, three of their more popular men turned out not to be straight. Their deception hadn't been malicious, but the damage to the studio could be real.

Niko had tried to keep it quiet, but that was nearly impossible when those men now lived their lives openly.

"Get on top of it. Talk to a reporter and give them our side.

The truth. That we didn't know at the time. That we continue to strive to provide our customers with the experience they desire. Blah, blah, blah. That's all we have."

"You don't think I tried that?" Sebastian's voice rose with his distress. "They want you. But I also don't think a lot of them care about the truth. There's a lot of crap going around on social media right now. Most untrue."

"It'll blow over. Don't worry about it. As soon as the next news cycle hits, it will all be about something else."

"I don't think this is going to die down."

"It will," Niko said, his confidence faltering. "It has to."

They said their goodbyes, and Niko approached the bar, shoving his phone into his pocket as he went. He retook his seat and glanced over at Vin, who had his own phone in his hand and a stupid, sexy grin on his face. He typed a response to whoever he was messaging on his phone, only glancing up when Niko cleared his throat.

The smile slipped and fell off his face as he clicked off the app and set his phone face down on the bar.

"Who was that?" Not that Niko had any right to ask, but that jealous part of him was more than curious who'd put that flush on Vin's face.

The phone vibrated, and Vin's eyes darted to his phone, but he didn't reach for it. "No one."

The phone went off again.

"No one?" Niko asked as it went off a third time, not three seconds later. "Sounds like someone."

Vin sat on his hands as if he needed the physical restraint to keep himself from reaching for it.

Buzz, buzz.

"For fuck's sake," Niko said. "Reply already."

Vin's face went full-on crimson, which said something. Especially when he'd been able to stare Niko down when they'd both had their hands on their dicks without blushing.

Snatching up the phone, Vin scrolled through the string of messages and started typing. Then he glanced up. "Um... What time do you think we'll be done shooting tomorrow?"

Niko crossed his arms. "Why?"

"Because I asked."

The first couple days would be lighter shoot days, and Vin knew this, yet still, he asked. "Early afternoon, if all goes well."

Nodding, Vin sent another message, that maddening grin plastered across his face again. When Vin put his phone down, Niko chuckled. It almost sounded real. "Hot date?"

Vin took a moment before he answered. "What if it is?"

Niko didn't quite know how to take Vin's question as an answer or deal with the sense of disappointment that curdled in his stomach like spoiled milk.

If Niko said he had a problem with Vin having a date, would Vin cancel?

And what reason would you have to make him cancel? You don't own him. And you'd made it more than clear that you didn't want him.

That rancid disappointment bubbled in his belly. He hadn't been pleased that he and Vin had to share a room, not knowing if his will was strong enough to resist Vin, but as Niko had lain in bed last night, he not only came to terms with the room sharing, he'd come to accept it.

Look forward to it.

Even if doing so would test his resolve to the breaking point. A streak of masochism, maybe?

Niko held up his hands. "Sorry. None of my business."

Vin stirred the melting ice into his Bloody Mary. "Exactly."

———

Vin awoke with his alarm at six the next morning. He'd laid off the booze the night before. With his mind clear, the only throbbing in his body came from the ache in his balls after he'd dreamed about his jack-off session with Niko.

Niko's bed lay empty, and when Vin knocked on the bathroom door, Niko wasn't in there either. He glanced around the room for a note, but only found the smart glass remote on the bedside table.

He picked it up, clicked the glass clear, and then back to opaque a few times, half tempted to leave it clear in the hopes that Niko would come in, and they could relive the previous morning.

But in Vin's heart, he knew that wasn't going to happen. Niko had left the room early for a reason. They weren't set to shoot a scene for a couple of hours, so Niko hadn't gone to prepare for the shoot, he'd left to avoid Vin and any possibility there would be a repeat.

After showering, he skipped the shave. One of the benefits of working behind the camera was that it didn't matter what he looked like.

Then why did you gel your hair and swipe on some cologne?

Because...

Just because?

He wasn't completely uncivilized.

And the fact that the cologne he used happened to be his favorite, as well as Niko's, was a big fat coincidence.

Liar.

The door opened, and Niko hollered out before stepping inside. "You decent?"

"Yeah."

Niko sailed in with a spring in his step, a wicked light in his eyes, and a tray of coffee and breakfast sandwiches in his hand.

"What's got you in such a good mood?"

If Niko were any other man, he'd be whistling and skipping across the room. "I have an idea."

Vin groaned and almost reached for his phone to cancel his meet up for later that night. He knew that when Niko had an 'idea,' it meant whatever scene they'd had planned had been scrapped, and they were shooting something entirely different and off the cuff.

Granted, those scenes usually turned out to be the best of all the content that Black Stallion released, but they tended to be time-consuming to shoot and needed the most editing.

Vin removed the lid from his coffee and blew on it before taking a sip. It was strong and black and shot a buzz of much-needed caffeine through his veins. "What's this genius idea of yours?"

"Eat up," Niko said. "I'll fill you in when I tell everyone else at this morning's pre-production meeting."

The piping hot breakfast sandwich almost singed the taste buds off Vin's tongue, but he was starving, so he suffered through the first bite. "I'm not going to like this, am I?"

———

WITH ALL OF THE CREW FROM BLACK STALLION IN VIN AND NIKO'S suite, it didn't feel so enormous. Cat had set up in one corner, doing Greer and Preston's makeup, while Vin set up lights for the first part of the scene... the first part of Niko's *brilliant* idea.

Which, from what Niko had told the crew in the pre-production meeting that had wrapped up not thirty minutes prior, would be a recreation of Niko and Vin's encounter that first morning. Of course, Niko left out the salient fact that this had been real life, not fiction.

And if Vin could keep the red from blooming on his cheeks, it would remain that way.

Everyone had been on board, especially when they saw the smart glass for themselves.

Niko walked up to Vin, the buzz of anticipation heating the space between them. "What's taking so long?"

Vin shut down Niko's complaint with a single look. "I want to get the lighting right. There's a lot of reflection off the glass. Keep your panties on."

Niko's brow rose, but he swallowed back a retort. Niko moved to step away, then edged closer, his voice low and unlikely to carry. "You okay?"

Vin had changed into his baggiest pair of cargo shorts before he started setting up because the thought of recreating and filming his and Niko's jack-off session, had given him a raging hard-on.

Filming it in tight shorts would be embarrassing and uncomfortable.

"You're the one who wanted to keep this a secret, and now you've brought everyone into our room and... and..."

"And what?"

Really? "You might as well have given them a tub of popcorn and front row tickets to our sex life."

"It's going to be hot as hell, and you know it."

Fuck if Niko wasn't right. "Give me five."

Backing off, Niko gave Vin the space he needed. When ready, Vin signaled and shouldered his camera.

Niko said, "Places, everyone."

Greer climbed into Niko's bed, naked instead of wearing briefs. The only difference so far to their morning yesterday. Preston dropped his robe and walked into the shower.

"Action."

Preston turned on the water and screamed.

"Cut."

"Oh, dear," Betty said. "Everything okay? I told you we should have put down one of those anti-slip mats."

"Sorry," Preston called out. "Water is freezing."

They waited until the water warmed, but made sure Preston kept it on the cooler side so the steam wouldn't fog up the glass.

Then they started rolling again. Filming Greer helped Vin relive the part of that morning he hadn't seen, the part before he'd turned around to find Niko standing on the other side of the clear glass, his hand down his briefs, his cock in his hand.

Fuck if Vin almost hadn't spouted off right then.

He'd never thought to ask Niko how he'd come to disable the smart glass.

Now it unfolded in front of Vin's lens, Greer raising the TV from the switch on the wall beside the bed, and accidentally using the smart glass remote instead of the TV remote.

Vin panned to the frosted glass and the barely-there shadow of Preston on the other side. The glass went clear. Niko had it play out the way Vin remembered, with Preston's back turned, Greer crawling out of bed, his hand stroking his already hard cock.

Everything the same.

The challenge in Preston's eyes mimicked the one Vin had given Niko.

With his inevitable hard-on, each step Vin took was uncomfortable. If he managed to keep the camera from shaking throughout the scene, it would be a miracle.

Then fiction veered away from reality. Instead of them both jacking off until they came, Greer stepped into the bathroom the way Vin had wished Niko would have.

"Cut."

Conversation in the room buzzed. Greer and Preston laid light hands on their dicks, keeping themselves aroused while

Vin repositioned lights, moved into the bathroom, and switched to his waterproof camera.

"You sure you don't want to change into your bathing suit?" Niko asked.

Considering all Vin had was a Speedo, the answer was a resounding *hell no*. He didn't want everyone seeing how aroused he was, especially Niko.

"No. It's okay if these clothes get wet. I'm not planning on getting that close."

Greer and Preston didn't take long to get going once Niko quieted the crew and called 'action' again. Greer sunk to his knees in the shower, water cascading over his body as he took Preston into his mouth.

Goosebumps erupted across Preston's skin, brought on by the sweet contrast between the cool water and the hot mouth, no doubt.

Fuck if Vin couldn't practically feel Niko's mouth on him as he eased closer to catch all the action. Behind him, Niko leaned against the bathroom counter, watching the scene unfold.

They had several more breaks for lighting adjustment and camera placement. Greer having gone from sucking Preston off to bending him over and eating his ass.

During one of those breaks, Vin took the camera off his shoulder and leaned against the wall, wishing he could excuse himself long enough to empty his balls. Then he'd be good to go for the rest of the day.

"Where the fuck did the condoms go?" Niko stepped into the suite. "Sebastian where—"

Niko cut himself off. Sebastian wasn't there. "Condoms? Anyone? Please tell me we didn't show up for a weeklong shoot without condoms."

"Oooh!" Betty dug around in her purse, which might have outweighed her by a pound or two. "Here they are." She toddled into the bathroom, her hands full of all different sized condoms, and held them out to Greer.

He reached for one but hesitated when he saw the look on Betty's face. "What's the matter?"

She glanced from Greer's dick to the condom. "I think you need a bigger size, dear. Hang on, I'll check my purse and—"

Greer chuckled, a deep, rolling, comforting sound like distant thunder. "This one is fine, ma'am."

She arched her penciled-in brow at him.

"Really."

"I don't mind checking."

"Thank you. But I'm good."

"Okay, dear." She turned to Niko. "He's so sweet."

Niko laughed and ushered Betty out of the bathroom. "Yeah, he is."

At least the condom interlude gave Vin half a chance for his dick to soften, though he could feel the dampness of his pre-cum soaked briefs as they brushed against his cock.

But Vin's reprieve proved short-lived, especially when Niko had Greer take Preston from behind, all that power and muscle pounding into that tight ass.

As he stared through the lens, he imagined Niko's hands on his shoulder, holding him in tight as Niko drove inside him, the musk of sex scenting the air, the snap and slap of wet flesh on wet flesh.

Fuck, Niko was killing him.

The water in the shower had long since run cold, and the frigid mist on Vin's face as he went in for a closeup didn't cool the beads of sweat forming along his brow.

The heated, smoldering look Niko cast Vin when he changed shooting angles didn't help. Was Niko also picturing the two of them together?

If Vin made it through the shoot without blowing his load involuntarily, he'd call it a win.

Always the perfectionist, Niko didn't leave the scene at that. As instructed, Greer lifted Preston in his arms, pressing the younger man's back against the shower wall, Preston's legs locked at the ankles behind Greer's back as Greer fucked him.

They had to break long enough for the hot water heater to kick back in. Steaming up the shower, Vin shot from the suite side of the room, Preston's back and ass pressed against the glass, the bathroom beyond hidden by the steam-fogged glass.

For the finale, Vin shot from inside the shower again as Greer stroked Preston to completion. Preston's head fell back, the cords in his neck taut, his breath hitching, and his moans making Vin's own balls tight.

Then Greer pulled free, lowering Preston to his feet and tossing the condom aside. Greer called out, a deep grumble and groan as Preston finished him off with his hands and his mouth.

As the last spurts of cum left Greer's cock, Preston lapped him from the underside with a grin and his flat tongue.

"Cut," Niko said. Cat tossed him a couple of towels, and he passed them to Greer and Preston as they came out of the shower. "Nice work, boys."

"Nice?" Cat laughed. "God, I love my job. It was hot as all fuck."

Preston and Greer toweled off, their goosebumps finally starting to fade as they warmed.

"Thanks," Greer said. Then to Preston added, "You good?"

Preston's grin turned shy. "I'm more than good."

Betty came into the room with a bottle of water in each hand. "Here you go, boys."

Fanning her hand dramatically in front of her face, she said, "Now I see why my friend and her husband are such fans of Black Stallion."

Niko laughed. "You weren't scandalized?"

"Sweetheart, I'm eighty years old. It takes a lot more than watching two men having sex to scandalize me."

She patted Greer on the arm. "When you two get dressed, come out to the balcony. I've had an early lunch sent up for you two."

"Sweet!" Preston kissed her on the cheek. "You're the best."

Betty blushed as she waved off the compliment and backed out of the bathroom.

"Hey," Chet said, "what about us? I'm starving."

"Hang onto your jocks, boys. The rest of the food will be up shortly."

Niko hung back as everyone vacated the bathroom, and Vin made a show of making sure his camera and lens were dry as he started packing them away. Truth be told, he needed a minute alone to strip out of his pre-cum soaked underwear before it showed through the shorts.

He'd rather go commando than have that happen.

"You going to grab some lunch?" Vin asked, not because he really cared, but it was something to say that got his focus off the scene they'd shot.

"What did you think about the scene?"

So much for Vin's dick deflating.

What was Niko playing at? He hadn't been shy about saying there could never be anything between the two of them. Then he goes and immortalizes their time together in a video.

Vin didn't know what to think, about the scene, or the underlying subtext of the question. He blew out a breath as Niko stepped into his personal space, not waiting for him to answer.

He leaned in, his mouth next to Vin's ear. "Everything we shot, everything Greer did, I wanted to do to you."

9

———

Later that afternoon, after they'd shot their scene with Hayes and Chet, Vin got cleaned up for his meet up with @dick-ful69, the guy he'd made a connection with on the *HotDix* app.

He'd half thought about asking Cat if he could use her shower to avoid all the thoughts that would be swirling in his head if he used his.

Especially with what Niko had said to him.

But Vin's imagination failed him, and he couldn't come up with a valid excuse that Cat wouldn't see through. Niko had headed down to the bar earlier and was probably drinking with Cat or Rose, so it wasn't like he could say that Niko was using it.

In the end, he leaned into the erotics of the day and let Niko's words wash over him as he stroked himself in the shower and found relief for his aching dick and his blue balls.

He dressed in his nicest pair of shorts and a short-sleeved island-themed button-up shirt hung open over his Bahama blue tank. He brushed his teeth, ran clippers over his beard—giving him that day-old beard look, instead of the three-day scruff he'd been sporting—and called it good.

Checking his watch, he had about ten minutes to run down

to the dock and make the water taxi heading to Nassau with Cat, Hayes, Greer, Chet, and Preston on board.

He slipped on his flip-flops, shoved his room key in his wallet, and headed for the door.

It opened in his hand.

Niko came up short over the threshold, Vin blocking his way.

"Where are you going?"

"Seriously? I'm not sixteen, Niko, in case you haven't noticed."

Niko leaned against the door jamb, the sun he'd gotten that day accentuated the laugh lines radiating from the corner of his eyes, and looked damn sexy on him. "I know that."

"Then, it's time you started acting like it." Vin opened the door wider and went to move past Niko, but Niko didn't budge out of the way.

"I need you to stay." The words came out low, and Vin never would have heard them if they hadn't been standing so close.

Had Niko changed his mind? More importantly, after what they'd been through—the auction, the date debacle, and Niko virtually running after their mutual masturbation session—did Vin want him to?

Vin cleared his throat to dislodge a word. "Why?"

Niko held his gaze, and for a moment, Vin got lost in Niko's dark brown eyes that held enough heat to warm him throughout an Arctic winter.

Vin felt himself leaning in, close enough to smell the spice in Niko's cologne and the sunscreen on his skin. His heart rate spiked, and a knot of anticipation squeezed his gut.

"I thought we could start the edits on the shower scene this morning," Niko said.

Vin stepped back, the door banging against the wall. "You've got to be fucking kidding me right now." He pointedly glanced at his watch and tried to brush past him again. "I'm going to miss the boat."

"You can reschedule."

Vin narrowed his eyes and studied Niko, but Niko's expression gave nothing away. Vin had a hunch he knew what this was about and called him on it. "You don't want me going on my date."

"This has nothing to do with that."

"Bullshit." Vin pressed a hand in the center of Niko's chest, felt the thump of Niko's heart beneath his palm. "Tell me I'm wrong."

After a second that warped into a minute, Niko stepped back, making room for Vin to pass. "Have a good evening."

Vin took the stairs down two at a time, determined not to miss the water taxi to Nassau. Fuck Niko and his head games. Vin needed a few hours away from his boss and everything Black Stallion to get his head on straight.

Whatever hesitation he had about meeting up with @dickful69 dissipated. One night of nearly anonymous connection might be just what the sex doctor ordered.

He jogged across the resort's grounds, past the pool and the expanse of green grass with the queen palms and coconut trees, down to the sandy beach and the long wooden dock.

The water taxi floated at the end, the engines churning, and the waves lapping at the hull. Cat glanced up and waved at him. He waved back, his footfalls sounding hollow on the wood planks.

"Hey, man," Chet said, "you made it."

"I bet Cat you wouldn't come," said Greer.

Why the hell not? Before he had the chance to ask, his phone buzzed in his pocket. He figured it was Niko and almost didn't check it, but he did.

@dickful69.

"Ready to go?" one of the dockhands asked. He had a dock line in his hands and one foot on the bow, ready to shove off.

Vin held up his hand to ask for a minute. He clicked through to the message center on the app.

@dickful69: *Gotta cancel. Something came up. Couldn't be helped. Reschedule?*

Vin blew out a breath, the disappointment hit harder than he'd expected. Especially considering he'd never met the guy in person.

"What's wrong?" Cat raised her voice over the drone of the engine.

"Plans changed. You guys go without me."

"Come on, dude." Preston wasn't having it. "Come out with us. It'll be an epic time."

"Yeah, thanks. I'm kind of jet-lagged anyway, but you guys have fun."

The dockhand shoved off and jumped into the bow. Cat held her thumb and outstretched pinkie to the side of her face and mouthed the words 'call me.'

Vin nodded, even though he had no intention of doing so. He was a big boy. He could lick his wounds all by himself.

As the boat pulled away, the bow bounced in the slight chop as the inlet led into deeper water. He watched until the setting sun hit the horizon, and his eyes watered as the boat disappeared into the sun's glare.

He leaned a shoulder against one of the pilings and noticed he had another message.

@dickful69: *Hope you're not mad. I really wanted to meet you.*

Vin: Same. Maybe next time.

@dickful69: *So there really will be a next time?*

Vin: If you still want.

@dickful69: *Oh, yeah. You're not just saying that? You're not going to catfish me, are you?*

Vin: Me? I thought you were the one who was flaking out on me.

@dickful69: *No, man. I just had this thing.*

Vin: So, you said...

Vin stared at his phone, awaiting the reply, wanting to ask what had come up, but it wasn't any of his business. His thoughts went to the obvious, that his hookup had found a better prospect.

Don't go there. Stay out of your head. There are a million legit reasons why he had to cancel.

Three dots showed up, then disappeared, then showed up, only to disappear again. He waited—longer than any sane person would—but nothing came through.

He walked back up the dock, the shadows from the trees getting long, the breeze kicking up with a hint of coolness that hadn't been there earlier.

The last thing he wanted was to have to sit in his room. It would be nearly impossible to ignore Niko in a confined space.

A crushed gravel path veered off to Vin's right, away from the resort, and he followed it. As darkness set in, strategically placed solar-powered tree and path lights lit his way. He climbed a set of stairs to a bench set at the highest natural point on the island, the dull thud of a headache forming behind his eyes.

He sat on the bench, staring out over the Caribbean Sea. From his vantage point, he watched as the waves crashed against the limestone on the windward side of the island, churning the sea to white foam and sea spray.

Near his feet, the low underbrush rustled. A lizard darted out at his feet, its curly tail curved over its back, and its beady eyes giving him the once over.

"Do I look as pathetic as I feel?"

The lizard cocked his head as if in thought, but then his tongue shot out and snatched up a spider.

"Taste good?"

"Making friends, I see."

Vin jumped at the sound of Niko's voice. Vin's heart lodged so tight in his throat he'd need a sledgehammer to knock it free. "You scared the shit out of me."

"Sorry." Niko shoved his hands deep into the pockets of his shorts, the wind whipping at his shirt. The moon started to rise, and the stars became visible against a blacking sky.

From their vantage point, the stunning view had the capacity to make you contemplate the world and all its wonders, but as Niko stood there, his gaze wasn't looking out into the sea, it focused on Vin. "Mind if I sit down?"

Vin scooted over, almost afraid to speak, thinking that if this were a mirage or a damn dream, he didn't want to spoil it by waking up.

When Niko didn't speak, Vin's heart climbed down and resettled in his chest. What was Niko doing out here? "Decided to go for a walk?"

Lame.

Jesus Christ. Just shut the fuck up, Andino. You're not doing yourself any favors here.

"I came looking for you."

Vin did a double-take. A witty comeback eluded him.

Niko bobbed his head toward the resort, and Vin glanced behind him. From where he sat, he had a direct line of sight into their lighted room. "I saw you sitting out here. Everything okay?"

"Sure. Plans changed."

"He canceled?" And why did Niko look pleased with himself?

Vin nodded.

"Sorry to hear that." Only he didn't sound contrite in the least.

Why had Niko sought him out? Maybe he was just trying to

fix that weird awkwardness that hadn't quite dissipated since they'd jacked off together.

Vin needed to steer the conversation to safer ground. All this internal conflict didn't help his headache.

"I guess I've got time now to work on those edits if—"

"I didn't come out here to put you to work."

"Why did you come out here then?"

Vin wanted the words back as soon as they left his mouth. He didn't like that they made him sound needy. Niko had been perfectly clear that nothing would happen between them.

Everything we shot, everything Greer did, I wanted to do to you.

Vin couldn't get the words Niko had said to him out of his head, the contradiction in Niko's words made his head spin, and his heart dare to hope. But he'd learned his lesson on the beach back in Cali.

He couldn't, wouldn't make the first move again.

Besides, if Niko knew about his past, about certain details of his life before he'd landed on the streets of southern California, Niko wouldn't want anything to do with him.

———

WHY *DID* HE GO LOOKING FOR VIN?

Valid question.

One Niko had asked himself the whole way there. As he took the stairs to the ground floor, as he passed Rose and Betty in the resort bar, as he made his way along the path that led to what he shouldn't want.

The funny thing about desire, it always seemed to seize control until your junk made you do things that your mind had already convinced you not to do.

"Can we talk?"

Vin eased away, the low-level light not hiding his wariness. Catching his hand, Niko said, "Don't run."

"No one's running."

The denial was a direct contrast to the tug of Vin's hand in his and the way Vin leaned away. He may not be conscious of what his body language said, but he was easy to read.

"Just say what you need to say and get it over with. I'm beat, and the couch is calling me," Vin said.

"I've been thinking about what I said to you, at the beach, and in our bathroom after the shoot. I want to apologize for sending mixed signals. You don't deserve that."

Some emotion flicked across Vin's face, and then it vanished. Niko pointed at him. "What was that?"

Niko expected Vin to deflect or say 'nothing.' Instead, Vin said, "I don't think you really know me well enough to say what I do and don't deserve."

What the actual fuck?

That hollowness, that defeat, in Vin's voice, Niko hadn't heard since the first months after Vin had come to live with him. It made Niko's lungs constrict, and his heart drop a beat. Were they even talking about the same thing anymore?

Niko stood to leave. "Maybe this wasn't such a good idea."

Vin tugged Niko back to the bench, their fingers now entwined. "Say what you came to say."

Did he dare? Was he just thinking with his dick? Would Vin welcome Niko's proposition?

This is an insanely bad idea, you know that, right?

It has regret *written all over it.*

Niko pivoted to face him. Here went nothing. "What I've said to you in the past still holds, there's no future between you and me, there can't be. But I can't deny there's a chemistry between us that defies everything I've told you."

Vin had one of those *you're just now figuring this shit out?* kind of looks on his face. He had the decency not to say it out loud and to wait patiently for Niko to spit out what he had to say.

"I'm fucking this up. This isn't coming out at all the way I heard it in my head."

Vin squeezed his hand. "It's okay. Just say it."

The fact that Vin hadn't let go of his hand gave him encouragement. Niko rubbed a sweaty palm down the leg of his shorts. You would think he'd never propositioned someone before. He winced at the word *propositioned* because that wasn't what he meant—it sounded too much like a shady business transaction —but he couldn't come up with a less sleazy word to slap on it.

"I thought... I thought that while we're here, we could explore the chemistry and see where it leads us. For the week, at least."

Vin dropped Niko's hand. Niko wanted to grab Vin's hand back but didn't. If Vin needed space to think, he'd give it to him.

"So, basically, you want to fuck around for the week and go back to the status quo when we get back to the States."

In a nutshell. "Yeah."

"Can you do that?" The challenge in Vin's words almost made Niko reconsider, but he'd denied himself for a long time, and now that he'd had a taste, he couldn't seem to get Vin out of his head, and worse, his dreams.

"That's how it has to be."

"You think we'll just get this all out of our systems?"

"I do."

Was Vin really considering his proposition? Thoughts pingponged in his head, and he couldn't come up with anything more intelligent to say besides, "I do."

"Does that ever work? Fucking someone out of your system?"

Niko couldn't help matching the tentative smile on Vin's face. "I'm willing to try."

"Our own mini gay Rumspringa out here in the cays?"

Niko barked out a laugh. "If you say so."

The insects chirped, and the breeze blew, though the humidity hung in the air—something you couldn't quite escape in the Bahamas no matter what time of year you went. In the distance, a yacht with its running lights on motored through the waters.

Niko forced himself to relax and prepared for the expected refusal. It wouldn't be the first time he'd been turned down, and it definitely wouldn't be the last. Waiting, his heart tripped into a rhythm that mimicked an old engine with a couple of bad plugs.

"Okay."

Niko shook his head. What? Had he heard Vin, right? "Okay, as in *okay*, okay?"

It was Vin's turn to laugh, a sound Niko had heard a thousand times before, but this time the sweet sound made the knots across his shoulders loosen, and the erratic, chugging beat of his heart settle into a soft purr.

"Yes."

Niko pulled Vin to his feet and hugged him to him. Gradually, the stiffness left Vin's body, and he eased into the close contact, his cock brushing against Niko's wood that he'd had one hell of a time taming all day.

With a forefinger beneath Vin's stubbled jaw, Niko bent his head, his eyes on Vin, when he lowered his voice to a sexy grumble. "I really want to kiss you."

Vin's nostrils flared, and his eyes widened, though the lighting was too low to see if his pupils dilated. "I'm not stopping you."

"Maybe you should."

"Maybe." Though Vin didn't make a move to put any space between them. "Or maybe you should get out of your head and kiss me already."

He liked the way Vin thought.

The first touch of their lips, no more than a brush, a silent acknowledgment of what was to come, and one last chance for Vin to change his mind.

Please don't change your mind.

The heat of their breaths mixed, and Vin slid his hands up Niko's chest, his pinkie finger skipping across the flat of his nipple, sending a spike of electricity straight to his dick.

If Vin wasn't careful, Niko would take him on the bench, not caring if one of the resort employees happened to stumble across them in the shadows.

Fuck if that idea didn't turn Niko on. A possibility for another night, perhaps. But tonight, he wanted Vin in his bed where they could take their time and shut out the rest of the world, if only for a night.

Threading a hand behind Niko's neck, Vin pulled him back into the kiss, his tongue skimming the seam of his lips. Niko opened for him, angling his head and deepening the kiss.

The musky cologne on Vin's skin reminded Niko of hot summer nights and simple, steamy sex.

A groan clawed its way up the back of his throat, and he couldn't care less that it escaped as Vin's tongue taunted and explored, the contact hot, not hurried.

Reaching back, Niko peeled Vin's hand from the back of his neck and broke the kiss. The worry on Vin's face knocked Niko back a step.

Tread lightly. You could hurt this man without trying.

"I don't want to do this here. I want you beneath me in my bed, and I want to do all sorts of things to you that would be better done without sand on our junk."

"I thought you'd changed your mind," Vin whispered.

Did Vin think Niko's desires vacillated in a matter of

minutes? Vin's admission nicked Niko's heart, and he hitched in a breath. "No."

That one word wiped the disappointment from Vin's face, and the sexiest, shyest tilt of his lips took its place.

Stepping back, Niko pulled Vin along with him. With the decision made, he couldn't wait to get back to the resort. Glancing up at their lit room, it might as well have been ten miles away.

On their walk back, Niko wanted to pick up the pace, but with the moon out and the stars high, he didn't want to rush the moment either. He liked the feel of Vin's hand in his and the way their shoulders brushed against each other, and how their strides synced up without effort.

When was the last time he'd walked hand in hand with another man, sinking into the contact, not wanting to let go?

Niko thought back over the years. Had he ever?

"What are you thinking?" Vin asked.

"You'll think it's sappy."

"Try me."

Niko raised their joined hands. "I don't think I've ever really held another man's hand before. Not like this."

Vin's grip loosened, but Niko tightened his. "Don't let go. I like it."

"It's okay," Vin said, "you don't have to say things like that just to get me to have sex with you. I already said 'yes.'"

Niko jerked Vin up short beneath the overhang of one of the resort's side entrances and pressed him back against the stucco walls. "I want to make myself clear. Just because this isn't going anywhere beyond what we make of it this week, doesn't mean I don't mean what I say or that I don't care about you. Got it?"

Vin's dry swallow made a clicking sound. "Got it. Now, are we going to stand out here all night, or are you going to take me upstairs and fuck me?"

10

———

Niko unlocked their door, the air conditioning crisp and refreshing against his skin as they entered the room. He flicked off the lights, the moon, and a far-off security light shining through their open blinds.

He dropped Vin's hand to go close them.

"Leave them open." Vin stepped over and stared out the wall of plate glass windows.

As Niko's eyes adjusted, he could make out the tops of the trees and even the outline of the bench where they'd met up. They might as well be the only two people on the tiny island.

"If someone stood out by the bench, they could see in," Niko said, though he wasn't telling Vin anything he didn't already know.

"With the lights off in the room, they'd only see shadows and silhouettes, if that."

Niko came up behind Vin, taking his hands and pinning them against the glass above Vin's head. He pressed his pelvis to Vin's ass, loving the way his cock settled into Vin's crack.

He nipped at the soft spot where Vin's neck met his shoulder and whispered in his ear, "You like being on display, do you? Are you an exhibitionist, Vin?"

Vin's lascivious chuckle zinged Niko's nerves, making his dick heavy and the need to take Vin against the glass door almost overwhelming.

"I'd be lying if I said I've never had fantasies of being taken in front of a window in a New York skyrise. That set we have back at the studio has featured in my dreams too many times to count."

"Except you don't want the set, do you, Vin, you want the real thing."

Vin lowered his hands, and his head fell back on Niko's shoulder, his words barely audible when he said, "Yes."

"Don't move." Niko peeled the unbuttoned shirt off Vin's shoulders and tossed it aside, then went back for Vin's T-shirt.

He took his time. They had all night, and as much as he wanted Vin's ass, wanted to hear him cry out his name when he came, Niko didn't want to rush. If all they had was this week, he wanted to draw out each moment and make it last.

Inch by inch, he raised Vin's shirt, catching Vin's reflection in the glass, getting off on the way Vin's eyes drifted closed as he lost himself in the quiet.

Vin's arms and hands came free of the fabric, and he reached a hand back, catching the back of Niko's head and pulling him in for an over-the-shoulder kiss.

Vin nipped and licked, keeping the kiss shallow at first before taking it deeper. Niko could get lost in that mouth, those lips. Forget the rest of what Niko wanted to do with Vin, he could stay there all night, tasting and drinking him in.

Niko wasn't one to compare lovers. Different people came together in different ways, which always made each encounter new and exciting, but never in his life had he kissed someone who put all of themselves into that intimacy, giving themselves over to the pleasure, living from one nip, one taste to the next.

Niko broke the kiss, catching his breath, but it wasn't just the lack of oxygen that made his head spin.

It was Vin.

And then, Niko saw his mistake.

They hadn't even had sex, and Niko found it hard to think about next Saturday, their flight back to California, and the real world crashing in.

"Hey." Vin turned around. "Where did you go?"

Niko laughed, rueful and perhaps a little wiser. "Contemplating my life's choices."

"That a good thing or a bad thing?"

"I'll let you know."

Niko reached for Vin's belt and released the buckle. The button of his shorts and the zipper came next. He hitched his thumbs into the waistbands of Vin's shorts and briefs and dropped them down to his ankles.

"Damn," Niko said. "You're a sight."

With a grin, Vin stepped out of his clothes and kicked them away. "Your turn."

Niko reached for his belt, but Vin batted his hands away. "My chance to have some fun."

Vin unbuttoned Niko's shirt, catching his arms in the sleeves and sliding the shirt down to his wrists, handcuffing them behind his back.

The air conditioning blew on Niko's skin, peaking his nipples. Vin ran his hands down the center of Niko's chest, through the short mat of dark hair and down his centerline, past his waistband to the burgeoning bulge between his legs.

Niko hissed out a breath, the touch tempting and torturous at the same time. He wanted flesh on flesh, not two layers of fabric between them. But Vin wanted his turn and, despite the urge to free his hands, gather Vin into his arms, and drop him on the bed, he'd let Vin have this time.

The flick of Vin's tongue across Niko's nipple and the stroke down his covered cock drew a muttered curse from Niko. "You need to hurry."

So much for taking your time.

"No chance." Vin's voice held a hint of delighted devilment. Straightening, Vin reached for the fastener on Niko's shorts and nipped Niko's chin. "I've finally got my hands on you. You're not getting out of this until I say so, or until you've come. If you want out, you'd better say so now."

Niko grinned and threw Vin's words back at him. "No chance."

Reaching around, Vin freed Niko's hands and walked him back until he hit the end of the bed. "Lose the shorts."

Niko obeyed Vin's command, intrigued by the domineering, take-charge side of him but also not wanting to wait a second longer to feel Vin's hand on his dick.

"Take hold of me." The thickness in Niko's words rumbled in his chest.

Vin chuckled as he reached up and gently pinched Niko's nipple. "It's gonna be a long night if we're both giving the orders."

"I don't have anywhere I need to be. You?"

———

Take hold of me.

Four little words that Vin never expected to ever hear coming out of Niko's mouth. As Vin took Niko's cock into his hand, he couldn't shake the feeling this was all a dream.

But his dreams had never been that concrete.

In his dreams, he couldn't smell the sea in Niko's hair, or feel the texture of the velvet-soft skin on Niko's dick, or hear their ragged breaths, or revel in the zing of his nerves as Niko nipped and sucked his way across Vin's collarbone.

Grazing his thumb over the head of Niko's cock and through the slick pre-cum, Vin started easing down to his knees, wanting to taste Niko again.

"Stop."

Vin's stomach knotted, and his hand stopped stroking Niko's dick. Had Niko already changed his mind? Or maybe Niko had to confess that Vin sucked at giving head.

"You don't like me going down on you? What do you like? I'll—"

Niko laughed. "Fuck no. As much as I've tried, I haven't been able to get the mental image of seeing you between my legs out of my head."

"Then what's the problem?"

"It's my turn to go down on you."

"This isn't tit for tat. I'm not keeping score. You—"

Niko pivoted, switching their positions and guiding Vin to sit on the edge of the bed. "I want to taste you. And then I want to fuck you. You good with that?"

Vin's hand drifted to his own dick. Smearing pre-cum over the head and down his shaft. "Sounds a-*fucking*-mazing."

Scruffing a handful of Vin's hair at the back of his head, forcing his head back, Niko leaned in, taking Vin's mouth and kissing the breath out of him. "Hang on. I'll be right back."

"Okay." The word came out more like a squeak than anything that resembled spoken language.

Vin followed Niko's movements. The play of moonlight over Niko's lithe form only made Vin harder. Vin's fingertips eased up and down his shaft as Niko rummaged around in his suitcase and returned with condoms and a travel-sized bottle of lube. He tossed them on the bed within easy reach.

Niko sank down to his knees, his hands skimming up Vin's inner thighs as Vin sat back, his weight resting on his hands behind him, his dick on ultra-high alert.

Hitching his arms under Vin's legs, Niko tugged Vin's ass to the very edge of the mattress. His balls drew up tight. Fuck, he was going to explode before Niko even got the chance to suck him off.

Niko dipped his head, and all Vin's thoughts and fears vanished as his mind zeroed in on the featherlight trace of Niko's tongue along the thick vein on the underside of his cock.

Vin's hand shot to the back of Niko's head, holding him in place as Niko held the base and swirled his tongue around Vin's thick ridge. Pre-cum leaked down his shaft, and Niko lapped it up with one long, warm, wet swipe.

"You're fucking torturing me." The words thick and guttural as Vin's hips flexed on their own, seeking Niko's mouth and all that it offered.

Niko's warm and wicked chuckle washed over Vin, kicking his heart rate into dangerous territory. If he red-lined, if this was how Vin left the world, it would be the best way to go.

"Tell me what you want." Niko's long, languid strokes teased and taunted.

Niko damn well knew what Vin wanted, but it steamed Vin's pipes knowing that Niko wanted Vin to say it.

"I want your mouth. I want your throat. I want to be balls deep tickling your tonsils until you can't take any more."

"*Fuck me*," Niko groaned as he pulled Vin down for a soul scorching kiss.

He tasted the salt of himself on Niko's tongue, the scent of sex, and musk heavy in the air. "Next time," Vin promised, taking Niko's epitaph as a command though he had no idea if Niko was verse or not. In all of the porn Niko had starred in, he'd always been the top.

"Hell, yeah."

Niko nipped and licked his way down Vin's sternum, pressing a hand to Vin's chest. "Lay back."

Vin obeyed, lacing his fingers behind his head and staring down his body at the man on his knees about to service him. Niko pressed his hands against Vin's inner thighs, spreading his legs wider and looping them over his shoulders.

At the first touch of Niko's tongue on his taint, Vin's eyes fell closed, and his head hit the mattress, shutting out all visual stimuli and heightening his other senses.

Niko licked and lapped and tasted his way from Vin's hole, across his taint, sucking first one ball and then the other into his mouth before releasing them both and taking a firm hand to the base of his dick.

His cock pulsed in Niko's grip, anticipating what was coming next. Niko gave the head of Vin's cock one last teasing lick before taking Vin deep to the back of his throat.

"*Aw, fuuuck.*" Vin squirmed, his hips thrusting to meet Niko's downward stroke. "Your mouth feels so fucking amazing."

He bumped the back of Niko's throat, but instead of pulling back, Niko relaxed and took him deeper. The lips, the tongue, the heat, the wet, all worked against Vin lasting like the porn stars he filmed.

His hand drifted to the back of Niko's head as Niko bobbed up and down on his dick. He locked his ankles behind Niko's back, holding him tight.

"I'm coming," Vin groaned as the first pulses started deep within.

Niko maintained a brutal pace. Vin had never been with a guy who drove a face fucking that hard and fast.

His climax hit. Vin cried out. The sounds of Niko sucking and swallowing ripped through him, making him come even harder.

Niko pulled off near the very end, finishing Vin off with his hand as the last of Vin's seed dripped from the tip of his dick. Niko ran a finger through the drop on Vin's belly and licked his finger clean with a mischievous grin.

"I love your cock," Niko said, scooting Vin up the bed.

Vin tried to help, but his muscles refused to comply. His nerves buzzed and tingled, and his brain remained offline.

Niko settled on the bed between Vin's legs, his dick still hard as Vin went soft. Resting his weight on his forearms, he kissed his way up Vin's body and burrowed his face in the crook of Vin's neck.

Nipping at Vin's pounding pulse point, Niko soothed the ache with his tongue, sucking in a deep breath through his nose. "Fuck, I can't get enough of your scent and taste."

As far as Vin was concerned, Niko could stay lodged between his legs for the rest of the night—hell, the rest of the week—their sweat mingling, their hearts thudding.

If Vin had his way...

Stop. You can't think like that. You accepted this week with Niko with your eyes wide open, knowing the pact came with an expiration date. Don't try to make it into something it isn't. You get to fuck your crush, count that as a win and move on.

Niko ground his cock against Vin's pelvis, chasing the friction. Reaching between them, Vin took Niko into his hand and repositioned Niko so that his cock ran down his taint and edged along his crack.

Within seconds, Niko's pre-cum had slicked Vin from behind his balls, past his hole, and all along the crease of his ass. Niko's slow strokes pressed against Vin's perineum, stimulating his prostate. Vin's dead dick started to come alive again. He needed Niko inside him. "You going to fuck me, old man, or what?"

"Who you calling old man?" Niko chuckled, rising on his hands. "I wanted to give you a chance to recover. Or beg off."

"I'm not backing out." Vin ground against him, flicking his thumbs across Niko's nipples, eliciting a sharp intake of breath. "I want you in me. Now."

Niko nibbled at his chin. "You kids these days. So impatient."

"Give me what I want." Vin caught Niko's face in his hands and forced Niko to look at him. "Less talking, more fucking."

Niko dipped his head, sweeping his tongue into Vin's mouth. "I love that demanding, dirty mind of yours."

"Prove it," Vin taunted.

Niko reached for one of the condoms and tore the wrapper with his teeth. "Careful what you wish for."

WITH SHAKY HANDS, NIKO COULDN'T ROLL THE CONDOM DOWN fast enough. When he finally got it seated, he reached for the lube, slicking his shaft and running a fresh bead along his finger to lube Vin's ass.

His dick strained, wanting to be inside Vin, but he couldn't do that without some prep.

He pressed the tip of one finger against Vin's hole, captivated by the eager way Vin pushed against it, his body begging for more.

He slid first one finger and then another inside, fighting back a groan—the wait to feel that tight ass around his cock, excruciating.

Vin's hips thrust, fucking himself on Niko's fingers as Niko's other hand inched up and down his thigh, enjoying the flex and strain of Vin's quads as he rode Niko's digits.

Vin blew out a breath, a hint of frustration in the sound. "I want your cock, not your fingers."

Niko leaned down and bit the tender flesh on the inside of

Vin's thigh. Vin yipped, and Niko grinned. "Give me a minute. I don't want to hurt you."

"On your back." Vin pulled away and pushed Niko into the mattress. "I'm not an ass virgin."

Niko barked out a laugh. "I never suspected you were."

Vin crawled on top of Niko, straddling his hips and guiding Niko's cock so that it slid up Vin's crack. "I know my limits. I know how to breathe. How to relax. And I don't need you handling me with kid gloves."

"You don't, do you?"

"No." Vin rose and wiggled until Niko's dick centered on his entrance. "I'm going to show you what I can take and how I like to be fucked."

The grin that overtook Niko's face couldn't be hidden or helped. He laced his fingers behind his head. "Be my sexy guest."

Vin shifted a fraction, and Niko's head breached that tight ring of muscle. The grip, the stretch, the groans—fucking phenomenal. Vin's eyes drifted closed, and the moan that erupted from deep down in Vin's chest had to have been the sexiest sound Niko had ever heard.

He wanted to grab Vin around the waist, hug him to his chest, and drive up into him, but as experienced as Vin claimed to be, he couldn't do that until he knew what Vin could take. There had been others who'd thought they could take all of Niko and had been disappointed to learn that they couldn't.

Vin's head fell back as he slid down Niko's cock inch by inch until he bottomed out. "You're so fucking thick."

Niko wasn't sure anyone had taken him that deep since his porn days. The grip that low on his dick made his balls tight and his head light. This could end a lot sooner than Niko wanted. Vin starting to move didn't help any.

"Slow down a sec." No way did he want this to be over before they got started.

"I told you, I don't need—"

"I do. Unless you want this carnival ride cut short, you're gonna have to give me a second."

Vin ran his hands up Niko's chest and back down his ribs, a naughty grin on his face.

"You're enjoying yourself, aren't you?" Niko said. "Knowing you have the control and the power to drive me over the edge, and I wouldn't be able to stop you."

Vin dove in for a kiss. "I'm not gonna lie. Holding the reins is intoxicating."

With the men in Niko's life, he'd been the one with all the control, and now, having the roles reversed, flipped the erotic script in his head that Niko hadn't known he wanted to write.

But holy hell, it worked for him—if the throb of an impending orgasm meant anything. Niko stilled Vin with his hands on his hips, but that didn't keep Vin from rocking back and forth.

Niko filled his lungs with oxygen, holding his breath until his impending climax retreated. Reaching around, he cupped one of the finest asses he'd seen in all of his career. It wasn't the roundest, or the most muscular, but those cheeks fit in his hands like they'd been made for him.

He started thrusting, slow at first, letting Vin adjust to the depth and angle of penetration, but Vin refused to let him drive for long.

Vin ramped up the speed, riding him senseless, their bodies slamming together, taking them higher and higher. Their breaths came fast as sweat sluiced off their bodies, the air conditioning incapable of keeping up with the heat they generated.

As much as Niko got a charge out of Vin riding him, laying

on his back, he lacked the leverage he needed to fuck Vin the way he wanted.

He wrapped his arms around Vin and reversed their positions. Vin went with the motion, hardly losing a stroke. Niko rose on his knees, throwing one of Vin's legs over his shoulder so he could pound into him the way he wanted.

He bumped past Vin's prostate over and over. "Oh, yeah, *fuck*. Right there. Christ, you're gonna make me come again."

Vin jacked himself as Niko's thrusts intensified and became erratic. With a hand on Niko's thigh, Vin encouraged him to speed up.

The air sawed in and out of Niko's burning lungs, hot and fast, the oxygen didn't have time to go where Niko needed it most.

"Aw, fuck, fuck, fuck." Vin's head fell back as he jacked himself with a frantic, furious rhythm. The cords in his neck went taut, and a groan ripped out of his throat as cum jetted onto his abdomen.

Vin's ass contracted around Niko, and he couldn't hold out any longer. He dropped down on top of Vin, sliding his arms beneath him and looping his hands over Vin's shoulders for leverage as thrust one last time.

Vin's arms wrapped around Niko's head, pulling him in tight to Vin's chest as the last sweet strains of his orgasm left his body.

Niko didn't know the last time he'd felt so utterly spent.

And wholly known.

11

———

"Don't go." Vin held Niko's hips as he started to pull away.

"I'll be back. I just want to take care of the condom."

Vin held tighter before letting Niko go. "I hate condoms."

"A necessary evil, unless we're fluid bonded, which..."

"Yeah. I know." No point and, more importantly, no time for Vin and Niko to be tested appropriately in the span of less than a week for them to enjoy condom-free sex. "You don't have to say it."

Vin's phone buzzed. *Go away, world.* He wanted to keep real life at bay, but with Cat and the rest of the crew still off the island, he couldn't ignore a text in case someone needed help.

With a groan, he slid out of bed and dug his cell out of the pocket of his shorts, his legs shaky, and his arms lifeless. Niko came out of the bathroom and tossed him a damp washcloth.

"You can't leave your phone for one night?"

Vin allowed the hint of censure in Niko's voice to roll off him. He understood the sentiment. Vin cleaned up the mess smeared across his abdomen. "I want to make sure Cat is okay."

"Isn't she with the others?"

Vin opened the message from a blocked number. "She is. I—"

Blocked number: *I need 150k or I'm going to the police with what I know.*

Vin's heart stalled.

His legs gave way, the bed catching him before he hit the floor.

"You what?"

Vin heard the question, but he couldn't form an answer. Niko came around the end of the bed and forced Vin to meet his gaze with a finger under his chin. "What is it?"

"I... I need to shower off." Vin pasted a jagged and raw smile on his face. "Give me a minute, yeah?"

"Everything okay?" Niko indicated the phone.

"Yeah. Wrong number." Vin stood, though how he managed to put one foot in front of the other was a mystery. His heart still hadn't found its rhythm, not with his world crashing down around him.

"You want company?"

Vin wanted distance. To get as far away from Niko as he could before Vin brought any trouble to Black Stallion's doorstep.

"No. I'll be out in a minute."

Vin ran his shower, letting the boiling water pound away at the knots in his shoulders, his stomach balled up tighter than a marble, while the crushing weight of an anvil sat on his chest, the oxygen fighting to get in.

He hadn't responded to the text.

Didn't know what to say.

How to act.

How to make it go away.

He should have known the past couldn't stay buried.

"Hey." Vin turned at the sound of Niko's voice. "Everything okay in here? You've been standing there for twenty minutes."

Vin slapped his hand on the lever, shutting the water off. "I'm fine."

He ducked Niko's gaze. If Niko knew the truth, he would not only want Vin out of his bed, he'd want Vin out of his life. Taking the towel Niko offered, he half-ass dried his legs and chest, wrapped the towel around his waist, and went searching for clothes.

He managed to slip a clean pair of briefs on before collapsing onto the couch and holding his head in his hands.

He was fucked.

Screwed.

His life as he'd built it, over.

Unless he got his hands on a hundred and fifty thousand dollars.

NIKO CAME OUT OF THE SHOWER TO FIND VIN SITTING ON THE couch, cradling his head in his hands.

What the fuck did you do, Stavros?

Vin had seemed as into the sex as Niko had been, but Niko knew all too well that when you're horny, your dick could lead you astray, and it was only in the aftermath that the regret and self-flagellation flooded in.

He'd been honest with Vin from the start with what he wanted and what he could give, but maybe that hadn't been enough.

"Hey." Niko sat on the arm of the couch. "That bad, huh?"

"Worse." The word came out thin, strangled.

"Jesus Christ, Vin." The words whooshed out of him, barely

a whisper. Niko pressed the heel of his hand to the ache at the center of his chest. He'd never wanted to hurt Vin.

He eased onto the cushion beside Vin and put his arm around Vin's shoulder. "You should have told me to stop. If I'd thought—"

Vin lifted his head but stared through the window into the darkness. "This isn't about the sex."

Niko waited him out. There had to be more.

"It's a personal thing. No big deal."

"Bullshit. I know you, Vin. Don't lie to me. 'No big deal' doesn't make you dissolve in front of my eyes."

Vin huffed out a caustic laugh. "You think because you had your dick in my ass that you know me?"

Niko squeezed the back of Vin's neck, light, but grounding. "We've been through a lot of shit together. Especially in those early years. Don't boil this down to a fast fuck on a hot night. If you need help, I'm here."

"I can take care of myself. I don't need to go running home to daddy."

Niko absorbed the verbal slap, knowing Vin didn't mean it. He was hurting like he'd been hurting all those years ago when Niko had first taken Vin in.

Chucking one of the throw pillows at the window, Vin hollered out, a guttural, haunting release of pent up rage. Slowly, the anger leaked away.

"Fuck me. That was rude," Vin said, meeting Niko's eyes. The fury had drained away but not Vin's distress. "Sorry."

Niko gave Vin's neck a squeeze again and tugged him over, pressing a chaste kiss to the side of his head. "It's alright. Don't push me away. I want to help if I can."

"I appreciate that. Truly. But you've done more than enough for me over the years. This is something I've got to handle on my own."

Niko understood the need to blaze your own trail. You couldn't build one of the more successful studios without standing on your own two feet against people who would love to see you fail.

Niko stood and held his hand out to Vin. "Come to bed with me?"

Vin sat up straight, running his hands down his thighs and giving Niko's outstretched hand a once over.

"I just want to hold you. Yeah?"

"Yeah. Sure." Vin blew out a breath and took Niko's hand.

Tossing the lube and condoms into the nightstand, Niko laid down and guided Vin onto the bed beside him, rolling him to his side and clamping an arm around his waist, tugging him in tight to his chest.

Niko's own heart thumped and thudded against his sternum. What wasn't Vin telling him? After all these years, why couldn't Vin trust him with his problem?

Niko tucked an arm under his head and traced soothing circles on Vin's hip.

"That feels good." Vin relaxed into the mattress and sank into Niko, seeming to absorb the comfort Niko willingly gave.

Planting a kiss in between Vin's shoulder blades, Niko said, "Get some sleep. I'm here. Tonight, and always, if you ever need to talk."

Vin didn't answer, but Niko didn't need him to. He'd offered. It was on Vin to accept.

All night long, Vin tossed and turned, mumbling in his sleep every time Niko changed positions or rolled on his other side until, finally, Niko laid flat on his back, and Vin snuggled against his chest. The steady rhythm of Niko's heart beneath Vin's ear, allowing Vin to sleep.

With the blinds open, they woke early with the sun, a shaft

of light slicing across the bed, shifting and sliding as the sun rose until it seared Vin in the face.

"I don't want to get up." Vin grunted and threw a protective hand over his eyes. Niko's hand went to Vin's back, trailing a light line up his spine.

Niko glanced at the clock on the bedside table. "Go back to sleep. We've got another hour before we need to meet everyone downstairs for breakfast."

Vin pushed up on an elbow, his cheek tugged on the skin on Niko's chest as it pulled free from where they'd stuck together. Vin swiped at the minuscule pool of drool on Niko's sternum, the flush rushing up to his cheeks. "Oops. Sorry about that."

"Not a problem."

Vin rolled out of bed.

"Where you going?"

"I gotta take a piss."

Niko needed to use the facilities as well, but his morning wood would make that nearly impossible. He'd just lay there for the next century or so until his dick flagged.

If he hadn't been concerned about waking Vin in the middle of the night, he might have done something about the mounting pressure in his balls, but Vin had needed the sleep more than Niko had needed to get off.

Vin returned from the bathroom naked, one hand on his dick, the strokes languid and lazy.

"I take it you're not going back to sleep."

Vin hitched his chin toward the tent in the sheets over Niko's cock. "I think the next sixty minutes would be better spent getting off. What do you think?"

As deep as Vin tried to stuff his troubles, it showed in the tightness around his eyes and the forced half-smile on his face. Sex wouldn't solve any of his issues, but it could take his mind off them.

"Well, if you can't think of anything better..."

"Fresh out of other ideas." At the foot of the bed, Vin eyed Niko like prey.

Niko, the hunted. Not the hunter.

The role reversal put a zap on Niko's head. Usually, he preferred to pursue the men he took to his bed, but... damn if he didn't love that dynamic with Vin.

Vin grabbed Niko by the ankles and gave a quick pull, dragging him down the bed. Kneeling on the end of the bed, he crawled on all fours until he straddled Niko's chest, pinning Niko's hands above his head with their fingers linked and Vin's knees on Niko's arms.

Vin's cock bounced a maddening inch too far away from Niko's mouth.

"What are you going to do?" Niko's words came out as a dare.

Waiting to hear what Vin wanted to do to him turned him way the fuck on. Pre-cum already dripped from the tip of his dick, and he squirmed under the delightfully wicked expression on Vin's face.

"Whatever I want."

"And what is it that you want? *Say it.*" This time the order came from Niko. The flip-flop of dominance and power a total cock-edging, cum-filling trip.

"I want to sit on your face. I want you to suck my balls, and tongue-fuck my ass."

Niko's hips flexed all on their own, and the devilment played in Vin's grin. He knew exactly what he was doing to Niko and got off on his power trip.

Where have you been my entire life?

Niko bit down on the traitorous thought before it got him into trouble. Just because they clicked sexually didn't negate the impossibility of a relationship extending beyond that week.

He was still Vin's boss.

And Vin was still that kid he'd pulled off the streets.

But there would be a time to dwell on that later. "Give me my hands."

Vin complied, and Niko scooted down farther on the bed, positioning his mouth beneath Vin's balls and looping his hands around Vin's thighs, guiding him into place.

The first lap of his tongue along Vin's taint brought a groan so low it resonated in Niko's chest, some sort of subsonic sex signal. He sucked and nibbled the delicate skin down there, his tongue forging the divide between Vin's balls.

Pressing a hand to Vin's chest, Niko made him sit up straight, so his tongue reached Vin's hole. He couldn't get enough of the musk and the scent and the taste of Vin.

Will you ever?

Doubtful.

Vin started grinding into Niko's face, and he pulled Vin down even lower, giving him the tongue fucking he wanted. Niko reached down to stroke himself as Vin reached up to grab his own dick, their breaths coming out in short, harsh pants.

As they both neared that cliff, Vin pulled away.

"What the hell," Niko said, his frustration impossible to cover.

Vin's lighthearted laugh made Niko's heart somersault, which turned into more of a tumbling dive in his chest as if he'd jumped out of the plane without a chute.

Total free fall.

He couldn't be falling for Vin.

Couldn't.

"I want us to come together." Vin scooted down Niko's body until their cocks aligned, bracing himself on his forearms. "Why do you look so surprised?"

It wasn't so much Vin's words as the vulnerability knocking around in Niko's chest at the realization Vin was more likely to hurt *him*—scratch that. *Break* him—than the other way around, because holy fuck...

This kid—

No, this *man* could easily steal Niko's heart and tromp all over it.

Niko deflected with the first comment that popped into his head. "I didn't expect it would matter to you."

And fuck if that wasn't the worst thing he could have said if the confusion and the hurt that flicked across Vin's features were any indication.

Niko needed to take the words back. "I didn't mean—"

Vin dipped his head, shutting him up with a kiss that put the exclamation mark on the notion that Vin would be his ruin.

He couldn't think with this man in his heart, in his head.

"Shut the fuck up, and let's come already," Vin said.

"Works for me."

Vin reached down between them, capturing both of their cocks in his hand, using their combined pre-cum as lube as he stroked them from head to root.

Niko thrust up into Vin's hand, the heat, the grip, the pressure, the friction, shooting him toward that inevitable precipice.

Vin's sharp intake of breath told Niko he was close. By the lightning zipping toward Niko's groin, he wasn't far behind.

He took Vin's hand away, locking their fingers together above his head, continuing the pump and grind, their bodies trapping their dicks between them.

Vin's head went back, his heart jackhammering against Niko's chest. Then his eyes locked on Niko's, his pupils almost blown.

"Fly with me," Niko said.

"Fuck, yeah." Vin shouted his release, muffling his words in the crook of Niko's shoulder.

Their cum spilled between them. A beautiful hot, sticky

mess. As the last shudders and twitches left their bodies, Vin collapsed on Niko's chest. Niko brought his arms around Vin, holding him tight.

His hands trailed down to Vin's ass, holding him close as he pressed up against him again, not wanting the contact to end.

As their breathing slowed, and the fog of sex cleared from his head, Niko laid there feeling wicked and wrecked.

And way the fuck in over his head.

———

Vin made it through to their mid-afternoon break between scenes, proud of himself for holding his shit together for most of the day.

He never would have made it that far if he hadn't shoved the blackmail text to the back of his mind and buried it under a blanket of denial so thick, no light could shine on it.

But that constriction in his chest wouldn't ease, and he couldn't draw in a full breath. Even moving the equipment and lights around had taken more out of him than it should have. If he'd been asthmatic, he would have reached for an inhaler.

He grabbed a cola and a finger sandwich from the spread of food the resort provided out by the pool. Not that he had an appetite, but he needed to keep up his strength to keep his head clear and to prevent others from seeing through the façade he'd erected.

The guys, as well as Betty and Rose, sat at the bar, eating and chatting away, while Niko had been MIA since the word 'cut' had left his mouth.

Vin found a lounge chair in the shade and out of the fray, directly in the path of a fan with one of those water misting attachments. It brought the air temperature down about ten degrees.

Closing his eyes, he took a long drag of the soda, waiting for the rush of sugar and caffeine to give him the boost he needed.

He took a bite of the sandwich. All the food at the resort had been top-notch, but he could have eaten a spoonful of sand, and he wouldn't have known the difference.

"Hey." Cat kicked one of the legs of his lounge chair. "What are you doing over here by yourself?"

"I needed a few minutes."

Cat's eyes narrowed, her head cocked to the side, assessing. He closed his eyes again, hoping she wouldn't be able to read him as well as she usually did.

"Want to try that again? This time without lying to my face."

Vin opened one eye. She had her hands fisted on her hips and if he thought she wouldn't deck him if the next words out of his mouth were 'I'm not lying,' he'd be dead wrong.

Cat scooted another lounger closer. The legs screeched as they skidded across the pool deck. The scraping sound sent goosebumps racing up his back, making his scalp tingle.

Plopping down, she stole the rest of his sandwich and stuffed it into her mouth.

"Hey, I was going to eat that."

"Liar." The bread muffled the word. She swallowed hard, then washed the food down with a swallow of his cola. "Something's been off with you all day. You should have come and hung out with us last night. We had a blast. Fuck that dude for canceling on you."

"It's not about that."

So many thoughts scrambled through his head. He'd need a solid month to sort them out. Only he didn't have a month. Hell, he didn't know how long he had before the blackmailer made a move.

Maybe you would know something if you weren't too chicken shit to text him back.

Fuck his life.

He'd come so far. Gone through and survived so much, and now some motherfucker threatened to take it all away from him.

"Then tell me what it *is* about."

Niko walked through the resort's double doors heading straight for the food table. He didn't glance Vin's way. Vin couldn't say the same. At least one of them could play it cool.

"Oh, my *gawd*." Cat's hands flew to her open mouth, the twinkle in her eye more mischievous than cute. "You totally fucked him, didn't you?"

How could she have guessed that? "I— We—" Vin sucked in a calming breath that had zero effect. "I didn't fuck him."

Cat eyed him down the length of her nose, her invisible antennae going up like some sort of human lie detector. "You're telling the truth."

"*Yeah*." He painted the word with a heavy shellacking of *duh*.

Nodding, Cat considered him from the short distance. He needed to get out of there before she figured out the truth. He went to get up. She snatched his hand and sat him back down.

"He fucked *you*."

The tinge of soreness in his ass didn't disagree. Niko had given him the pounding he'd wanted and needed, and he was trying desperately not to beg for again and again and again.

The look he shot her didn't dissuade her, even though he'd added a touch of heat to throw her off the scent.

She leaned in. "How was it?"

"I'm not—"

"Don't give me any lip about not kissing and telling, that's total bullshit, and you know it."

Vin crossed his arms over his chest. "If you breathe a word—"

Zipping her lips closed, she tossed the invisible key over her shoulder. "You know Fort Knox only wishes it were as secure as all the secrets in my head. Whatever you tell me will be triple-locked, razor-wired, and guarded with my life. Now spill."

"Okay. Yeah. We spent the night together."

Cat threw her head back and laughed so loud the others stopped talking and glanced their way.

"Would you keep it down?"

"Sorry. 'We spent the night together.' Puh-*leese*." Cat shook her head at him, her scowl full of parental disappointment. "Even Betty wouldn't describe a night with Niko like that."

"We had sex. That's all."

Vin didn't want to go into any details. Not that he hadn't shared details of his sex life with Cat before. And if he'd hooked up with @dickful69, they would be having an entirely different, more detailed conversation. But what he and Niko had shared had been... singular. The connection... incomparable.

And he wanted to keep that experience all to themselves.

"And..."

"It was great."

Cat crossed her arms over her chest. "But?"

He had to toss her a bone. Even if it had little meat on it. Maybe it would be enough to shut her up if she had that to gnaw on. "It's only for this week."

"You've got to be fucking kidding me." Cat shot to her feet, the red racing up her neck and landing on her face. Vin yanked her back down to the lounger before she stormed over to Niko and threw a punch.

"It's okay," Vin said.

"It's not okay."

Vin glanced over to the group by the bar. *Jesus.* All eyes were on them. He leaned toward Cat, his voice a rough stage whisper. "Keep your voice down, everyone is looking."

"It's not *okay*, Vin," Cat repeated herself. This time she

managed to keep her voice from carrying, but barely. "You've had this massive crush on Niko for a long, long, long—"

"I know. I get it."

"*Long* ass time." Cat kept going, not caring that she mowed over his comment. "Whose brilliant idea was this anyway?" And by *brilliant*, Cat's tone said *stupid as shit*.

Vin couldn't look at her when he admitted, "His."

Cat glared over her shoulder at Niko. He was too far away to hear what they were saying, but he raised his hands at her as if saying *What's the problem here?*

She flipped him the bird and turned back around.

"Haven't you ever had a bucket-list fuck?" Vin asked.

"Who doesn't?"

"Well, Niko's mine. I took his offer because it's what I want to do. Good or bad, this is my decision. And, as my friend, I'm asking you to respect that."

She reached out and squeezed his hand. "You're going to get your heart stomped, you know that, don't you?"

"I'm not an idiot."

"Fuck, but you're acting like one." She reached over and pulled him into an awkward hug. "I love you. If you ever need to talk, I'm here."

"Thanks."

Besides a home and a career that he loved, Vin owed Niko for the fantastic friends he had in his life. He didn't have a biological family he could count on, but he'd built his own around everyone at Black Stallion.

Not how he'd once seen his life going.

It was better.

12

Niko set his half-empty drink down, excused himself from the conversation he was having with Rose and Betty, and headed over to the loungers where Cat and Vin sat in deep conversation.

He walked a circuitous route beneath the shaded porch overhang, scrolling through his email as he walked.

A message came through from Sebastian, stopping Niko: *I had to silence the phones at the studio. Reporters won't stop calling. They want a comment from you. For the love of God, call them and give a statement. Not all publicity is good publicity. Download rates have dropped almost by half.*

Hell. He hadn't even given the story that broke more than a passing thought, figuring the story would blow over while they were gone. Guess he'd been wrong.

Niko: *I'm back in six days. I'll handle it then.*

Sebastian: *Call them now. Before it does real damage to your bottom line.*

Niko sent a non-committal: *Thanks for the heads up.*

He had enough to deal with between the shoot and Vin and—

"You're going to get your heart stomped, you know that, don't you?" Cat's voice carried.

Between that statement and the middle finger Cat had shot him from across the pool, he had no doubt she knew he and Vin had had sex.

Glancing behind him, he couldn't see the bar from where he stood, and the tall planter with the leafy green foliage shielded him from Cat and Vin's view.

He caught a couple of other words. *Idiot* being the one that stood out most. But he wasn't going to stand there and listen in on their conversation again. Dropping his phone into his pocket, he walked over to them, not able to drum up any anger about Vin telling her about them. Cat was a vault. If anyone else found out about him and Vin, it wouldn't be from her.

And really, Vin having someone to talk to could be a good thing.

His inner voice laughed at him, almost maniacal. *You're the one who's going to need someone to talk to after this week is up. A friend. A therapist, maybe? Because, sure as shit, you're fucked up in the head for starting this... this whatever the hell you want to call it.*

Niko shoved his hands into his pockets and stepped between Cat and Vin's loungers. "Everything all right over here?"

"Just peachy." The amount of saccharine Cat poured over those two words could kill a whole lab full of mice in an instant.

Cat stood, the top of her head hitting him mid-chest, but that didn't stop her from jabbing her index finger into the center of his sternum. "You hurt him and I'll—"

Gently, Niko closed his fist around her hand. "I have no intention of hurting him."

"That's what I keep trying to tell her," Vin piped in.

She glanced from him to Vin and back again, her plump lips going flat and her brown eyes going dark. "You're both knuckleheads. This isn't going to end well. You know this, right? It's fucked up and messy, and I'm the one who's going to have to pick up all the pieces."

Niko employed his most reasonable voice. The one that usually calmed people and set them at ease. "We're both adults—"

"Adults, my ass." Cat dropped her hands to her thighs and started walking away, muttering to herself. "You're not adults. You're nothing but a couple of horny kids being dragged around by your dicks and your hormones. Of all the stupid, idiotic…"

Cat walked out of range, the muttering continued, and the words became unclear. Niko got the gist. He turned back to Vin. One corner of Vin's lips turned up as he watched Cat retreat.

"She's worried about me."

"Ya think?"

Vin chuckled, like Niko hoped he would, the awkwardness ratcheting down from Defcon 5. Vin rubbed at the muscles on the back of his neck as his smile slipped.

"Look," Niko said, "we can call this whole thing off. Just say the word."

Vin's eyes caught his. "You gonna let her objections dictate our sex life?"

"She's got nothing to do with you and me. But that doesn't mean she's wrong."

Vin stepped closer, the space between them all but disappearing. "Pretty arrogant of you, assuming I'm the one who's going to get hurt, don't you think?"

A quick glance at the bar told Niko no one was paying them any attention. Niko laid a hand on Vin's shoulder and guided him back, step by step until the shrubbery and the porch overhang concealed them.

Vin stopped when his back hit one of the support columns. Niko ducked his head, brushing his lips against Vin's and taking the kiss deeper as Vin's mouth opened in invitation. The contact shot right to his groin, and he couldn't wait to get Vin alone in their room again.

Breaking the kiss, he whispered in Vin's ear. "A couple days ago, I might have thought that was true, but now I'm not so sure." Niko straightened, leaving his hand on Vin's hip. "There are a lot of things I'm unsure of right now. Who's going to come out on the losing end of this thing is one of them."

Vin shook his head and stared at something over Niko's shoulder. "This isn't a zero-sum problem. There doesn't have to be winners and losers. We're just two adults fucking each other out of our systems."

Niko chuckled. "I like the way you think."

Vin tracked something in the sky as the low hum of a helicopter engine, and the whomp of rotor blades drew nearer. He stepped out into the sun, shielding his eyes with a raised hand. "They're flying awful low, aren't they?"

Niko joined him to get a better look. The helicopter turned, revealing its tail number. "That's the same asshole who flew over us during our beach shoot this morning."

"What do they want?"

The helicopter descended lower and lower as it circled the island, the rotor wash making waves in the pool as it passed by and headed for the on-island helipad.

"I have no idea." Niko clapped Vin on the back and started for the landing area. "But it looks like we're about to find out."

The two-seater helicopter landed as Niko and Vin approached the pad. The rest of the Black Stallion crew scrambled to keep up. The pilot cut the engine, and the rotor blades started winding down.

"Why does that guy have a camera?" Cat asked.

"We expecting anyone, boss?" Vin took his fingers out of his ears.

The little thrill Niko got when Vin called him 'boss,' he let pass. As much as he didn't like being called that on the set, hearing it in the bedroom might be... interesting.

The passenger door of the helicopter opened, and a man jumped down, a camera with a telephoto lens in his hand that he quickly refitted with a shorter one.

"A fucking reporter." This had to have something to do with the leak Sebastian had told Niko about. "Someone get Knowles."

"He's already here." Greer stepped aside for the resort's manager to pass.

"You can't be here," Trevor Knowles said. "This is private property."

The reporter raised his hands. "I'm Dylan Wilson. I'm a reporter with *Queer-y*."

"Jesus Christ," Vin said.

"What are those mother fuckers doing here?" Cat asked.

More importantly, Niko wanted to know how they knew where to find him. "It's a long story."

"I just need a minute," Dylan said.

Dylan put his camera to his eye, but Knowles put a hand over the lens. Dylan lowered the camera but didn't step back. Knowles was a slight built native Bahamian, but he stood with his arms folded across his chest, blocking Dylan's way.

"Okay. Fine. No pictures. Just give me a couple minutes, and I'll be on my way."

"The only thing I have to say is, 'no comment.'" Niko couldn't make it any plainer than that. He turned to his crew. "You all head back inside. We're filming in thirty minutes."

Knowles shifted his attention to the pilot, his words rapid, laying his accent on so thick that Niko had no chance of understanding a word, but by the gesticulations, Knowles was pissed, and the pilot caught the brunt of it.

Everyone beat it back to the resort, except Vin.

"You can go, too," said Niko.

Vin shot him a look. "Not likely."

With Knowles's attention diverted to the pilot, Dylan edged closer. His hands out at his side in supplication. "C'mon, man. I'm just trying to do my job here. Free speech and all that."

"One," Niko said, "you're trespassing. And two..." Niko laughed at the absurdity of this guy landing at their resort. "'Free speech' my ass. You've got a lot of nerve. You work for *Queer-y*. Ninety percent of what you print is pure fabrication, the other ten percent is lies."

"Then talk to me." Dylan didn't argue Niko's point. He knew the truth about his employer. "Give me something to print."

"And have you twist my words until what's printed doesn't remotely resemble what I said? No, thanks." Niko turned. "Let's go, Vin. We've got—"

Dylan's hand landed on Niko's arm and brought him up short. Fun fact: the bedroom was the only place Niko didn't mind a little manhandling. "You're going to want to let go."

The pilot shouted out to Dylan and made a 'come on' motion with his arm. Dylan muttered a curse, dropping Niko's arm and jogging back to the helicopter. "What's your deal, man? I paid you..."

Whatever else Dylan had to say was lost when he climbed back into his seat and closed the door behind him. Knowles stepped over to them and ushered them back down the path toward the main resort as the whine of the helicopter's engines spooled up.

"They won't be bothering you anymore," Knowles said, his accent less pronounced as he spoke to Niko. "We'll make a special dinner for your people tonight. Drinks are on us."

Niko clapped Knowles on the back. "It's fine. That's not your fault. I appreciate you getting rid of them for me."

———

HALF-STARVED FROM HIS STRESS-INDUCED LACK OF APPETITE earlier in the day, Vin swallowed a mouthful of the pulled pork and scooped his fork into the peas and rice. He washed it all down with a gulp of his Kalik beer.

The entire crew sat in the resort's dining room that evening at one big circular table, overlapping conversations and laughter brought the noise level in the room overlooking the water well past a dull roar.

Vin's phone chirped in his pocket. The light buzz he had going on had him reaching into his pocket without a second thought.

Tick-Tock.

The hops soured on his tongue.

Blocked number. Vin didn't have to be Stephen Hawking to formulate a theory as to who the text came from. Sweat beaded along his hairline that had nothing to do with the temperature in the room and everything to do with having no fucking idea where he could get his hands on a hundred and fifty thousand dollars.

Vin hadn't responded to the first text, hoping he could come up with something, *anything*, that would make it all go away, but it was as if the text had obliterated all higher thought. He had no plan. No money.

You could run.

The cops can't lock you away if they can't find you.

Vin glanced around the table at the smiling faces, at his friends, at his *family*.

He couldn't start over again.

Better than sitting locked in a cell.

He thumbed out a reply: *I don't have that kind of money.*

The return message came back immediately: *Find it.*

Followed by: *Or else.*

Yeah. Fuck. He knew what else. Having a good idea Stu was

behind the texts didn't help. And that was only a guess. The blackmailer knew what he knew. Confronting him wouldn't make him forget it.

"Vin… *Vin*." Greer laughed, a conch fritter dangling in his hand. "Preston asked what it was like sleeping with Niko."

"Excuse me?" Vin's voice squeaked. The heat rushed in, and his cheeks ran hot.

How did everyone find out? He glanced at Cat, who shook her head. Whatever they'd heard, it hadn't come from her.

Niko cleared his throat, wiping his mouth and hands on a napkin. No way Niko had said anything. "We've lived together before. Not much has changed."

Except for the sex.

Niko's expression gave nothing away, but his eyes held a warmth meant only for Vin. Those eyes. *Fuck*, they would be the end of him if the cops didn't get him first.

Vin cleared his throat, determined to play along with the teasing. "True. You still snore like a freight train, and you can't sing worth shit, even in the shower."

Niko threw his head back and laughed, easing the mounting tension across Vin's shoulders. "Touché."

"How's that ass, Preston?" Hayes asked. "You going to be up for your scene tomorrow?"

Vin tuned out. The conversations went on around him as he tried to figure out how to diffuse the atomic bomb that had landed in his lap. If it blew, he didn't know how he'd survive the fallout.

The next thing Vin knew, the waiters came through, clearing plates. "You finished with this, sir?" one of them asked.

His pork remained half-eaten, and the rest of it he'd hardly touched. "Yeah, I'm finished. Thanks."

Vin pushed away from the table as Niko walked around to his side. "You ready to work on those edits?"

Betty came up to Niko and threaded her arm through his. "Now, now. Don't work the boy so hard. It's been a long day. Besides, you promised an old lady you'd escort her around the island."

Niko patted Betty's hand. "I did."

"Glad there's someone who can ride roughshod over him," Cat said. "The evening is too beautiful to spend it holed up in a dark room bent over a computer."

Preston rubbed a hand over his full stomach. "I'm headed to the pool."

"I'm right behind you," Hayes said as they filed out of the dining room.

Chet laughed, the dimple in his cheek popping out with his huge grin. "Haven't you spent enough time behind Preston already today?"

"Christ," Greer grumbled, "can't you guys get your minds out of the gutter for a second?"

Vin fell to the back of the group, planning on finding a small corner of the world to curl up in and wish his troubles away. He'd thought about calling Sebastian, but he couldn't keep a secret. Where Cat was a vault, Sebastian was a sieve. He didn't mean to spill secrets, they just flowed out of him.

They all went their different ways, Cat catching up to Vin near one of the beach paths. "Oh, hey," Vin said. "What are you doing here."

"I came to find out what the actual fuck is going on with you."

"I don't know what you're talking about."

Cat sighed. Big and dramatic and way over the top. "We're not going through this again today, are we?"

"What?"

"Where you insist you're fine when everyone around you can tell things aren't copacetic." They followed the walkway around the pool bar to the footpath that led to the beach. "What did Niko do this time?"

"This has got nothing to do with him."

Cat stopped and turned him to her. The look she shot him would have had him confessing the truth if he'd been lying. "Okay." Cat retook his arm, and they continued down to the beach.

The sun sank near the horizon, and the evening breeze had picked up, swirling Cat's hair around her head until she had to gather it up into a shorty ponytail to keep it from whipping across her face.

The path dipped down to the beach, and they shucked their flip-flops where the grass ended and sank their feet into the hot white sand. She turned around backward, taking both of Vin's hands and pulling him to the water up to their knees.

Sand shifted beneath their feet, but the refreshing water felt good against his skin. They started walking along the shore, heading into the sun.

She pulled a phone out of her pocket and waggled it in front of his face. "Does this have anything to do with why Niko had to stop the shoot twice today? Because you forgot to start filming when he said 'action?'"

Not *a* phone. *His* phone.

He tapped the pockets of his shorts, though clearly, his phone wasn't where it belonged. "How did you get that?"

"You left it on the table at dinner. I picked it up."

Vin frowned. He snatched his phone back, but she gave it up without a fight. "And cracked my lock code and snooped around in my messages."

"Seriously. If you don't want someone looking at your messages, you need a better PIN than 6969. That's as bad as Sebastian's 1234."

"It's still a violation of my privacy and—"

Cat busted out a laugh. *"Violation of my privacy."* Cat did a half-decent job mimicking his voice, so he couldn't fault her on that. "You practicing to be a lawyer or something?"

"I'm just saying—"

"What's a violation here is your propensity to keep me at arm's length and not trusting me when you're in trouble. That's the friendship violation, right there."

"I'm not in trouble. I have it handled."

"So, you what? You got a Swiss bank account you never told me about? A grandmother who died and left you her inheritance? A bank you robbed? A mob boss you killed?"

That last one landed square in his chest. Too close for comfort. His legs wobbled, and he had to plop down on a sun-bleached log embedded in the sand to keep from falling on his ass.

Cat eased down beside him, her hand rubbing his back as he lowered his head between his knees before the tiny black spots in the periphery of his vision turned into a full-on faint.

"Slow your breathing," Cat ordered.

Yeah, well, if he could do that he wouldn't be on the verge of hyperventilating.

"Cup your hands in front of your mouth. We don't have a bag, so that will have to do."

He followed her orders. He didn't want to pass out and risk Cat going to Niko and telling him everything.

By the time his breathing finally slowed, and the spots disappeared, the lower edge of the sun-splashed down into the sea, the oranges, reds, and yellows painting the horizon. A bird tiptoed around in the shallows, spearing the sand with its beak over and over again.

Cat's arm held tight around his waist. "You going to tell me what's going on?"

"You read the messages?" Vin asked, though Vin already knew the answer.

"Yeah."

"Someone is blackmailing me."

"I got that much." Cat kissed his shoulder to soften the harshness of her tone. "I'm wanting to know what you planned on doing about it."

Vin laughed, the fabric of it threaded through with hysteria. "Try to come up with the money is all I've got."

"What about the police? Maybe they could figure out who it is and—"

"No police. And I have a pretty good idea who's behind it."

"This isn't something you can, cowboy. You gotta go to the police and—"

Vin shot to his feet. "I can't go to the fucking police, okay?"

Cat slowly stood, reaching out a tentative hand as if afraid he'd bolt. "Okay. No police." She took his hand and sat him back down. "Just tell me what's going on. You're scaring the shit out of me."

Elbows on his knees, he plucked a strand of dried seaweed out of the sand and tore it into pieces bit by bit. He glanced up at her. "Niko can't hear a word of this."

"Obvs."

"I can't report it because I'm being blackmailed with the threat of going to the police. So, the police can't know, and they can't help me."

"It can't be all that bad."

Vin took a deep breath. Prepared to say the words he'd only uttered once before. His heart did a swan dive, belly-flopping at the bottom of his chest, a quivering mass of muscle and blood that had forgotten how to function.

The world spun, and Vin fought to keep it upright.

"I killed a man."

13

———

NIKO AND BETTY WALKED COUNTERCLOCKWISE AROUND THE
island. On the dirt path cutting through the grass on the far side
of the island, then down to the sand when the rocks gave way.

Niko carried both his shoes and Betty's in his hands. For an
old lady, she had twice the stamina of anyone else on his crew,
and her kind heart, fast-thinking, and wicked wit had quickly
endeared her to him and everyone else as well.

Which made him understand more the lengths Grant Hardy
had gone to to make sure this woman, his grandmother, had a
roof over her head.

Lying about being straight had cost Grant his job with Black
Stallion, and if the latest download reports from Sebastian were
correct, it was costing the company tens of thousands of dollars
in lost daily downloads from the backlash when news surfaced
that Grant was gay.

But he'd gladly face down any helicopter riding, camera-
carrying, online rag mag of a reporter any day if it meant Betty
still had her home.

"You're quiet tonight," Betty said.

"Got a lot on my mind."

She patted his arm. He could almost hear the 'there, there' behind the touch. She made him want to grab a bag of cookies and a glass of milk and spill all his problems.

"Is it boy problems?"

Boy. Yeah. That was the problem.

"I don't think you want to hear about my sex life."

"I'm eighty years old. I've pretty much seen and heard it all. And what I hadn't seen before, these nice young men this week have filled in the blanks. At this point, there isn't a whole lot that you can say that will shock me."

Since Niko didn't have a clue how to dig himself out of the hole he'd made for himself, maybe Betty would have the answer. If not, would he really lose anything besides a little privacy?

"There's this guy that I'm... well, let's just say I'm kinda into."

And would be *into* at that very moment if Betty hadn't wanted to take a walk. Not that he held that against her. The night was still young.

"Does Vin know that you like him like that?"

"I didn't say it was Vin."

She patted his arm again, making him feel simpleminded. "You didn't have to, sweetie. You can't take your eyes off him. And when you do, when he's out of sight, you're always looking for him."

"That obvious?"

"Only if you're breathing."

Niko slapped a hand to his face. "It's not supposed to be like this."

"Love never is."

"I'm not in love."

"Okay." Betty's agreement made his skin feel too tight and prickly. He'd expected her to argue with him, not let him sit with his statement and let it itch like a bad rash.

"It's just..." Niko struggled to put his thoughts into words. "I don't see the point. It can't work."

"You two fight?"

"No."

"You don't have good conversations?"

"It's not that."

"Are you sexually incompatible?"

Niko laughed, shaking his head. "It's not that either."

"Then call an old lady crazy, but I don't see what the problem is."

"I'm his boss."

Betty looked at him with her penciled eyebrows raised above rheumy eyes that had seen a lot of the world, the good and the bad they seemed to say. "As long as you don't use that power to hurt him or others, I don't see what the problem is."

"And he's just a kid."

"There's not a kid on this island, sweetie. He's an old soul. He's lived a lot of life in the years that he's had from what I've heard. And that *man* knows his own mind."

They kept walking, and Niko stewed on her words. When the resort came back into view, and no more had been said, he figured the discussion had ended.

She stopped him with a gentle tug on his arm. In the distance, the laughs and shouts of Preston and Chet filtered through the trees.

"My husband and I had quite an age difference ourselves."

"How much older was he?"

Her eyes lit, a smile coming to her lips that made the years fade away, and he saw her as a young woman in love for the first time. "I was sixteen years older."

"Cradle robber."

She laughed and threaded her arms through his again. "Don't you know it, dear."

"What are you trying to say?"

"By the standards of the time, I was practically an old maid. But that made no difference to him, not one lick. Made no difference to me either. I guess what this old lady is trying to tell you is don't run from happiness. 'Cause it always has a hard time catching up."

VIN SQUEEZED HIS EYES CLOSED, WAITING FOR CAT'S SHRIEK—OR A punch or what, he didn't know—bracing for Cat's reaction.

He had no idea what to expect.

What do you say when your friend tells you someone died because of them?

Or she could turn away and not speak to him ever again. Might be the best option. No one wants to be besties with a killer.

"*Okaaaay,*" Cat said. "Wow. Yeah. I mean... Um... That's not where I thought you were going with that, but..."

She leaned into him instead of sprinting away. Maybe that was a good sign. "Like *killed* killed?"

Vin stared out into the sea. The roar of the waves mimicking the blood rushing behind his eardrums the same way it had way back then in Chicago. Rushing. Rushing. That night a blur of shouts, of racing hearts, of bruises, and pain, and the unrelenting certainty that that was the night Vin would die.

"*Killed* killed," Vin confirmed.

"Like... with a car. An accident. A—"

Vin held his hands up in front of him and stared at the backs of them. "With my hands. With a bat, but with my hands." He met her eyes. They weren't fearful. Wary maybe. Concerned certainly. Were the worry lines on her forehead for him or for her? "It wasn't an accident."

"Who was it?"

For years he'd tried to put that bastard out of his mind. Sometimes he stayed gone for a while. Mostly, he didn't. "My old man."

"You get in a fight?"

"We were never *out* of a fight. Not really. Not after he found me fucking the high school quarterback I'd been tutoring my freshman year."

He thought back to those times. To the dilapidated house, the scent of beer and piss always heavy in the air like a backwoods biker bar that streetwise people didn't dare enter.

Cat didn't prod. She waited him out, giving him the space to breathe. The space he'd never had growing up.

"My father had his suspicions about me way before then. Couldn't talk my way out of it that time. Easier to dismiss when it's rumors and whispers. Kinda hard to ignore when your kid's caught balls deep in some dude's ass. I don't even remember the guy's name. He jumped out the open window, taking the screen with him, leaving his pants, his books. I tried to run, but I wasn't fast enough."

Cat rubbed his back as she leaned against him, resting her chin on his shoulder. "What did the police say?"

He blew out a breath, releasing some of his pent-up stress, relieved that she didn't ask for more details. Some things you can't unsee or unhear. What would he do if his friends abandoned him? Not that he would blame them one bit.

"Dunno. I lit out that night. Never went back. Or gone anywhere near Chicago ever again. There's no statute of limitations on murder. That's how I met up with Stu. We were both riding the rails. Took up traveling together until we jumped off in LA. We got real close real quick. Until he ditched me. He's the only person I ever told, until now."

"Not even Niko?"

"Are you kidding? He put a roof over my head when I didn't have one. Kept me from resorting to survival prostitution. I couldn't tell him. I couldn't take that chance back then."

"Sounds legit." She fell quiet, but they'd been friends long enough for him to know she had more to say. "Everything you told me, though, if it went down the way you said, it sounds like self-defense to me."

"I wasn't keen on waiting around long enough for the cops to make that determination."

"What about now? You could go to the police yourself and—"

"And what? I've got no way of proving anything. No. It's better that I pay this guy off and try to move on with my life."

"Surely they're not still looking for you."

Vin shrugged. Honestly, he had no clue. The case had to be cold after ten years, but if someone, AKA, the blackmailer, went to the police with information, that could change in a heartbeat.

Cat pressed a kiss to his cheek. "You may have killed someone, but you aren't a killer. That's not who you are."

His heart clogged his throat and, even after he tried clearing it twice, it refused to budge. He nodded and dried his eyes with his sleeves.

Don't you fucking cry now, you scrote.

Pushing to her feet, Cat brushed the sand off her ass and held out a hand to him. "Come on. We'd better head back before they send a search party for us."

Vin allowed her to help him up, and they walked back to the resort, stumbling in the uneven sand in the near dark. They had to use the flashlights on their phones to find their shoes.

At the outdoor shower near the beach, they washed the saltwater and sand from their legs and feet, their flip-flops making squishing sounds as they walked up the path.

"You should talk to Niko about this."

Vin laughed, the humor falling flat. "That would be a 'no.'"

"He's got a crapton of money."

"No."

"That you helped him make."

"No."

"You could pay him back if that makes you feel—"

Vin stopped in the middle of the path, blocking her way, the security lights reflecting off the frown on her face and the trench between her brows. "He can't know."

"But—"

"Promise me." That plea in his voice? No fake manufacturing required. "Don't make me regret telling you."

"Fuck, Vin. I'd never rat you out, you know that."

"Promise me, then."

His heart thudded in his chest—this slow, methodical beat, like the big bass drum in a marching band. *Boom... boom... boom*, the reverberation making his marrow shake as he waited for her answer.

She held up her pinkie for him to take.

Vin ran a hand through his hair and huffed out a laugh. "A pinkie promise?"

"They're unbreakable."

He locked his pinkie with hers, and they shook on it. The excess moisture in her eyes glistening in the light. He pulled her into his chest, kissing the side of her head. "Why are you crying?"

She made a noise, part chuckle, part sob. "I don't know."

When her breath stopped hitching, she pulled far enough away to see his face. "What are you going to do if you can't come up with the money?"

"Fuck if I know." *Yeah, you do.* "Run, if I have to."

———

Where had Vin and Cat run off to? The island was too small to get lost. They should have been back to their rooms already.

Niko turned away from the window. Vin wasn't on the bench where Niko had spotted him the night before.

Go find him. You're not going to be able to relax until you do.

What are you worried about? He can't get into any trouble on the island. He could have stopped for a drink or got pulled into the volleyball game at the pool that had been in full swing when Niko had headed up to the room.

He rubbed at the hairs on the back of his neck. Something had been off with Vin since they'd slept together, and he couldn't put it out of his head.

Find him. He doesn't even have to come back to the room if he doesn't want to. It's not like working on the edits wasn't more of an excuse to be close to him without everyone else around.

Niko swiped his keycard off the dresser and strode for the door. As soon as he knew Vin was okay, he'd—

The door opened in his hand, and Vin smacked him with the door.

"Sorry," Vin said as Niko stepped back and let him in.

"I was just going out to look for you."

"Miss me?" The smile Vin shot him over his shoulder as he walked into the main area of the suite almost looked genuine.

But it fell fast, and the hairs on Niko's neck took notice.

"Yeah, actually."

Vin turned to face him, this smile more real. "Really?"

Niko thought about pointing to the computer and the crude editing area he'd set up on the desk and saying, 'really.' Instead, he did the dumbest thing he'd ever done.

He walked over to Vin, laid his hands on Vin's hips, and stepped into his personal space, their lips almost touching when he said, "Really."

Leaning in to kiss him, Vin stopped Niko with a finger on his lips. "Careful, you're going to make me fall for you if you keep saying shit like that. We can't have that, can we?"

Was it too late to change the rules?

Because that irrational, infatuated part of Niko's brain liked the idea of Vin falling, tumbling because Niko had felt the shudder of the unsteady ground beneath his feet. One wrong step. One wrong move and he'd be falling, too.

"I guess not."

Niko backed away, went to the mini-fridge, and dumped a tiny bottle of Jack into his coke. "Want one?"

"That would be great. Mind if I shower off real quick before we get started on the edits?"

"Go ahead. I've got some emails I need to attend to."

He would love to join Vin in the shower—wanting to recreate that scene they'd shot—but Vin didn't invite him. And Niko didn't ask.

When Vin returned, they sat down at the desk in the two office chairs, one of which he'd swiped out of Betty's room with her permission.

They started with a scene they'd shot with all four men. After reading Sebastian's update on the studio's decreased download numbers, as well as the drop in subscription memberships, the sooner they released new content to help bolster their numbers, the better.

Vin worked hard cutting and splicing scenes until the flow felt right. Adding in some background music and cutting out any of the voice directions Niko had given that had made it into the final cut.

"Fuck. This one's shooting straight to the top of the 'most viewed' list," Vin said.

"I think so, too." Niko had watched enough men having sex to last several lifetimes. You'd think he'd be immune, but watching Greer and Hayes take on Chet and Preston gave Niko a severe case of blue balls.

And the two of them sitting that close, the scent of the resort's coconut body wash wafting off Vin's skin, turned Niko's semi into a full-bore hard-on.

After this trip, the erotic association between coconut scented soap and sex would make it impossible for Niko to smell coconuts ever again without getting aroused.

"The daddy/twink thing is really hot right now. We should have been shooting more of these a lot sooner," Vin said.

Yeah, except every time he shot an age gap scene, he couldn't get Vin out of his head and all the crazy things he wanted to do *to* him and *with* him. He'd never wanted to give his brain enough leash to go there.

It had been easier to mostly avoid shooting that genre than have the memory of those scenes rattling around in his head.

But he'd finally given in and set up this trip to get a bunch of those scenes in the can. He'd theorized that doing a bunch in one go, instead of one here and there spread out over the months, would keep his thing for Vin compartmentalized.

That compartmentalizing thing... not exactly working for you, is it?

"You're right, we should have made these sooner."

Thirty minutes later, the edits were nearly done. "Ready to run through the whole video one last time?" Vin asked. "If it's good, then all I'll need to add are the title and the credits."

"Sure." Niko straightened in his chair and scrubbed his face with his hands. His lids scraped on his eyes as if they'd gone rusty, and his stubble scratched his palms. He really needed to shave. "What the hell time is it anyway?" Seemed like they'd been going at it half the night.

Vin pulled his cell phone out of his pocket. "Twelve-forty."

"Yeah. One last run-through, and we can worry about the

rest tomorrow. We'll be completely worthless in the morning if we don't get some sleep."

"You won't get an argument from me." Vin set down his phone. "I need a bio-break, and I'll be good to go. Unless you need to go first."

"Go ahead, I'm good."

Niko watched Vin go, his first few steps stiff from sitting so long. Vin swung his arms around to get the circulation moving again as he disappeared into the bathroom.

Niko tilted his head from side to side, working out some of his own stiffness. Vin's phone buzzed, and a message appeared on the lock screen.

He shouldn't look.

It would be an invasion of privacy.

Don't do it.

@dickful69: Tomorrow night. Wanna meet up?

The message was followed up with a peach and an eggplant emoji.

Niko's boner shriveled, and his chest went tight at the thought of Vin with another guy.

He and Vin had made no declarations of exclusivity. Vin had every right to see who he wanted. Still, Niko would have rather not seen that.

Serves you right for snooping.

14

———

Vin came out of the bathroom with a longing glance at the couch. He needed sleep. Maybe when he wasn't so exhausted, he would be able to come up with a plan that would satisfy the blackmailer.

Plopping back into his seat, he got a good look at Niko. "What's wrong?"

"Why would anything be wrong?"

"You tell me. I left, and everything seemed fine, and now you're Eeyore with a dark cloud hanging over your head. Is it the stuff with the reporters?"

"Not really." Niko clicked play on the video.

Vin took the mouse and hit pause. "Tell me."

"You got a message while you were taking a piss. The phone was face up."

A message from his blackmailer? That vibration in Vin's marrow turned into a quake. Did Niko know?

Niko cleared his throat and, instead of an apology for reading Vin's message, he said, "What are you going to do?"

The amount of air in Vin's lungs barely supplied enough

oxygen to maintain consciousness, much less speak. His words sounded hollow when he said, "I haven't decided yet."

"What's there to decide? It's just a hookup, right?"

Wait. What? Vin grabbed his phone and read the message. Not the blackmailer. *Phew.* "Um... yeah. I guess."

Vin unlocked his phone and messaged the guy back, basically fobbing him off as politely as he could.

"So? When are you guys meeting up? I think we'll be done early tomorrow night if you—"

"I'm not seeing him."

"Why not?"

"Because I'm seeing you." It came out more like a question.

"I mean, yeah, I understand, but..." Niko scrubbed his hands down the legs of his shorts and tossed back what was left of his drink, which amounted to melted ice and a couple drops of diluted alcohol. "You don't owe me anything. If you want to see him, see him. I don't want you missing out on a connection just because you and I are fooling around."

"F—" Vin choked on the word. "*Fooling around.* Is that what the kids are calling it these days?"

"Fuck, Vin. I don't know what to call it." The exasperation leaked into his words, his sigh a harsh exhale of breath. He made a 'gimme' motion with his hand. "Let me see this guy. See if I approve."

The tilt of his lips said he was kidding about the 'approval' remark.

"You wanna see this guy's profile?"

"I do."

"You sure your ego can take it, old man?"

Niko laughed, the sound calming Vin in a way that shouldn't be possible considering his dire circumstances. "I'm not sure at all."

"All right. If you end up curled in a ball in the corner of the room, don't blame me." Vin clicked through the app until he found the profile and handed the phone to Niko.

He thumbed through the photos one by one. The standard naked torso, an ass, a couple of impressive dick pics. "Maybe Black Stallion should recruit this guy."

"I doubt he wants the world knowing who he is. He never gave his real name, and there are no pictures of his face. He could have the face of a troll for all I know, or—"

"Or he's a closet case."

"Or married. He's from the LA area. He could be a famous actor, trying to get some dick on the down-low."

"LA, you say?"

"Yeah."

Niko returned the phone. "You should see him. Maybe he's not a troll, or a closet case, or an actor looking for discreet dick. Maybe he's a good guy. You two could hit it off and—"

Sounded like Niko couldn't get rid of Vin fast enough.

"LA is in our backyard. I can always look him up later."

The 'after we stop seeing each other' Vin left unsaid because frankly, he hated being reminded that the clock determined their time together.

"I thought this app was for people looking for a little strange while out of town," Niko said. "Stands to reason if he's looking here, he may not be down for anything once he gets back home. You know, so there isn't a violent collision of his two worlds."

"Then, it would never amount to anything anyway." Vin dropped his phone into his pocket and turned his attention to the computer. "Let's finish this so we can get to bed."

Niko pushed his chair back and stood. "I think we've done enough for one day. I'm beat."

"Same."

Vin saved the file, and they both headed to the bathroom to get ready for bed. Vin finished first because all he had to do was brush his teeth. He left Niko to his shower, and Vin dropped his T-shirt and shorts in a heap by the couch, fluffed up the pillow, fell onto the cushions, and pulled the lightweight blanket over the top of him.

He closed his eyes, but his thoughts raced. Get the money or run. Hell of a choice. He had some money saved, but not nearly enough to pay the guy off, and he had little to sell besides his motorcycle and his truck.

Could he qualify for a loan?

Or find a loan shark?

There had to be some in the valley if he looked hard enough. At least that would buy him some time.

Time enough for you to default when the interest ate your lunch and have them come to break your kneecaps.

Do they do that anymore?

Or they could just end you. Use you as an example for other loan seekers of what not to do...

Or you could run.

Vin cradled his head in his arms.

Start all over again.

The Jack and Coke sloshed around in his stomach, which should have been impossible since it had been hours since he drank it. Acid bubbled up the back of his throat, and he swallowed the burn down before he made a complete mess on the tile floor.

"You awake?"

The coffee table in front of the couch creaked under Niko's weight. Vin pulled his arms away from his head. "I'm awake."

Niko held out his hand. "Come to bed."

As much as he wanted to take Niko up on the offer of sex and oblivion, if only for a short time, he doubted even Niko's dick—Niko's glorious, magical dick—could drive away his demons tonight.

Vin rose on his elbow. "Yeah. Look, man, it's late. I'm not really up for—"

"I just want to hold you. That okay with you?"

More than okay. "Actually... that sounds amazing."

Niko helped him up, climbed into bed, and brought Vin down beside him. Vin's back to Niko's front, and Niko's strong arm snugged tight around Vin's waist.

Too tight to fall apart. Too tight to run.

Vin settled into the pillow, Niko's steady breathing ratcheting Vin's heart down to a safe, sustainable level. Even his stomach settled, and that quaking from deep within calmed to a mild shudder.

Niko pressed a chaste kiss to the back of Vin's shoulder. "Get some rest."

Closing his eyes, Vin laid his hand over Niko's, his thumb absently rubbing across a knuckle. Niko nuzzled Vin's neck, breathing him in, a muttered, breathless *fuck* spilling from his lips. "I wish we could lay like this forever."

Vin didn't respond immediately. Finally, he said, "Do you ever wish things had turned out different?"

That I wasn't the kid off the street.

That I wasn't someone you won't let yourself have.

"No." Unequivocal. No hesitation.

Niko opened his fingers, and Vin slotted his in between. "Everything we've lived and survived brought us here. We wouldn't be in this moment if our lives had turned out any other way. And right now, there's not anywhere else I'd rather be."

———

Vin groaned in his sleep. The sexiest sound Niko had ever heard. He'd been awake most of the night, not wanting to miss any second of the time he had with Vin.

Niko reached over and silenced the alarm before it had the chance to go off, thinking of much better ways to wake up.

Vin rolled, throwing his leg over Niko's, his morning wood pressing into Niko's hip as Vin started dry-humping him in his sleep.

Which did nothing to ameliorate the raging hard-on between Niko's legs.

Must be one hell of a dream.

He shook Vin awake. They didn't have much time before they needed to be down for breakfast to meet with the rest of the crew and go over the production schedule for the day.

The humping stopped, and Vin slapped a hand over his face before glancing down at the way he lay sprawled over Niko. "Sorry about that."

"I'm not." Niko placed a staying hand on Vin's hip. "Tell me what you've been dreaming about."

And if Vin took that as an order, all the better.

Niko chuckled and placed a finger under Vin's chin to force him to meet his gaze. "Your cheeks pink up like that, and I *definitely* need to hear it."

"Me. You." The words came out shy and thick with sleep. A low rumble that settled in Niko's chest, a gentle flame warming him like the first fire in the fall. "And all the things I want you to do to me."

Vin rolled on top of him, aligning their cocks as he nipped and sucked at the sensitive flesh at the crook of Niko's neck. Niko laid his hands on Vin's hips, stilling him.

Maybe Niko should have woken Vin sooner, but Vin had been physically wrecked when they'd gone to bed the night before, and whatever had been eating at him made everything worse. He'd needed the sleep more than they'd both needed the sex.

"We don't have time. We've got to be downstairs in—"

"You going to make me run around and film all day with a semi?" Vin rested his chin on Niko's chest and stared up at him with a sly tilt to his lips. "We can make it fast."

Niko rolled Vin to his back, and rested his head on his upturned hand, looking down at Vin as he lay stretched out beside him. "How about I get you off while you tell me all about your nasty little dream."

"Deal." Vin chuckled, wasting no time shoving his briefs down to his ankles and kicking them off. They landed somewhere on the floor with a soft swoosh.

"What about you?"

"This isn't about me. Besides, between scenes, I'm going to enjoy thinking about all the things you're about to tell me. And all the things we can do to each other tonight."

Niko cradled Vin's head and reached for his cock. With so much pre-cum dripping out of Vin's dick, he didn't even need to reach for the lube.

Each wicked, lascivious, devilish, mischievous, and downright dirty thing Vin said landed direct hits to Niko's groin, like sexy heat-seeking missiles. If Vin kept that kind of talk up, Niko would come without a hand being laid on him.

As Niko stroked Vin, he paid close attention to the ridge of the head that got Vin groaning and writhing beneath his hand. Niko loved the power. The control. Loved knowing *his* hands brought Vin to the very edge.

Within minutes, Vin's words faded, his breaths hot and heavy against Niko's neck as he nipped Niko's shoulder.

Vin fisted his hand in Niko's hair, pulling him in for a brutal kiss. Niko couldn't get enough and was two seconds away from scrapping the shoot for the rest of the week and locking them both in the room and saying to hell with it all.

But he didn't do any of that.

He had to do what was *best*.

Even if what was *best* wasn't what he wanted anymore.

Niko added a couple of firm strokes, his thumb working Vin's slit with each pass. He swallowed Vin's cry as he shattered in Niko's arms, Vin's cum coating Niko's hand with warmth.

Vin's head fell back, and Niko ran a line of kisses across his collarbone.

"That…" Vin didn't finish the sentence, his breathing too harsh to talk, and really, the satisfaction on his face said it all.

Niko climbed out of bed to get a towel for cleanup. After washing his hands, he threw a warm washcloth across the room at Vin. It landed with a wet plop on his belly.

Vin wiped himself off while Niko watched from the bathroom, which wasn't helping Niko's own hard-on in the least, but if they were going to get any work done that day, they needed to get moving.

Standing on wobbly legs, Vin stumbled. Niko reached out and caught him. Vin thanked him with a tonsil-teasing kiss.

"You gotta quit that," Niko said. "That's playing dirty."

"All's fair in love and lust."

Niko rapped him on the ass as Vin slid by and started the water in the shower. "Hurry up. We don't have all day."

Vin leaned out of the shower stall, dripping water all over the floor. "Damn, you're a Grumpy Gus when you don't get any."

"Grumpy Gus?" Niko folded his arms over his chest, but couldn't keep the grin off his face.

"Yeah," Vin ducked back under the spray and squirted body wash into his palm, raising his voice to be heard. "But don't worry, old man. I'll take care of you tonight."

If Niko made it until that night. He'd hate to have to run back up to the room during a break and rub one out.

Instead of getting dressed like he should, Niko cleared the smart glass, watching the steam billow up and the water sluice down Vin's body. Down Vin's defined shoulder blades, down the cords of muscles on either side of his spine, down the crack of his ass, down his hamstrings, to the back of his knee, and along the curve of his calf.

Vin chuckled, and Niko glanced up. *Caught.* Not that he had any intention of apologizing.

"Thought you were in a hurry."

"Yeah, yeah," Niko said as he turned for his closet.

Only four more days to get Vin out of his system.

Good luck with that. A little advice? Don't take those odds to Vegas.

By the time Vin finished dressing, whatever had been on his mind the day before came roaring back, casting a cloud in his eyes and wrinkling his forehead.

Vin reached to open the door, with Niko one step behind. Niko caught it with his hand before Vin could make his escape.

He leaned in close, though no one else was around to overhear. "You ever going to tell me what's eating at you?"

Over his shoulder, Vin glanced back at him, the corners of his mouth angled down as his chin came up. "Not if I can help it."

———

THEY ALL TOOK BREAKFAST OUT BY THE POOL. CAT HAD PULLED UP a chair and joined Vin and Niko at their table. Vin welcomed her company. Niko had been stewing since they'd left the room after Vin admitted that he had no intention of confiding his problems to him.

Having a buffer between them would hopefully keep Niko from pressing the issue.

Knowles came out as Vin cut up the last of his sausage.

"I'm sorry, sir," Knowles said to Niko, "but there's a private boat approaching the island. I think you have more visitors."

Niko balled up his napkin and tossed it onto his half-eaten food.

"Want me to go with you?" Vin asked.

"No. Finish your breakfast."

"I could send Cat. She could probably kick their ass better than I could."

Cat stood, a *you bet your ass* grin on her face, but Niko sat her back down with a firm hand on her shoulder. "Stay. I don't think I'm going to need that kind of help. Though if it's the same people, they're persistent little fuckers."

Cat hooked her heel on the front of her seat. "Next, they'll be making an underwater approach with a team of SEALs."

Vin tried on a smile that didn't feel too artificial. "I'm sure you could take them, too."

"Awh." Cat leaned forward and kissed him on the cheek. "You're so sweet."

Niko clapped Vin on the shoulder. "I'll be back."

Vin finished the rest of his sausage to find Cat staring at him, her arms around her legs, her chin on her knee. The morning sun sparkled in her all-knowing eyes.

"What?" Though he doubted he wanted to hear her thoughts.

"Someone looks well fucked."

Vin choked on his coffee, burning his sinuses. He coughed. "Would you keep your voice down?"

He glanced around at the other tables. Betty and Rose were going on about some TV show, and Preston, Hayes, Greer, and Chet were too busy eating and cracking crude jokes to notice.

"It wasn't like that," Vin said. "Last night was..." Vin didn't know quite how to describe it. "I hadn't expected the tender, empathetic side of Niko. He knows something's wrong, and he took me to bed and held me. It was..."

Cat's eyes got glassy, and she swiped a finger under her nose.

"Oh, my God. For someone so tough, you're such a sap."

"I'm a sucker for love. What can I say?"

"It wasn't love."

Cat raised one brow. The brow with the piercing that somehow added sarcasm to the disbelief. She could think whatever the hell she wanted.

Vin knew the real score.

"I do think he cares, though," Vin said.

Not enough.

"No shit, Sherlock."

"Don't go making this into anything it isn't. I jumped in with both feet, my eyes open, and my hard dick in my hand. It's gonna suck when it's over, but I can live with it."

"If you say so."

"I just did. Can we change the subject, please?"

"Sure." Cat sat back and tossed the rest of her orange juice to the back of her mouth and swallowed. "Why don't you tell me what you're going to do about the blackmailer?"

Greer threw his head back and laughed, though appropriate to the situation, he couldn't have overheard. The hairs on Vin's arms danced, and he rubbed his skin, brushing the unnerving sensation away.

"I was thinking about asking him to meet. Negotiate in person, maybe. There's no way in hell I can come up with that kind of money, no matter how much time I have."

"Do it. Before he gets tired of the silence and goes to the police with the information."

Vin pulled out his phone and composed his message: *I'm out of town. I want to meet in person. How's Sunday evening?*

The phone buzzed in his hand before he could set it on the table: *Sunday. Rick's Coffee shop. Eight a.m.. Don't be late. You don't come, I'll be at the police station by nine.*

Fuck me.

"You going to reply?"

"Not much to say to that. At least that buys me a couple of days to make phone calls and see how much money I can pull together."

"If I tell you something, will you promise you won't be mad?"

His lungs seized, and the air backed up in his bronchioles until it forced its way out. "What have you done?"

"Just remember I'm only trying to help you and that you're one of my besties and I love you and—"

Vin grabbed her wrist as she started talking faster and faster. "Just tell me."

"I talked to some of our mutual friends."

Vin's insides felt like they were melting into a quivering mass of nothingness. He slapped a hand to his face. How many of his friends knew? What would they think of him? He might as well take off now and—

And leave Niko behind? You really ready to do that?

It's not like Niko had made Vin any promises.

Except for the promise their humpfest would be over by Saturday.

"How many people know?" He coerced the words out of his mouth, not having the force of anger and betrayal to back them up, not when all he felt was empty.

"What? No. Nobody knows. Not like that." She leaned forward and grabbed his shaking hands. "I didn't tell anyone. Not the details. I swear. I only told them you were in a bind and if they had money to lend—"

"I don't know how I can pay that kind of money back. Niko pays me well, but..." They lived in California where you could buy a house the size of a park bench and be out a million dollars.

He feared asking how much she'd managed to come up with, but his curiosity got the better of him. "How much?"

"Between everyone I could reach last night, I came up with almost twenty-five grand."

They didn't have that many mutual friends. His heart vibrated in his chest, his eyes welled, and he had to sniff back the snot.

Fuck, what a mess.

With his elbows on his knees, Vin leaned forward and rubbed his hands down his face, looking at Cat over the top of his fingers. "That's a lot of money."

One look at his face and Cat's own went red around her eyes and nose.

He swallowed hard. "Don't you cry on me, Cat. Or I'm going to fucking lose it."

"A lot of people love you," was all she said.

"This is insane. I can't believe I'm contemplating this. I know who you would have called. They don't have that kind of money lying around. That kind of money would empty out their savings accounts. I can't ask them to do that for me."

"You didn't ask. *I* did. And no one hesitated. If you ask me, I still think you need to go to Niko, but if you don't want to, I get it. On top of what I could raise, you're welcome to everything I have."

Vin shook his head, pulling Cat onto his lap and hugging her tight. He pressed a kiss to the side of her face. "I don't deserve you."

"You do. You deserve all of us."

Niko returned. His head cocked at the sight of them, but Vin interrupted whatever it was Niko had planned to say. "What was that all about down at the docks?"

Hands on his hips, Niko shook his head. "Same reporter that came in the helicopter. Can you believe that guy? I mean, sure, Black Stallion is taking a hit, but I never expected the rag magazines to make that big of a deal about it."

"You're forgetting Pierce Hatchett owns *Queer-y*," Cat said, still perched on Vin's lap, her arms around his neck.

"Fuck. Of course. He'd die with a permanent stiffy if he took down Black Stallion and me with it. Well, it's not going to work."

Niko motioned at both of them, the downturn of his lips tugging up. "Something you two wanna tell me?"

Cat hopped up and kissed Niko on the cheek. "Take care of this guy, he's one of the good ones."

Niko turned and watched her walk away. When he turned back around, he asked, "What was that all about?"

"Nothing." Vin gathered up their dirty dishes. "Everything is fine."

"That's what you keep telling me," Niko said as Vin dropped the dishes in the busboy's tub. "But I still don't believe you."

15

———————

"Where have you been?" Vin asked.

Niko returned to the room later that night. Vin lay in Niko's bed, reading a paperback, the sheet across his hips, exposing the V angling down from his abdomen. Niko's eyes followed the trail of hair, knowing the treasure beneath.

Walking over, he left a bread crumb trail of clothing to the bed as he stripped off his T-shirt, dropped his shorts, stepped out of his flip-flops. The stress melted away as soon as he stretched out beside Vin. He trapped one of Vin's legs beneath his as he curled an arm around Vin's waist.

He buried his face in Vin's chest and breathed in through his nose. "I love the way you smell."

Vin chuckled. It rumbled in his chest against Niko's cheek. "Like chlorine, sweat, and seaweed? I rinsed off and jumped in the pool after that scene we shot in the water. Still, haven't had a proper shower."

"No. Like sun and surf and sex." Niko lifted his head and gave Vin the stink eye. "You jack off without me?"

Vin laughed and dropped his book. "You were gone for a while."

Niko growled, and Vin scrambled to get away, but he wasn't fast enough, especially with all the laughing. Without much effort, Niko pinned Vin to the mattress. "I'm going to make you pay for that."

"Goody." Vin grinned up at him, and Niko's heart tripped. Niko caught it before he fell completely for the man trapped beneath him.

"That was a long call to Hatchett. You two get things settled? Is he gonna call off his dogs?"

"That fucker." Niko rolled to his back, linking his hands behind his head. "The call lasted less than ninety seconds if that. He's had it in for Black Stallion for years, ever since we surpassed him in memberships and monthly downloads."

Vin scooted over and laid across Niko's hips, his head in his hand. "He doesn't like being second best?"

"A far, far back second best. And me winning you at the auction chapped his ass."

"I'm glad you won me." Vin leaned in and brushed a kiss against Niko's lips.

He caught Vin with a hand to the back of the head. "Do that again."

Vin kissed him again. Tender and sweet. Niko had always been a hard-loving guy, but with Vin, they could lay there and enjoy each other's company as well as have stellar, galactic, out of the world sex.

Other lovers of his had known his history in the sex industry and had expectations that Niko usually was all too happy to fulfill, but it was also nice to be with a man and just... *be.*

Fuck, Niko hoped he knew what he was doing with Vin. Letting him go at the end of the week was the right thing to do.

Right?

Hell, he didn't even know anymore, now that the lines had blurred.

Blurred? More like obliterated now that he's under your skin.

"If the call didn't last long, what did you do for the rest of the time? You've been gone over an hour."

"Nothing much. Went for a walk to cool off. Stared out at the ocean mostly."

"Find any answers?"

"Not really."

Vin brushed his thumb over the groove between Niko's brows. "You know, I like a threesome as much as the next guy, but Hatchett is the last person I want in bed with us." Vin scraped his teeth along Niko's stubble. "What do you say we kick him out?"

Niko gripped the hair at the back of Vin's head and guided him in for a kiss. "I think that's the second-best idea I've heard all week."

"And the first?" Vin asked, the grin knowing. But if Vin wanted to hear Niko say it out loud, he would.

"Taking you to my bed."

They both avoided the whole *what's going to happen at the end of the trip* thing. He doubted either one of them needed the reminder of the built-in self-destruct button.

"Rather inspired. I guess that is the wisdom that comes with advanced age."

"Advanced age, my ass." Niko rolled them, reversing their positions, their bodies and cocks grinding together when their bodies aligned. "I've got the stamina of a man half my age."

Vin reached for a condom and the lube he'd had at the ready on top of the bedside table. He tore the corner off the packet and held the condom out to Niko. "Prove it."

Niko woke Friday morning—their last full day on the

island—before the sun came up and the birds started twittering. Even before a couple of roosters that herded a loose flock of chickens all over the island crowed.

Careful not to wake Vin, Niko crawled out of bed and eased out to their balcony, the security light in the distance illuminating the bench where he'd first found Vin sitting.

How could the week already be over when it seemed like only five minutes ago that he'd found Vin out there by himself and made the stupidest, bravest deal of his life?

Could Betty be right? Could he put his and Vin's early years into perspective and accept Vin as the autonomous, grown man he was today?

Or would their previous relationship forever paint any future one?

Niko didn't know the answer, and there wasn't one blowing in on the mild morning breeze either. He'd left the door cracked open, and the air conditioning rushing out cooled his skin.

But no matter which way he turned the situation over in his head, he couldn't see his way through, unable to think with Vin so heavy on his mind.

Niko's father had always told him that when your mind was muddled, and your thoughts were unclear, stick with the decision you made when you had your head on straight.

Which meant they needed to stick to the original agreement they'd made—back when he was only thinking with his dick—and his heart and his emotions hadn't factored into the mix.

When the time came to leave the island, they'd leave all this nonsense behind.

You're a fucking idiot if you let that man out of your life.

But Vin wouldn't be out of his life.

He'd see Vin almost every day. Between the pre-production planning, the shooting, and the editing, they already spent more time together than they did apart.

Yeah. That's exactly the same thing as taking him to your bed and into your heart.

Into your life.

There are other men out there to fill that void.

Not one of them has yet. Coincidence?

Fuck fuck fuck fuck fuck.

Niko grabbed one of the bistro chairs off the balcony, raised it up over his head, reared back, and...

The chair caught on something.

Niko glanced around. Vin's hand gripped one of the chair's legs.

"Come back to bed," he said, before letting go and disappearing back inside.

Niko dropped the chair and scrubbed his hands down his face. What the hell was wrong with him? Vin had his emotions tied in a rat's nest and try as he might he couldn't tease any one of them free.

He followed Vin back to bed, where Vin had stretched out, holding the covers open for Niko. He slipped beneath the sheet, and Vin pulled him in, hugging Niko's head to his chest.

Did Vin feel it, too? Every beat in his chest, like the hollow tick of the clock as it winds down.

Niko pressed a kiss to Vin's sternum, right over the thud of his heart. Vin pulled back, his hands on either side of Niko's face. "You okay?"

Not even the slightest.

The truth spilled out. "I want you."

Maybe too much of the truth.

Vin's soft smile made the guilt lay heavier as if gravity had tripled. "I want you, too."

Did Vin mean it the same way Niko did? For now, and for always?

But Niko had a deal to stick to. One they'd both agreed on.

Niko shifted until he had Vin beneath him. They didn't have all the time in the world with three scenes to film before the day finished, but he would take every last minute, every last second, and make the best of it.

Vin reached down, relocating Niko's dick until it grazed Vin's taint and glided against his crack. Vin ground against him, his hands grabbing Niko's ass, maximizing his leverage.

Niko threaded his arms under Vin's shoulders and cupped the back of his head, kissing his way from the pulse at the base of his neck to the stubble on his jaw.

Vin's arms locked around his chest, holding him tight as if Niko was his world, and Vin refused to be spun out of Niko's orbit.

Their lips met, soft brushes and gentle nips. Tongue and teasing, breathing each other in.

"You're on top of me, but you still feel a galaxy away," Vin said. "I want you closer. I want you in me. I want..."

"What *do* you want, Vin?" Niko pulled back enough to see Vin's face. The eminent sunrise graying out the room enough that the vulnerability in Vin's eyes, shredded and ripped through Niko's chest like a sharp knife.

"Truth?"

Niko nodded.

"What I know I can't have."

Did Niko have to repeat their agreement? *Do you think having Vin say it will make the deal harder to break?* "We made a d—"

Vin scruffed the hair on the back of Niko's head. "Don't say it. Don't say *anything*. Just fuck me until I forget. Yeah?"

Niko did as Vin ordered. He didn't speak. He grabbed a condom and rolled it down his dick while Vin slicked himself with the lube.

Vin squirted more lube into his hand, coating the condom

and stroking Niko. *Fuck, that felt good.* Vin had a way with a handjob.

Vin chuckled.

"What's so damn funny?" Though Niko couldn't help returning Vin's smile.

"I love that moment when I make your eyes roll up, and I can see all conscious thought evaporate."

Vin continued his strokes. Long and languid. "Just you and me."

From the tip, down down down his shaft, cupping his balls and giving them a tug, not enough to really hurt, but enough to inject a quick nip of pain swirling with the pleasure, just the way Niko liked it.

"Whatever you say."

Niko playfully batted Vin's hand away and pressed the head of his cock against Vin's hole.

"Hang on." Vin grabbed a clean hand towel from the bedside table and wiped the lube off his hand before running his fingers down Niko's back, taking a handful of each butt cheek. "God, I love this ass."

Vin groaned and released a breath as Niko eased inside. "I love that cock, too."

Niko seated himself, balls deep inside Vin. It had only been a day since they'd had sex, but Niko had to hold himself steady to tear himself away from the ledge, his impending climax standing on the edge, one foot hanging off, ready to jump.

But Niko didn't want a quick ending.

Or the fast, pounding fuck that Vin enjoyed so thoroughly.

For once in his adult life, he wanted to go slow and draw the pleasure out, even as the rest of his world seemed to be spinning out of control.

Niko braced his weight on his hands, resting his forehead on

Vin's as he thrust in and out, his body shaking with the over-whelming urge to go faster.

With his hands on Niko's thighs, Vin urged Niko to increase his speed, but Niko kept up the steady, easy pace. "Faster," Vin ground out.

"Not going to happen."

Vin sucked in a breath, his response part groan, part chuckle. "I'm dying here."

"That's the point."

"You're a sadistic, evil bastard." Vin ran his hands up Niko's back and hooked them around Niko's shoulders, trying to gain leverage. Niko held his ground.

"I love you like this." Niko buried himself again, allowing Vin's leverage to take him deeper.

"What? Walking the knife-edge of insanity? You plan on paying the deposit on my rubber room?"

"If I must."

Niko kissed his way across Vin's jaw, the prick of hair against his lip, his face, drove him. Down Vin's neck, he licked and sucked, Vin's rapid breaths and muttered curses coaxed him.

Vin's hands roamed all over Niko's body. His hips, his ass, his nipples, his hair, Vin's body writhing beneath him as he raced toward his release. But by bracing his body over Vin's, Vin didn't have the rub and the grind of his dick on Niko's abdomen to get him there.

Vin's head thrashed side to side. Niko reached between them and took Vin's straining cock in his hand.

"Just like—*fuuuck*."

Vin's head fell back against the mattress as Niko worked the head with his thumb and his palm, with the same slow, deliberate consistency. Vin's eyes squeezed tight against his impending orgasm.

Niko's own orgasm built, watching the pleasure play across Vin's face, took him to the brink. "Look at me."

Vin thrust up into Niko's hand, his eyes fluttering open, a tinge of pink heating his cheeks, and the depth of the lust in his eyes enough for Niko to drown in.

Christ, he was going to miss creating that look in Vin's eyes. No one had ever looked at him that way. Like he was the only planet in the universe, something to be cherished, and not a means to an end.

They only thing Vin seemed to want from him was his presence. Not the fancy cars, or the mansion, or all the things his fat bank account could afford. It wasn't as if Vin could see past it, it was as if Vin didn't see it at all.

"Are you ready to come?" Niko asked.

"What's the matter?" Vin's voice came out thin and airless between pants. "Don't wanna see a grown man cry?"

Niko chuckled, lashing Vin's nipple with a flat swipe of his tongue before he rose up on his haunches and wrapped his arms around Vin's legs, changing the angle.

"Fuck, yeah." This time when Vin gripped Niko's hips, he went with the motion, rocketing them skyward. Vin jacked himself, his strokes mirroring the pounding Niko now gave him.

Vin only lasted seconds before his orgasm hit, his ass tightening around Niko's cock. No way Niko could last. His climax hit, a shock to his body, a zapping of his nerves, a blinding of his sight.

Niko collapsed into a sweaty heap on top of Vin, his body shuddering with the aftermath as his brain came back online, his thoughts flickering and fleeting like an old neon sign.

Vin wrapped him in his arms, kissing the top of his head. "You still alive?"

"Not sure yet. I think my world went supernova."

Vin chuckled, and it sounded light and carefree. "I'm pretty sure only stars can do that."

Niko glanced up, resting his chin on Vin's chest because his arms shook, and his legs complained too much for him to hold himself up or roll off. "Then maybe I'm dead, and all that bright light was the shine off the pearly gates."

"Well, if this is the afterlife, I think I'll be happy here."

Vin straightened his legs with a groan, and Niko pulled out and ditched the condom before he made a mess. Vin wiped the cum off his belly and swiped at the smears on Niko's, but neither one of them moved to get off the bed.

"You know," Vin said as he glanced toward the frosted shower wall. "We still haven't done it in the shower."

"That's because I like having you in my bed too much. But we can take advantage of it tonight if you want."

"Seems a shame to waste the opportunity."

Niko's shower back at his house was bigger and more luxurious. It didn't have the smart glass, but everything else was top notch. But that was back home. Vin would never see it, and they'd never have sex in it. "Yeah. Wouldn't want to waste it."

When Vin made a move to get up and hit the shower, Niko caught his hand and pulled him back down to the bed.

"What?" Vin asked.

Niko pressed a kiss to Vin's lips. "Thank you."

Vin's grin went lopsided at the same time his brows rose. "What for?"

"For this week and the time we've spent together. I—"

"Stop." Vin's lips went flat, and he glanced up at the ceiling as if all the answers could be found up there. Then he pinned Niko with a harsh look, the muscle ticking in his jaw. "You think I was doing this as a favor?" Vin's voice tripped as it climbed up the octave scale.

"No. That's not what I meant at all."

"Then what did you mean?" Vin scraped the back of his knuckles across Niko's cheek, and Niko closed his eyes and leaned into the touch.

Niko shook his head. "I'm going to mess this up."

Vin pinched Niko's chin between his thumb and forefinger. "Try me."

"This week meant a lot to me in many ways. And I'm thankful for the time we had together. I won't forget it."

Niko had more to say, but he stopped there, not trusting he could get it out without being misunderstood or spilling too much of the truth. He certainly couldn't say it without his voice cracking.

Vin smiled, the façade faked, the smile not even getting close to his eyes. "Still have twenty-four hours. It's not over yet."

"What do you have in mind?"

Vin flicked a glance at the smart glass.

"In addition to the shower."

"Have dinner with me tonight." Before Niko could answer, Vin added, "Not here. Nassau. I can find a nice restaurant. Make reservations."

In all the years Niko had known Vin, he'd never been a difficult man to please. "That's all you want?"

"Not even close. But it's what I'll settle for."

"Okay, then."

Vin's eyes lit. "Yeah?"

Niko cupped a hand behind Vin's head, bringing him in for a kiss. "Yeah. It'll be fun."

16

Near the end of the day, Vin jumped into the pool to cool off and play volleyball with Cat and the rest of the guys. The warm water felt like a bathtub, but the sea breeze cooled his wet skin.

Cat kicked her way across the pool, her arms around the volleyball, using it as a makeshift flotation device. "Are you and Niko heading over to Nassau with us tonight? You gotta come. You two have been stick-in-the-muds. Even Betty and Rose are going."

Vin grabbed for the volleyball, and she went under in the ensuing struggle, spitting water in his face when she resurfaced. He wiped the water out of his eyes. "We're going, but you guys will have to survive without us."

"Cannonball!" Preston shouted as he launched himself into the deep end, the wave of water raining down on Cat and Vin, as well as everyone else.

Cat squeegeed a hand down her face. "Where are you two going?"

"Dinner. At Alonzo's. I've got reservations at eight."

"Oooh. I saw that place the other night. *Fancy*. And romantic."

Vin rolled his eyes. He didn't want Cat getting the wrong idea. She knew the score as well as he did. "It's just dinner."

"If you say so."

"Hey," Chet called out from the other side of the net. "Are we going to have a game, or are you two playing footsie all night?"

Vin laughed and chucked the ball over the net. "We get Greer."

Greer swam under the net and surfaced.

"Why do you get Greer?"

"Because after this week, I'm pretty sure he'd rather have a chance to kick your asses than fuck them."

Greer gave Vin a high five. "You're not wrong, brother."

Vin, Cat, and Greer spread out. While Chet, Preston, and Hayes did the same. Rose and Betty watched from a couple of loungers, sucking down fruity umbrella drinks.

"Okay, Chet," Greer said, "let's see if you can serve it as well as you can take it."

Chet laughed, tossing the ball in the air as he prepared to serve. "Your funeral."

By the time they'd finished their second game, the full-body exhaustion had made Vin's limbs weak, and his chest billow as he sucked in air. Considering how much water he'd ingested during the game, he was lucky he hadn't done a full Titanic.

The alarm on Greer's watch went off. One of those clunky black watches with the extra-large faces that had more buttons and dials than a nuclear submarine. "We'd better call it a night if we're going to get cleaned up and head out. We have the water taxi scheduled to show up at seven."

Vin's stomach flopped, either from all the chlorinated water sloshing around down there or from nervousness. Vin heaved himself out of the pool, drenching the deck as he went for a towel.

The rest of them followed, Cat coming up to him with this stupid, sappy smile on her face.

"What's up with you?"

"I'm happy and excited for you, that's all."

Vin scrubbed the towel over his head and worked his way down his body. "Why? Nothing is going to come of it. If all the sex and the time alone together hasn't changed Niko's mind, dinner isn't going to make a difference. He doesn't want me. At least not like that. I've made my peace with it."

"Have you?"

Vin ignored her skepticism.

"I don't think Niko's issue is a question of him not wanting you."

"Maybe. Doesn't change anything."

"I'm sorry."

Fuck if he wasn't, too. "Don't be. We had our fun." Vin wrapped his arm around Cat's neck. "Come on, we've got one more evening in paradise. Let's not spoil it."

They all took the same elevator, splitting off on different floors, Cat, Betty, and Rose getting off on the third.

"See you in a bit." Cat pointed at him. "Don't be late."

"Bye, dear," Betty said.

"Bye, Betty. Bye, Rose."

The doors closed, taking him up to his room on the fourth floor.

He found Niko on the balcony, pounding away on his laptop. Vin opened the door, pulling his damp towel from around his hips and wiping away stray drops of water.

"I thought you were getting ready?"

Niko barely glanced up before returning his attention to whatever he'd been working on. "Yeah. I'll be right there."

"The boat leaves in twenty-five minutes."

"Twenty-five," Niko repeated. "Got it."

Vin left him to it, bringing his one nice change of clothes with him into the bathroom. He showered off in a flash, brushing his teeth, gelling his hair, and spraying on a touch of cologne before slipping on his slacks and a light-blue button-down.

Cat would probably laugh at him when she saw what he'd chosen to wear. The clothes didn't say 'casual dinner with a friend' they said 'date.'

Still no Niko.

Maybe he'd already showered and only needed to get changed. Vin rolled his sleeves up his forearms as he went to find him.

Vin found Niko on the patio, still in his shorts and a tank, his cell phone plastered to his ear. Vin stepped out.

"Hang on a minute," Niko said to whoever was on the other end.

Vin swallowed back his annoyance and kept his voice light. "We've got five minutes. Can you wrap it up and—"

Niko muted the call. "Yeah. About that. I'd better stay. Some stuff came up and..." Niko shrugged his shoulders and passed Vin a wan smile. "You know how it is."

"You've gotta be fucking kidding me." Vin didn't hold back. "We made plans."

"And I have to cancel them. It can't be helped."

"Sure, it can't." Vin's hands went to his hips, his head hanging between his shoulders as he tromped down on the urge to blow up at Niko.

He's not yours. You have no control over him.

"Look. I'm really sorry."

Vin glanced up. Niko's contrition seemed sincere, the bull-shit reason about not being able to go, not so much.

"It's better this way," Niko added.

Without replying, Vin turned to go, refusing to argue or beg. He did have some pride.

"Hey, Vin." He turned back as Niko reached into his wallet and pulled out several one-hundred-dollar bills and held them out to him. "You guys have some fun on me tonight."

The anger drained away, sucking sadness into the void, making Vin's chest hurt and his throat tight. "I don't want your money, Niko." His words were little more than a rasp, but that couldn't be helped. "In fact, I don't want anything from you at all."

He retreated into the room. Niko called out after him, but Vin grabbed his wallet and his room key and strode for the elevator before Niko had a chance to catch up with him.

He jammed his thumb into the elevator's call button over and over again. Not that it helped get the elevator there any faster, but it gave him something to do besides glancing back at the room to see if Niko would come after him.

Niko didn't.

———

Vin jogged to the boat. Everyone else was on board and ready to go, their voices over-loud and excited for their last night on the town.

"One more coming?" the dockhand asked.

"No," Vin said, "I'm the last one."

He stepped on the gunwale and jumped in as the captain shifted the boat into gear, and the dockhand shoved off.

Vin took a seat by himself at the back of the boat, still trying to catch his breath from the blow Niko had landed.

Stupid. Stupid. Stupid.

He might as well have handed Niko the two-by-four to beat him with.

Cat walked toward him, her steps faltering. She adjusted to the movement of the boat as it bounced across the light chop. The bow hit a boat wake, and she landed hard beside him, threading her arm through his and resting her chin on his shoulder. "Hey."

And fuck if those large eyes and that ghost of a sympathetic smile didn't add the weight of a freight train to what already lay on his chest, pushing his heart into his throat.

"Don't," Vin managed.

"Love you."

He gave her hand a light squeeze in acknowledgment as Cat leaned in and kissed his cheek, before leaving him alone the way he'd wanted.

Fuck Niko and fuck the stupid deal.

He didn't need Niko to have a good time. Retrieving his phone from his pocket, he thumbed through to his *HotDix* app, pulled up @dickful69's profile, and opened up their message thread.

Vin: *You still want to meet?*

Better than a *sup*, though not much.

The reply came immediately: *The Sand Bar. Already here.*

@dickful69 pinned his location on Google Maps and sent it to Vin.

Vin: *Be there in fifteen.*

@dickful69 sent back a thumbs up and two eggplant emojis.

Yeah. Just what the doctor ordered—hot, anonymous sex to burn off the searing emotions.

Too bad he didn't really feel up to it, but he'd be damned if he would spend his last night in the Bahamas pining for a man that could take him or leave him.

More like leave, but—

Yeah, yeah. He didn't need the reminder.

The boat slowed as they approached the dock in Nassau. Chet, Hayes, and Preston jumped out first, giving a hand to Betty and Rose. Greer joined them on the dock, and Cat hung back with Vin.

Already having second thoughts, Cat took his hand and tugged. "Come on. We're going to eat, and we found this awesome nightclub with the hottest guys." She waggled her brows. "You and I could both get lucky."

They climbed out of the boat, following the others as they walked toward the street. According to the map, The Sand Bar was within easy walking distance.

Vin held up his phone and gave it a weak shake. "I'm meeting someone."

Cat whooped. The others glanced back but kept going. She held up her hand for a high five. "That's what I'm talking about, baby. You go get you some."

Cat's contagious enthusiasm eased the pressure on his chest. "Thanks. I think I will. Don't wait up, Mom."

Cat laughed and gave him a hug.

He watched the rest of them leave before heading in the opposite direction.

Following the map on his phone, he passed all the tourist shops with their conch shells and Bahamian flag shirts, and the restaurants overlooking the water. He turned down a narrow street, a couple golf carts full of half-blitzed, half-naked tourists buzzed by, laying heavy on their ineffective, clown horns.

He passed brightly colored clapboard buildings. Curly-tailed lizards ran along the sidewalks, jumping into the brush. The crowd drinking and mingling outside The Sand Bar made it easy to spot.

Vin shouldered through the crowd. He had no idea what @dickful69 looked like and had no likelihood of spotting him unless he'd shown up naked. Unfortunately, The Sand Bar wasn't that kind of place.

He glanced around, but since no one caught his eye, he bellied up to the bar and ordered a shot of whiskey with a beer chaser. The bar was full but not overly crowded. Handing over his cash, he took his drinks to a two-top table in the far corner with a view out the screen at the canal beyond, as well as a direct line of sight to the front door.

A few people gave him a look up and down, but they didn't approach, so he chalked it up to being overdressed. This wasn't a casual Friday wear kind of place. This was a T-shirt and flip-flops and bathing suit cover-up kind of dive.

Picking up his shot, he tossed it back, closing his eyes against the burn. The blazing trail snaked down his esophagus and settled into his stomach.

He should have bought two.

Slapping the shot glass on the table, he opened his eyes. "What the fuck are you doing here?"

Dylan Wilson, the helicopter riding, trash writing reporter from *Queer-y*, held his hands out to the side, a beer in each hand. "I brought you a beer."

Vin held up his bottle. "I've got one."

Dylan took the seat across from him and passed Vin the beer anyway. "Mind if I have a seat?"

"Actually, I'm meeting someone."

Dylan stopped with the bottle half-way to his lips. The *I hate to break it to you* expression on his face had Vin muttering a curse.

"I can't fucking believe this," Vin said, "you're @dickful69?"

"The one and only."

Vin stood, his chair scraping the concrete floor, and Dylan laid a staying hand on Vin's wrist.

"Let go."

Dylan released him, but Vin wasn't finished with him yet. "How long have you known who I was? Who I worked for? From the start?"

Dylan held his gaze. "No."

"Then, when?"

"After the helicopter. I had no clue who you were until then."

"Yet, you kept wanting to meet up."

"I don't have a problem mixing business with pleasure."

"You're a piece of work. You're trying to destroy Niko and fuck me."

Dylan got one of those clueless frat-boy type smiles. "I'm not seeing the issue here. I've got nothing against you."

Only the man Vin loved.

Love. *Christ.*

He'd loved Niko for many years, that love shifting with time from platonic to something much more.

Vin shook his head, not believing the drivel coming out of Dylan's mouth, and not believing how he'd allowed himself to be dragged into something with Niko that he'd been told from the start could never be.

Vin carefully laid his beer bottle on the table when all he really wanted to do was throw it across the room and watch it shatter in the same way Niko had shattered him. "I'm out of here." Then he leaned in, dropping his voice. "If you're smart, you won't follow me."

Turning on his heel, he strode toward the exit. Dylan called out, but Vin ignored him, though he'd half expected Dylan wouldn't heed his warning and would take out after him. Wanting the sex or the story, Vin didn't know. Didn't care. Dylan would get nothing from him.

Determined to blow off steam, Vin walked around town, down busy streets and narrow alleyways, from the touristy parts of town to the parts of Nassau he figured few tourists ever saw.

The sun set, the stars came out, and a night breeze blew in gauzy clouds. Vin kept walking. And walking. Until his feet ached, and his legs grew weary. Finally, he made it back to the docks, sat down on a bench and sent Cat a quick text, letting her know his plans to head back to the resort.

She didn't answer right away, but he hadn't expected her to. He just didn't want them wondering where he'd run off to.

He stood as a group of guys walked by, some of them holding hands and laughing, dressed for a night of clubbing. Was there a gay bar on the island? He hadn't even looked.

Vin fell into step behind them, street after street until he lost his bearing, and they disappeared inside a building. Nothing on the outside gave away what kind of place lay inside besides the bouncer at the door and the thump of bass drifting out each time the door opened and closed.

"Hey," the bouncer said. He had a kind face and a ready smile for someone big enough to knock heads together. "You goin' in?"

Vin glanced from the door, back down the street in the direction he'd come from. To hell with Niko and Dylan. Vin refused to let either one of them ruin his last night.

"Yeah, sure. Why the hell not?"

———

SOMETIME AFTER LAST CALL AND THE MUSIC HAD STOPPED, AND the lights had come back on, Vin stumbled out of the club, his ears ringing, the world spinning, and the thump of the bass still vibrating in his bones.

"Oops," Vin said as he bumped into the bouncer. "Which way to the docks?"

The bouncer pointed to his right. "Where's your shirt?"

Vin glanced down at his bare chest, at the sweat drying on

his skin, and spun a slow circle around him. "It should be here somewhere. Have you seen it?"

The bouncer chuckled and waved him off. "Naw, man. I ain't seen your shirt." At least that's what Vin thought the man had said. The accent so thick that Vin couldn't be too sure, or maybe Vin was too drunk to understand.

"You need an Uber?"

"No. The dock's not far."

Vin started walking, but the man jogged up to him and caught his arm. "Other way."

"Right." Vin's tongue felt thick in his mouth, and he had to concentrate to enunciate. "Thanks."

Vin trudged down the street, working his way back to the docks, tripping over a low hedge twice and vomiting in an alley once. The tourists had cleared out, and the streets were mostly empty. It wasn't until he'd passed the sign with the giant shark twice that he realized he was lost.

Think. Think. Think.

Phone. Map. He could find his location and get back to the dock. He reached into his pocket, but no phone. He searched his other pockets. Wallet, cash, credit cards, but no phone.

Fuck.

God, he needed to take a piss.

He slipped down a darkened alley, the security light at the end cast it in shadows. Leaning against the dumpster, he scrunched his nose at the stench of rotting shellfish, and undid his pants, catching his balance on the brick wall in front of him.

As he zipped up his pants, he heard the scrape of a shoe on the concrete behind him.

"Hey," someone called out.

The world tilted, and Vin closed his eyes to keep the twirling at bay. Here he was on his last day in the Bahamas, and he was probably about to be busted by the cops for public indecency.

Rough hands grabbed his shoulders and spun him around, tossing him against the brick wall. "Okay, okay. Sorry, I had to go, I promise I—"

"Give me your wallet, man."

Wait. Vin's eyes refused to open on their own. He had to hold one open with his fingers to see. "You're not the police."

The man shoved him against the wall again. "Your money."

"Is this a stick-up?" Which came out sounding like 'thiz a stigup,' but it was the best Vin could do. "'Cuz I gotta boat..." Why did he have a boat again? Right. "Gotta boat to catch—"

"Look, man, I ain't playin' witcha."

"That's good, 'cuz I'm not... not havin' fun. I—"

Vin never saw the fist coming. Pain erupted in his jaw, spinning him around and sending him sprawling. Stumbling, he pitched headfirst into the corner of the dumpster.

The bolt of pain shooting around his skull replaced the throb in his jaw. He spat out blood as the stars swirled, and darkness descended.

17

NIKO LAID IN BED, AWAKE WHEN THE CLOCK CHANGED TO midnight, one in the morning, two. By three, he got up and started pacing.

He texted Vin again, though all of his previous texts and voicemails had been ignored. He didn't expect an answer this time either but hadn't given up hope.

Niko: *I really am sorry.*

Vin: ...

Niko: *I fucked up.*

Vin: ...

Niko: *I get that you're mad. I get that you don't want to speak to me. Just let me know you're okay, and I'll leave you alone.*

Vin should have returned already. Even with having to take the water taxi to the resort, with the clubs closing at 2 a.m., he'd had plenty of time to get back.

You think he wanted to spend his last night in the hotel room locked up with you?

Vin still should have called. Or texted back and let Niko know his plans.

He probably crashed with Cat and Rose, or one of the guys.

Or he hooked up with a rando.

Happy now?

No. Not even a tiny bit.

In fact, he felt like a complete asshole. He'd thought it would be better if they ended the farce. And going to a nice restaurant with Vin as if they were on a date, as if what they had could possibly go anywhere when they both knew that it couldn't…

He hadn't been able to go through with it.

And now he'd hurt a man who meant more to him than Vin ever should have. If they couldn't salvage a friendship or at least a working relationship after this, Niko wouldn't forgive himself.

And that was the exact reason why he had the 'no fucking the employees' policy.

So that's what you're most concerned about? Losing your cameraman?

He dropped down on the coffee table, his face in his hands, cold sweat beading between his shoulder blades, and a black-smoke-spewing excavator digging cavernous pits in the lining of his stomach.

Vin had been an integral part of Niko's life for the past ten years. He couldn't picture his life without Vin in it.

He had to fix this.

And to fix it, he had to find Vin and apologize. Not on the phone. Or by text. In person.

He picked up his cell to call Cat to try and locate Vin, but he only had thirty minutes before he was supposed to meet everyone downstairs to take the water taxi to Nassau for their early flight back to the States.

And Vin hadn't packed.

He'd waited this long to speak to Vin, another thirty minutes wouldn't make a difference.

He pulled out Vin's suitcase, scrummaged through all the drawers, and tossed Vin's clothes in the case. Then he packed up

Vin's computer and his other electronics in his backpack and called down for a porter.

How the hell had it ended up being Niko's job to get Vin packed for the trip home?

The porter came, and Niko followed him down to the lobby, where the rest of the crew stood around with their luggage and all the filming equipment.

"There you are." Cat pursed her lips and filleted him with a scathing look.

Niko counted heads. Rose and Betty were getting cups of coffee to go. Cat stood with her hands on her hips and venom in her eyes. The four guys hung onto the luggage carts, their eyes heavy as they rubbed at their foreheads, keeping their voices low. Niko could almost see the alcohol vapors wafting off them.

"Where's Vin?" he asked Cat.

The scowl slipped from her face. "What do you mean, *where's Vin*? You're the one he's rooming with."

"He didn't come back to the room last night. I thought he bunked with you or one of the guys."

"No. He texted me last night and said he was coming back early."

Fuck. Niko planted his hands on his hips. Where the hell could Vin be? He understood that Vin was pissed at him, but if they didn't get on that boat soon, they'd miss their flight.

Niko whistled, getting everyone's attention. Preston grabbed his skull as if the high-pitched sound had nearly shattered bone. "Hey, anyone seen Vin since you guys left last night?"

Everyone shook their heads.

Betty stopped stirring her coffee. "Oh, dear."

"I'll talk to management and see if anyone from the resort has seen him," Rose said.

"Sir," a porter came up to Niko. "The boat is here."

"Okay. Take the bags. I'll be right behind you." To the rest of them, Niko said, "I'll talk to the boat captain, you guys see if Vin crashed on one of the loungers or a bench somewhere."

Everybody spread out to search, except Cat. No surprise.

"This is your fault, you know that, right?"

"I get it. Go look for Vin. You'll have plenty of time to bust my balls later."

"We're not done with this conversation," Cat tossed back as she headed for the pool area.

Niko jogged down to the boat, but after speaking to the captain, his fear grew. He called Cat as the porters loaded up the boat. When she answered, he said, "Get everyone together and come on down to the dock."

"What did the captain say?"

"Just get down here, then I'll tell everyone what I know."

Niko paced the dock until everyone arrived, his footsteps on the wood boards sounding as hollow as his heartbeat.

"What did the captain say?" Greer asked when they'd all assembled.

"Vin never got on the boat back."

"That's not good," Chet said.

Understatement.

"He probably got a room in Nassau for the night." Preston leaned against Chet. Hard to tell who held who up. "Or he got lucky and went home with someone."

"I sent him a text and a voicemail telling him to meet us at the airport. I'm sure he'll beat us there." Niko tried to infuse his words with confidence.

He didn't want anyone to panic, though the burn in his veins from the steady rise of adrenaline in his system and the double-time thump of his heart told him his own panic lay just around the corner.

"Oh, dear," Betty said again. It seemed to be her go-to statement.

When Niko found Vin, he'd… he'd… scoop him up in his arms and tell him he damn well better not scare the shit out of him ever again.

And then you can apologize.

Grovel, if you must.

With all the gear loaded onto the boat, they climbed aboard, and the dockhand shoved them off.

Niko stood at the stern, watching the resort fade away in the distance. The week had gone by in a flash. The shoot was just supposed to be an ordinary, on-location kind of thing. Yet it had turned into so much more.

As darkness began to fade, worry seeped into his bones. There had to be a way to find Vin. Niko worked his way to the bow, his hip ramming into one of the seats when the boat dropped into the trough of a wave.

Cat sat alone, staring out the front windshield. Niko sat down beside her, the anger gone from her face when she said, "I'm really worried."

He held out his arms, and she scooted over, wrapping her arms around his waist. He hugged her in tight and kissed the side of her head. "Me, too."

She sat up and turned in her seat to face him. "He's got to be out there somewhere."

"Do you know where he went when you guys split up?"

"I don't, but he said he was meeting up with someone."

"The guy from the app?"

She cocked her head at him, that pierced brow raised. "You know about him?"

"Yeah. Do you think it was the same guy?"

"Most likely." Cat brightened. "I've got an idea. Download the *HotDix* app. We can log into Vin's account and maybe message this guy and see if he knows where Vin is. I'd do it, but my phone's out of data."

"You're brilliant," Niko said as he pulled out his phone.

After the app downloaded, he typed in Vin's email address and glanced up at her. "I don't know his password."

"Try 6969. That's the unlock PIN for his phone."

Niko typed in the number. "Nope."

"You could try his birthday or..." Cat's voice drifted off as she thought about it. "Try seven-five-zero-nine."

Niko started typing the numbers in. "How do you know—" *Seven-five-zero-nine.* "I've seen that number. It's tattooed on the pulse point of his right wrist."

Cat nodded.

"A date?"

Cat nodded again.

"July fifth, two-thousand and nine." He thought back. *Fuck.* "That's—"

"That's the night you picked Vin up off the streets. The night you changed his life."

Niko rubbed his eyes with his thumb and forefinger and pinched the bridge of his nose. It did nothing to alleviate the pounding behind his eyes.

"Vin's looked up to you—loved you—for a very long time."

"I never meant..." Niko shook his head, staring down at the fiberglass deck, his phone dangling in his hands between his knees. "I never wanted to hurt him. I thought this was something we both wanted. I truly want the best for him. And what's best for him, isn't me."

She rubbed his back. "I know I've been busting your chops, but not all the responsibility falls on you. He's an adult. He made his own decisions. He thought he knew what he was getting into. I just don't think he knew how hard it would be to give you up."

The captain cut the engines back to idle, then put the boat into reverse, easing to a stop against the dock. Once the deckhands secured the boat, they began offloading all the luggage and equipment. Niko left the younger men to it while he logged into Vin's account.

Niko showed the screen to Cat. "They had plans to meet. There's a pinned map."

"What are you going to do?"

"The van is here," Betty said. "Are you two coming?"

"Coming," Cat said.

Niko stood, and Cat followed him off the boat. "It's not far from here. I could check it out and—"

"I'm going with you."

"No. You go to the airport with everyone else. Text me if he shows up. I can always hurry back. I'll rebook my ticket if I have to."

The driver of the van honked his horn.

"Go," Niko said. "Vin's probably already at the airport waiting for us."

———

NIKO DROPPED ONTO THE BENCH AT THE HEAD OF THE DOCK AND used an app to summon a car service. The bar wasn't far to walk, but not having to search on foot would speed things up.

While he waited, he messaged @dickful69. Hopefully, Niko would drive up to this dude's hotel and carry a hungover Vin to the car. If they hurried, they'd still make the flight.

Pretty optimistic.

Maybe. But it was something he could hold onto to keep his mind from wandering to all the places it could go, all the terrible, frightening, gut-wrenching reasons why Vin wouldn't, or couldn't, answer his phone.

The guilt ate at Niko. It had been small nibbles at first, but now those bites grew bigger, chewing him up from the inside out.

Niko: *Is Vin with you?*

@dickful69: *Who is this?*

Niko: *A friend. Look, I don't have time to explain. Just answer the question.*

@dickful69: *No, man. We met. Didn't hit it off. I don't know where he went.*

Niko: *You sure?*

@dickful69: *You think I'm lying?*

Niko: *Do you know where he could have gone?*

@dickful69: *I'm not his keeper.*

Niko clicked out of the app as his car arrived. Now what? His one lead ended in a dead-end. *Think, think, think.*

The driver rolled down his window. He was an older Bahamian man, hardly tall enough to see over his steering wheel. "Mr. Niko?"

"Yeah. Mind if I ride up front?"

The man smiled and gestured toward the front passenger seat. "Yes, yes."

Niko climbed in and shook the man's hand. The driver's credentials said his name was Erris. "I need a favor."

After telling the driver that Vin was missing, he explained that he wanted to hire him so that he could look for Vin. "I can pay, I don't care how long it takes or how much it costs," Niko said. "I just need to find him."

Erris dropped the gearshift into drive and pulled away from the curb. "No worries. We will find your friend." The soft rolling sounds of his accent and the assurance in his driver's voice almost made Niko believe they would.

He tried Vin's phone again, but it bounced to voicemail.

"Have you called the police?" Erris asked.

Niko rubbed a hand over his jaw. He hadn't even considered that Vin had gotten arrested. "No, that's a good idea. What's the number?"

Even as Niko said that he redialed Vin's number one last time. It answered on the first ring. Relief. Anger. Frustration. Elation. They all flooded in. A tornado of dizzying emotions.

"Pull over. Pull over." He pointed to the parking lot of a grocery store and answered the phone. "Where the ever-loving fuck have you been? Do you know how wor—"

"Who the hell is this?" The deep voice on the other end of the phone asked, his light accent not Bahamian. Jamaican, perhaps.

"I'm looking for the man who owns this phone."

"He's not here."

"Where is here?" The man started rattling off an address, but Niko had no clue where that was. "Hang on, tell my driver."

He handed the phone to Erris. The man nodded. "Yes, yes. I know where this is." He hung up and gave the phone to Niko, his eyes a little too wide, and his smile gone.

"What's the matter?"

"Is gay club."

"I just need to pick up my friend's phone and talk to the guy, you don't have to come in. You don't even have to wait if you don't want to. Just get me there. I'll hop out and—"

"Is not that. You can not walk down there."

Niko's impatience grew, as his temper ran short, he finally had something to go on, a place Vin had been. Maybe someone had seen him. "Why the hell not?"

"Bad part of town. Really bad."

The sun breached the horizon, and the island had begun to wake. People walked around, starting their day. Locals mostly. Niko figured the tourists were sleeping off the effects of the night before.

"I will take you. You must be careful."

Jesus Christ. What had Vin gotten himself into?

Erris pulled out of the parking lot and headed for the club.

Each street they turned onto took them deeper and deeper into a seedy part of town that even in the daylight, Niko wouldn't feel safe walking down.

And Vin had gone there at night. Alone?

Niko had to find him. He couldn't lose Vin. Not now. They had too much they needed to talk through. And Niko had too much apologizing to not be able to say it.

And you never got a chance to tell him how you really feel.

What if you never get to?

His gut tumbled, and he swallowed down the slick, bitter taste of bile.

"How much farther?" Niko's knee bounced up and down, and he didn't even bother suppressing it.

Erris pointed straight ahead. "Less than a mile that way."

A golf cart pulled out in front of them, doing half the posted speed limit, and Erris stomped on the brakes to avoid hitting them. The seatbelt cut into Niko's shoulder, and he grabbed the handhold in the dash.

Then Erris made a sudden right turn, away from the direction they needed to go. "Wait, where are you going?"

The narrow one-way road they turned down went behind rows of clapboard houses with dilapidated chain-link fences and overgrown vegetation, the street barely wide enough for the car to scrape by without taking out some of the garbage cans left out for pickup.

"This is a shortcut to the boats. Maybe your friend walk this way."

Niko wanted to grab the old man by the ears and plant a big fat smacking kiss on his lips. Instead, he said, "I like the way you think."

They turned from narrow street to narrow street. Some of them dirt, some of them paved. Potholes dropped Niko's stomach down to his knees and jarred his spine. Erris slowed as they scanned every alley as they passed, the stray dogs pawing and chewing their way through some of the trash bags left beside full dumpsters.

A group of kids came down the alley toward them on their bikes, barefoot and shirtless, living the island life. Erris eased by them, then slammed on his brakes.

Niko grunted, his stomach already in a world of hurt between the worry and the guilt.

Erris backed up and threw the car into park. "Is that him?"

———

SOMETHING POKED VIN IN THE CHEEK. SHARP. THE GROUND beneath him unforgiving and lumpy. His head throbbed, his jaw complained when he yawned, and his stomach rolled and retched.

He clamored to all fours, his abdomen heaving until he vomited. The jackhammer thumping at his temple morphed into a pile driver. He tried to open his eyes, but the bright sun seared his retinas, and he squeezed them closed again, spitting the rancid taste from his mouth.

His arms shook, and he maneuvered to the side. At least when his arms gave out, he didn't land in his puke.

If the world decided to swallow him up, he'd consider it a personal favor.

A car door slammed, but Vin couldn't be bothered to glance up. Shoes slapped on the ground, and Vin covered his head with his arms in case his attacker had come back.

"Vin. *Vin.*"

"Ni—" Vin coughed. Arms came around him, and he laid there, ragdoll limp, as Niko hauled him into his lap.

Vin rubbed at one eye until he brought Niko into focus.

He came for you.

Vin choked back a resentful laugh, not daring to read anything personal into it. Niko probably didn't want to have to search for a new cameraman.

Pretty cynical.

Vin's head and stomach ached too much to argue with himself. At least Niko had found him. He'd worry about Niko's motivations later.

"What the hell happened to you?"

"Fuck if I know." Vin's words came out gritty as if his vocal cords had rusted in the humidity overnight. "Pretty sure I was robbed."

Niko brushed pebbles off Vin's bare chest and abdomen that had embedded themselves into his skin.

Niko glared down at him. "You're lucky to be alive."

At that particular moment, Vin had a hard time feeling so lucky. Maybe after a shower, and after his skull no longer felt like shattered glass.

Niko's fingers probed Vin's forehead.

He flinched. "Ouch."

"Hold still, you big baby. I'm trying to see how deep this gash is."

Vin caught Niko's wrist. "I'll live."

"Yeah, well, we'll see what the doctor says. Come on." Niko shifted and locked his hands around Vin's chest and hefted him to his feet with help from Vin.

"I don't need a doctor. I just want to go home."

"Tough. You need a doctor. You can barely stand. You could have a concussion."

"It's just as likely that I passed out. I'm fine. Really."

As long as Vin didn't move fast, the world didn't tilt or spin. He let go of his hold on Niko and took a tentative step on his own. He didn't fall. Turning, he looked back at Niko, as proud of himself as if he'd scaled Mount Everest without oxygen tanks. "See?"

A car reversed down the alley, and a man scrambled out and opened the back passenger door.

"Our chariot?" Vin asked.

Niko threw an arm around Vin's shoulder and pulled Vin tight into his side, pressing a kiss to Vin's temple. "You scared the fuck out of me."

Vin allowed himself that moment to absorb Niko's strength and compassion. "Let's get out of here."

The driver popped his trunk and handed Vin a bottle of water out of a cooler. "Thanks."

He took a swig, swished it around in his mouth, and spit it out before swallowing a few tentative sips to see if they'd stay down.

When he felt like he wouldn't barf in the car, Niko helped him into the back seat and slid in from the other side.

"Can you take us to a doctor or a hospital?" Niko asked the driver.

"Babe," Vin said, "seriously. All I need is a shower, some steri-strips, and some ibuprofen. Not necessarily in that order."

"And a shirt."

Vin chuckled. His head whimpered like a whiny kid. "And a shirt."

Slouching in the seat, Vin laid his head back and closed his eyes. In what seemed like no time, Niko had retrieved his phone from the club, picked up some first aid paraphernalia from the pharmacy, and had checked them into a hotel so Vin could clean himself up.

Vin dropped onto the closed toilet seat while Niko ran water in the tub. A shower would have been preferable, but the thought of standing that long seemed daunting.

"You good by yourself?"

"Yes, *Mom.*"

Niko cut him a look but let Vin's sarcasm slide. He really should cut Niko some slack. He had come riding in on his white horse to save Vin when he could have left him in a foreign country without so much as his wallet or ID.

Well, not a white horse. A faded blue Chevy with questionable air conditioning.

"Get washed up. Take your time. I'm going to head out. I've got a few things I need to take care of."

By the time Niko made it back to the room, the analgesics had started to kick in. Vin leaned against the bathroom counter with a towel around his waist as he steri-stripped the gash on his forehead. It only took two.

Niko leaned into the bathroom and handed him a bag.

"What's this?" Vin asked as he opened it.

"Some things to tide you over until we can get you home."

Vin riffled through the items. A swimming suit that looked like a lightweight pair of cargo shorts, a Kalik Beer souvenir T-shirt, and a travel-sized toothbrush and toothpaste. He grabbed Niko's arm before he could disappear back into the room. "Thanks. I really appreciate everything you've done for me. I know I've been an enormous pain in your ass."

Niko stared at the tile floor, then met Vin's eyes. "This isn't all your fault. I could have handled things better."

By *things*, Vin knew Niko alluded to what he'd said the night before and how he'd canceled dinner, effectively ending their week together early.

While Niko might have had a bit of responsibility for the shit-show of the night before, the majority of it fell on Vin. "Same."

"I'd like to talk if—"

Vin pulled a face. "I really don't feel like talking." Not now.

Maybe not ever. As much as he didn't like to, he could take 'no' for an answer. "Can we drop it?"

Niko blinked a few times, his jaw working side to side as if chewing on Vin's words. "For now."

Stepping back, Niko let Vin pass. "I re-booked our flights. We've got a couple hours before we need to leave for the airport. Get some sleep."

Vin dropped the towel and climbed under the covers, his head barely hit the pillow when a realization hit. "Fuck."

Niko sat on the love seat by the window, his phone in his hand. "What's wrong?"

"I don't have any ID. How am I going to get through security and customs?"

Niko reached into the back pocket of his jeans and pulled out two passports. "I've got your back, Vin. Always have. Always will."

18

———

Midnight had come and gone by the time Niko pulled up in front of his house with Vin dozing beside him. "Cat dropped your bags here. I can bring them to your place tomorrow if you want."

Vin's color had improved during the plane ride home, but he'd hardly eaten, and the bruise on his jaw continued to turn varying shades of purple.

Popping the door latch, Vin said, "I'd rather get them now and be on my way."

Niko didn't want Vin to leave. A part of him thought that if he convinced Vin to stay long enough—at least until they got some sleep and both of their heads cleared—then they could sort everything out. He had a lot of things to say, and he wanted to make sure Vin was recovered enough to process his words.

"It's late. Why don't you stay? You can have your old room and—"

Vin slammed the Jaguar's door. "Are you fucking kidding me right now?"

Vin didn't stick around for the answer. He stormed off,

entered the code into the keypad on the door, and shoved the door open. It bounced off the wall and smacked his shoulder.

Niko jogged to catch up. Having just said the absolute stupidest thing that he'd ever said in his entire adult life proved that now was not the time to have a heart to heart.

At least you got that part right.

"Would you stop?" Niko caught Vin's arm and spun him around.

"Fine." Vin crossed his arms over his chest, the challenge flashing in his eyes. "Why don't you tell me the real reason you don't want me to leave?"

"I think anything we need to say is better said after we've both had a good night's sleep."

Vin didn't budge, his eyes drilling holes through Niko. If he didn't say anything convincing, Vin would be gone, and with the way things were going, Niko honestly didn't know if Vin would ever return.

He stepped toward Vin, backing him up until the wall stopped him. So many things swirled in Niko's head. All his thoughts, all his feelings. The horror, the panic, of seeing Vin laid out in the alley, not knowing if he were alive or dead.

All of it mixed in with his internal struggle with their history together, and what it meant for their future.

"We never got to have our last night together." Niko cringed. Where the hell had that come from?

Of all the things that could have spilled out—I'm sorry, forgive me, I love you—that's what you go with?

Vin blew out a hot breath, shaking his head. "Whose fault is that?" Holding up a hand, Vin said, "You know what. Don't answer that. It's too late at night for confessions and half-truths."

"Don't be difficult," Niko said.

Vin's shoulders straightened, the glare he shot Niko more lethal than a missile strike. "You mean like a kid?"

Niko took a step back, rubbing his forehead. His hands going to his hips as he collected his thoughts. Fuck, he couldn't say anything right tonight. He dropped his voice. "That's not what I said or what I meant."

Vin shouldered past Niko and headed for the open front door. "I'm out of here. Keep my shit for all I care. I don't need anything bad enough to put up with your horseshit."

"Vin," Niko called out, but Vin just grabbed his car keys out of the bowl on the hall table where he'd left them before their trip and kept on going. "*Vin.*"

Should he go after him?

He wanted to.

You're only going to make things worse.

It took everything Niko had to stand in the doorway and watch Vin drive away.

Finally, Niko closed the door and walked down the darkened hallway. The light he'd left on over the stove illuminated his way to the bar and the whiskey.

He added a couple of ice cubes to his glass, poured himself two fingers, then added two more, collapsing onto one of his bar stools at his kitchen island. His relationship with Vin wasn't irreparable. They just needed some sleep, some perspective, and a whole lot of groveling on Niko's part, and everything would be better.

Or Vin could never come back.

Pierce Hatchett had made it perfectly clear on numerous occasions that Vin had a job waiting for him at PornU. Vin never had to step another foot over Black Stallion's threshold if he didn't want to.

Niko rolled the cold glass against his forehead to soothe the throbbing headache. He pulled out his phone, his thumb hovering over Vin's name on his favorites list before thinking better of it.

He scrolled back up through the list, hitting his cousin Demetri's number instead. Yeah, it was late. Yeah, the alcohol was going straight to Niko's brain, but Demetri was more like a brother.

And a voice of reason.

If anyone could talk him out of showing up on Vin's doorstep in the middle of the night, it would be Demetri.

When his cousin answered, Niko said, "I fucked up."

Demetri groaned. It came out thick as if he'd been asleep for a while. "This in general, or something in particular?"

"I slept with Vin." The silence drifted on. Niko heard Demetri breathing, so he knew the call hadn't been dropped. "Did you hear me?"

"Yeah. I just can't think of something to say that doesn't sound condescending, or judgy, or like *I told you so*."

"Hit me with it. I'm a big boy."

Demetri blew out a breath, part chuckle, part disbelief. "Are you out of your mind? Why the hell would you do that?"

"I think I love him." Niko glanced at his near-empty glass, trying to blame his honesty on the liquor fucking up his inhibitions, but even as exhausted as he was, he hadn't had enough alcohol to blame it on that.

"Aw, fuck, man."

Niko waited, but Demetri didn't add anything else. "That's all you've got to say?"

"What do you want me to say?"

"I don't know. It's fucked up, right?" Niko didn't know if he was looking for validation or absolution. "I mean, I took him in when he was a kid. He works for me. It's a line I shouldn't have crossed, and now that I have, I don't know how to walk it back, or erase it and draw another."

"What does Vin say?"

Niko laughed and sucked down the rest of his drink before

heading to the bar and pouring another—just as generous—one. "He's not exactly talking to me at the moment."

Demetri held his hand over the phone and spoke to someone else. Fuck. Demetri had company. No wonder he'd been keeping his voice low.

"I'm sorry. I should have known you wouldn't be alone on a Saturday night." Niko heard sheets rustling and Demetri fumbling with the phone.

"Maybe you need to start from the beginning." Demetri spoke in his normal voice now. He must have left his date in the bedroom and gone into the kitchen because he heard the refrigerator open and close and the hiss of a pull-tab being yanked.

Niko spilled his guts. Telling Demetri everything, knowing that Demetri would tell it to him straight, not hold punches, or sugarcoat anything.

When Niko finished, he said, "Have I shocked you into silence, or have I bored you to death?"

"I don't know where to start. I guess it's not a surprise. He's always been someone special to you, and Vin's been carrying a torch for you for years. I'm thinking something like this was bound to happen."

"Special, but not like that. It's not like I preyed on a little kid or something."

"Fuck, Niko, you don't think I know that? That's not what I'm saying. Vin's an adult. You two have a strong friendship and history together. It just stands to reason a time would come that you two would explore the relationship beyond those parameters."

"You don't think it's wrong?"

"You had power at a time when he had none. You're his boss now. I think you have to be introspective. Interrogate your desires and make sure you're pursuing him for all the right reasons. If your feelings for him are true, then I don't see a problem with two consenting adults who clearly dig each other to have a relationship if they want. And you shouldn't either."

"What makes you think he didn't pursue me?"

"Because I know him. More importantly, I know *you*. But after you've thought this through, assuming that he's willing to speak to you again, I think there's something else you need to consider."

Niko swirled the bits of ice remaining in his glass. "What's that?"

"Maybe there's more from you that Vin wants."

Demetri's tone had Niko's hackles rising, Niko's voice more of a warning than a question when he asked, "How so?"

"Don't act dumb," Demetri said. "A guy with your kind of wealth can't dismiss the possibility that money could be part of the reason someone is interested in you."

"Not Vin. He's not like that."

"If you say so."

"Of course, I fucking say so." Niko slammed his glass down on the marble island, a thread-thin crack spreading up the side of the glass. "It's a battle to get him to accept a raise. He's driving a piece of shit. I offered to give him my old Mercedes back when I bought the Jag."

Niko blew out a few calming breaths. He shouldn't take what everyone would think about their relationship out on Demetri just because he wasn't afraid to tell the truth. It wasn't like Niko's money hadn't been what had attracted boyfriends in the past. This wasn't a new concern.

"Sorry," Niko said. "Any other guy and I would agree with you, but we're talking about Vin."

"Okay," Demetri said, in that *we can agree to disagree* way people have. "Just keep it in the back of your mind moving forward."

"I don't think there's any moving forward from where we are. And if there is, I'm not seeing it."

———

VIN SLEPT THROUGH HIS FIRST ALARM AND HIT SNOOZE TWICE ON his second. Why the fuck had he set the alarm for the morning after he returned from the Bahamas?

Oh, shit. Vin popped out of bed and stumbled into his bathroom to take a piss.

He had a meeting with Stu. Or the blackmailer, if they weren't one and the same.

He wrinkled his nose at the stench of his urine, the concentration so high it had practically formed a solid. He flushed and gulped water straight from the faucet, downed an inappropriate amount of analgesics for the headache he couldn't seem to shake, and jumped into the shower.

In less than fifteen minutes, he zipped out of his apartment complex twenty minutes away from a meeting at a coffee shop that he had ten minutes to get to.

"Come on, come on, come on." Vin honked, and the guy in front of him flipped him off. Probably deserved, considering the light was still red.

He tapped out a quick text, letting Stu, or whoever it was on the other end, know he was on his way but that he was stuck in traffic.

No reply came.

Would the guy still be at the coffee shop when he got there?

If he wants his money, he will.

Vin could only hope. There had to be a way to come to some sort of agreement. Lower the amount of money. Come up with a payment plan. *Something.*

You can't afford a new car payment. How are you going to make payments to a blackmailer?

Pierce Hatchett.

He might pay.

He'd offered Vin a stupid amount of money at one point to go work for him. The offer probably came more because Hatchett wanted to stick it to Niko than because Vin was aces with a camera and a natural in the editing room.

But at that point, Vin's ego didn't care. Whatever kept him out of jail.

Rick's Coffee shop was in the corner of a strip center that had its glory years more than a decade before. It didn't have a cute, hipster name. The signage had faded, and the cracked glass in the door hadn't been replaced.

Vin walked into the nearly empty shop and headed straight for the man sitting with his back to him at a table in the corner.

Vin slid into a chair and sat opposite him. "Why isn't this a surprise, Stu?"

"If you're trying to insult me, it's going to take a hell of a lot more than a snide remark to get the job done."

"What the hell happened to you?" Stu asked when he got a good look at Vin's face.

"You're not the only one after my money."

"Why did you want to meet? My message was clear."

"Where do you think I'm going to come up with that kind of money?"

"You were always a crafty kid. I'm sure you can figure it out."

Vin needed to take another tack. "Look, it was self-defense. My old man tried to kill me."

"Boo-hoo." Stu shoved the last bit of a greasy donut into his mouth. Vin's stomach grumbled.

"No jury would convict me."

Stu laughed, spewing crumbs all over the table that he didn't bother wiping up. "If you believed that, you wouldn't be sitting here right now. You'd have told me to go fuck myself."

"A good lawyer—"

Stu leaned in. "A hundred and fifty thousand dollars for your freedom sounds like a deal to me. You'd spend that much on lawyer's fees alone trying to prove your innocence. Besides, if you aren't guilty, why did you run?"

"I was a fucking *kid*. Scared out of my mind. What the hell was I supposed to do?" The barista spared him a glance at his outburst, her lip curling up and her eyes rolling at the drama.

Stu slouched as if bored with the whole thing. "You paying me or not? Because I got nothing better to do today than spend it with a detective."

"I. Don't. Have. The. Money."

"Get it." Stu stood, and whatever appetite had been returning to Vin, vanished again. He caught Stu's arm.

"I'm going to need a month at least."

Try a decade.

"I'll give you a week."

"Fuck, man. You might as well go to the police now because I won't have it by then."

Stu narrowed his eyes and chewed the inside of his cheek. "Two weeks. If you don't have the money by then, say goodbye to all this beautiful California sun, because you won't be seeing it again for many, many years."

Stu caught the barista's eye, pointing to the table. "He's paying." He slapped Vin on the arm with the back of his hand. "Don't forget to leave a tip."

Vin dug a five and a couple singles out of the pocket of his jeans that must have been in there from the last time he'd worn them. Now that the hangover had mostly worn off and he could think more clearly, he made a mental note to cancel his cards and make a list of all the other things he needed to do on Monday, like get a new driver's license.

Stupid fucker.

You talking about you, or the guy who took your wallet?

Both. Definitely both.

He pulled out his cell phone—at least he didn't have to buy a new one. Thank God for small favors—and sent a five-word message to Hatchett: *Is your offer still good?*

"YOUR JAW IS LOOKING BETTER."

Vin glanced up from one of the Bahama videos he'd been editing. He really wanted to get all those scenes finalized and to Niko before he left.

Not Black Stallion.

California.

He hadn't heard back from Pierce, and it had been three days. He'd already gone through his things at his apartment, deciding what he could fit into his truck to start his new life and what he could live without.

The way he had things, he could leave at a moment's notice, but he didn't want to disappear and leave Niko in an editing lurch.

"My jaw's fine. Sorry I missed the press conference. How did it go?"

Niko eased into the chair beside Vin, one of the scenes with Chet and Hayes paused. "As well as anything like that can go. Alex, Elijah, and Grant came through for me and spoke on Black Stallion's behalf, explaining their situations and how I hadn't known they weren't straight. Between that, my mea culpa, and the generous discount for present and returning members, I don't think Black Stallion is going to suffer any long-term effects from Hatchett's veiled attempt to take us down."

At the mention of Hatchett's name, heat climbed up Vin's cheeks. Thank God he kept the lights in the editing room dim, so Niko had little chance of noticing.

"That's great." Vin put the headphones on his ears and turned his attention back to the computer.

Niko pushed one earpiece off. "Speaking of Hatchett..."

Vin yanked the headphones off his head and tossed them onto the desk. His stomach dropped. He figured Niko would find out about the text to Hatchett at some point. The porn world was a small one.

Vin refused to play dumb. "Hatchett told you?"

"He was very proud of himself. He crowed like an old rooster."

Vin wrapped and unwrapped the headphone cord around his finger, unable to look Niko in the eye. He had nothing to add to the conversation.

"Why did you contact him? Was it because of our fight?"

Vin didn't want to get into their personal shit. And for Niko to suggest that Vin's loyalty would crumble because of a disagreement felt like a betrayal all on its own. Yeah, Vin shouldn't have contacted Hatchett, and a part of him had been glad when he hadn't heard back, but Vin had been desperate.

"The money's good."

"If you need the money, you should have said something. I tried to give you a raise last month and—"

"I don't want any more of your money. You pay me a more than a fair wage, and you've already done more than enough for me already."

"But you'll take Hatchett's money."

"He never contacted me. Besides, I'd already decided I

wouldn't take a job with him, even if he'd offered. I sorted every-thing out already."

Vin reached for the headphones again. Maybe Niko would take the hint.

"Are you just going to keep ignoring me?"

Vin stood and stepped to the doorway, getting some distance and hopefully some perspective. He couldn't think with Niko that close, with his cologne, his *presence*, filling every inch of the room. He had to get away before he did something stupid, like kiss him.

"I don't know what you want from me."

"I just want to talk."

Vin gestured toward the computer, though he doubted he'd get any more work done tonight. It was late, and he still hadn't recovered fully from everything that had happened on the trip. Kicker of it was, the robbery and the gash on his head hadn't been the worst of it.

"I'm working. You got what you wanted. You wanted us to end. We ended. Now we're back home, and it's back to status quo. Correct me if I'm wrong, but last I checked, heart-to-hearts weren't in my contract with Black Stallion. You definitely don't pay me enough for that."

Niko pushed to his feet, yanking a wad of hundred dollar bills out of his wallet and stuffing them in Vin's front pocket, his eyes dark and dangerous. "How much of your time does that buy me?"

The lump that formed in Vin's throat was bigger than the wad of cash. He dropped the money on the floor, his voice cracking when he said, "I'm not fifteen anymore. I don't go looking for people to screw me over for cash."

Vin turned and headed down the hall, digging his keys out of his pocket as he went. Fuck the editing. Fuck Black Stallion.

And most of all, fuck Niko.

With his truck all packed up, nothing was keeping him in the valley. Why bother staying another day when he knew he had to leave?

"God damn it."

Vin heard the slap of Niko's Italian loafers on the studio's concrete floors as he jogged after Vin.

Niko caught up to him on the stair landing between the basement and first floor and rushed ahead to block Vin's ascent. Vin came up short and took a staggering step back. "Let me go, babe. *Please*."

"*Babe*."

Fuck.

"You called me that in the Uber as well."

Vin turned to go back the way he came. He could go out the emergency exit at the back of the studios. It would set the alarm off, but he didn't really care. Niko blocked his path again, and Vin stared down at a chip in the wallboard.

"This isn't finished between us. I know it isn't. Deep down, you know it isn't either. Stay."

Vin glanced up, the desperation in Niko's eyes made Vin's heart stall and the blood back up in his chest until he couldn't draw a breath.

"Please. Now I'm the one who's begging."

Vin had no defenses against this side—the vulnerable side —of Niko.

Sensing Vin's wavering determination, Niko held out his hand for Vin to take. Vin hesitated before entwining his fingers with Niko's.

He'd hear Niko out.

He could always leave town tomorrow.

19

———

Niko led Vin up the back stairs to his private wing at Black Stallion, expecting Vin to change his mind at any second and pull away. Though the grip he had on Vin's hand would make that rather tricky unless Vin wanted to leave some of his fingers behind.

He flipped on lights as they entered his home, not dropping Vin's hand until they stopped in the kitchen. "Want a beer?"

"Oh, God, no." Vin's lip curled up, and he turned an interesting shade of green. "I don't think I'm ever drinking again. At least not in this century."

Niko pulled a beer out of the fridge for himself. "How about something to eat?"

"I'm starved." Vin came around the island and pulled out the menu drawer. "You want me to call something in? Chinese? Thai? Italian?"

Niko took the menus out of Vin's hands. He didn't want any interruptions, even for the time it would take to pay the delivery guy. "How about an omelet?"

Vin visibly brightened. It had always been one of his favorites. "With peppers and onions?"

Niko smiled. "And fresh spinach and ham. And I think I have some of that hot sauce you like, too."

Would it be weird if you told him you buy it and use it because it reminds you of him?

Shut up.

"What was that?" Vin asked as Niko retrieved the omelet pan from one of the bottom drawers. Vin's head cocked to the side, and a smile spread across his lips. "Did you just growl?"

Niko turned to the fridge so Vin wouldn't see the red rising up his face. "I don't know what you're talking about."

Niko gathered all the ingredients, and Vin went for the plates before grabbing an extra knife and cutting board to help Niko cut up the veggies. Like they'd done many times years ago back when Vin had lived with him.

It felt like old times but also felt new. Niko waited for that twist in his gut, telling him how wrong it was, but... nothing. Maybe Demetri was right. Vin was very much an adult. A grown man with a grown man's body, a grown man's autonomy.

A grown man's desires.

Maybe he needed to bury his and Vin's old relationship and use the week they'd shared in the Bahamas to start anew. God knew he wanted to.

Now if he could only get Vin on the same page and quit putting his own foot in his mouth and screwing things up. He wasn't used to having someone turn him in such knots that he couldn't articulate what he felt and what he wanted without making a complete ass of himself.

They chopped, cooked, and ate in companionable silence, Vin not taking no for an answer when it came time to clear the table and put the dirty dishes in the dishwasher.

Niko leaned back against the counter, watching Vin for the few minutes it took to clean up. "You finished? You wipe that counter again, and you'll wipe the color clean off."

Vin turned with a dishtowel in his hand. "You saying I'm stalling?"

"That's exactly what I'm saying." Niko stripped the towel out of Vin's hand and backed him against the counter, blocking him in with his hands on either side. "It's time we talked."

Vin groaned and ground against Niko as Niko eased closer. "Can't we skip the talking and go straight to the fucking? We both know that's where this is headed."

"Maybe." Niko eased back, just enough so that having Vin's cock rubbing against his wouldn't rob him of his thoughts or make him change his mind about clearing the air. "But I've got things to say, and I want to make sure you hear them."

"Fine." Vin blew out a breath and boosted himself onto the counter. "I'm listening."

With so many things Niko needed to apologize for, with all his thoughts and feelings and concerns and worries, he couldn't pinpoint the best place to start.

"First, I need you to know that I'm sorry. Not only for what I'd said tonight but the night we got home as well. This isn't an excuse, but seeing you motionless in that alley…"

The visions from that moment came roaring back. For a second, Niko was transported back in Nassau, scrambling out of the car and making a mad dash down the alley. He wasn't a religious man, but he'd prayed to every god there had ever been on his race to get to Vin.

Niko cleared his throat, it felt like a lump of granite had lodged there, all sharp and jagged. "Seeing you lying there sent me into a tailspin. One that I'm just now climbing out of. All my emotions are on the surface, and I can't keep what could have happened from popping into my head during the day and into of my nightmares when I sleep."

Vin's chuckle held a hint of derision, but he'd gone red

around the eyes. "Keep saying shit like that, and I'm going to think you care."

"I *do* care."

Vin's lips went flat, and if Niko hadn't been standing so close, Vin might have crossed his arms over his chest. Vin didn't believe him.

Or maybe he's afraid to. Don't clam up now. Keep talking.

"But most of all, I want to apologize for proposing the deal to begin with."

"I'm not sorry about that. And if you say you regret it, I'm walking out that door."

Niko eased closer, cupping Vin's cheeks and forcing him to meet his gaze. "I don't regret it." He said it slow and precise so that even the not-so-bright kids at the back of the room could understand.

Vin scrunched his hand in Niko's hair and hauled him in for a kiss, haunting in its hunger. Vin pulled away first. "Then why are you apologizing for it?"

"Because I should have manned up and asked you out on a date. Not fabricated some rule-bound, back-room bargain that on the surface allowed me to check my emotions at the door."

"So how did that work out for you? Coat-checking your emotions?" The barest hint of a smile played across Vin's lips as if he knew the answer to that. Frankly, they probably wouldn't be standing there in the kitchen together if Vin was clueless.

"It didn't. When we started, I didn't think this could be real." He motioned between the two of them as Vin held Niko between his legs, his wrists looped over Niko's shoulders.

"Feels pretty real to me."

"Same."

Vin leaned back and looked down at Niko. "What are you saying?"

"I'm saying I want to give us a shot. One shot to prove that what we have is the real, long term, messy, strings-attached deal."

"What changed your mind? It was my ass, wasn't it?"

Niko laughed, appreciating the way Vin lightened the mood and cut the tension. "It certainly goes in the plus column."

"We're really doing this?"

"Yeah."

"Okay." Vin wrapped his legs around Niko's waist and pulled him in tight, his cock already hard and pressing into Niko's belly.

Niko leaned in for a kiss, loving the way Vin opened for him, inviting him in. Vin tasted of sweet peppers and hot sauce all mixed in with a passion that had Niko lifting Vin off the counter, preparing to carry him up to his room.

He pulled back, far enough to see Vin's face. The smile bright, but a flash of sadness crossed Vin's eyes that Niko didn't understand. He'd circle back to that later.

Niko hefted Vin higher, getting a better grip around the finest ass that side of the San Gabriels. Between now and forever, he planned on proving himself to Vin.

Proving he was worthy of the second chance.

And proving to them both they could have a life together.

He carried Vin up the steps, almost dropping him when Vin ducked his head and whispered in his ear what he wanted Niko to do to him.

Niko groaned.

"Can't you climb these stairs any faster, old man?"

Vin gathered up his cameras and began returning them to their cases. Niko walked up behind him, laying a proprietary hand on Vin's lower back. He leaned in and pressed a kiss to Vin's jaw.

Niko had been doing that in the last few days since they'd made up and decided to make a go of it. Small displays of affection not only while they were out and about town, but in the studio as well. He'd been discreet but also didn't jump away if Rose or Cat or Betty happened by.

At times, Vin still felt like he lived in an alternate universe. But it was all too real, especially their nights, to be fiction.

"You almost done here?"

"You got something planned?" Vin was coming to appreciate Niko's plans. They usually ended with them both sated and satisfied.

"Demetri's popping over. We're going out for a few drinks. You want to meet me for dinner after?"

"I could cook something."

Niko pulled a face. "You've worked your ass off enough today."

"I can call in for delivery."

Niko put a finger to Vin's chin, turning his face enough that their lips briefly met. "We can go to that sushi place. I'd kind of like to show you off."

Vin grinned. Niko wanting to take Vin out and not hide him away in his home told Vin that Niko was trying. While he may not be entirely comfortable yet with their history, he was making a good faith effort to push through his misgivings.

"What will all your friends say?"

"Probably that I'm a lucky bastard." Niko's hand drifted to Vin's ass and gave it a squeeze. "And they'd be right."

Vin glanced down at his jeans and T-shirt. "I'm not exactly dressed for it."

"I don't care what you're wearing as long as you're there."

From the back of the studio, they heard the clomping of feet as someone hurried down the back steps. "Vin. *Vin.* Where the hell are you?"

"Back here," he called out.

Niko gave him one last peck. "See you later."

"I'm looking forward to it."

Cat marched into the studio as Niko disappeared up the other stairway to his wing. Vin could practically see the contrail of fury wafting in her wake.

She stopped in front of him, her hands on her hips. "Why is everything you own packed into your truck?"

"It's not everything."

"Don't be a dick. What's going on?"

"Contingency plan."

Her eyes narrowed, and her brain whirred, he practically heard the gears grind and shift. She thumped him in the shoulder with her palm. It mostly didn't hurt. "You haven't told Niko, have you?"

"Not exactly."

"Which means not at all." She spun around and started pacing. "You're together now. He needs to know."

"No." Vin made sure he enunciated clearly so there wouldn't be any chance that she would misunderstand. "He doesn't need to know."

"You've found a way to come up with the money? Or do we need to go rob a bank?"

Vin figured Cat was only half-kidding. "Neither. I'm not paying, but I'm also not sticking around."

Cat dropped into one of the director's chairs. "What the actual fuck, Vin?" The hurt clear in her voice like he'd gone out of his way to destroy her. "You weren't going to tell anyone you were leaving, were you?"

"I didn't want anyone talking me out of it. It's for the best, for me, for Niko, for the studio."

"But you're still here."

Vin let his head drop between his shoulders and leaned

against the table. "I just..." He glanced up at Cat. "I wake up every morning in Niko's bed, thinking today is the day I'm going to leave. After my shower, or after lunch, or after that scene, or after the next time we have sex, and then I go to bed telling myself I can leave the next day or the next. But I'm running out of days."

Cat stood, a frown on her face. Vin couldn't tell if it was disappointment, disapproval, or what. "Gimme your hand."

When Vin hesitated, she made a give-it-here motion. Vin complied, and within a second, she spun him around and pinned his arm behind his back, licks of pain radiating through his shoulder from the bind she'd put him in.

"Ow, ow, ow. What are you doing?"

"Don't fight, and it won't hurt so bad," Cat said, then added, "I'm doing what I should have done a week ago when you told me about this nonsense."

She shoved him toward the back stairs, toward Niko's wing, keeping a steady pressure on his arm. Not enough to drop him to his knees, but enough to keep him from fighting her. "I'm going to make you tell Niko."

———

A KNOCK CAME ON THE DOOR JAMB OF NIKO'S OFFICE. "YOU ABOUT ready?" Demetri asked as he walked over the threshold without waiting for the invite.

Glancing up from his computer, Niko said, "Give me a minute."

He needed to send some instructions to his website guy for the membership discounts he'd be offering. If Hatchett wanted to take Niko down, he'd need to try a hell of a lot harder.

"Is it official?" Demetri asked as he sat on the leather sofa on the other side of the room.

"It is." Niko kept typing.

"It's going okay? You and Vin. No problems, no—"

"What are you getting at?" Niko stood, his email forgotten as he walked around to the front of his desk and sat on the corner.

"I'm concerned is all. This is the honeymoon phase. They don't start asking for more until they've got their hooks in you."

"Where is this coming from? You *know* Vin. He's nothing like all the other men I've been with. Frankly, I'm getting tired of your insinuations."

"If they are only insinuations, then maybe I'm not making myself clear."

Niko shook his head. Demetri meant well. He'd always had Niko's back, and he figured Demetri felt like he was only doing more of the same. But Niko wasn't going to put up with Demetri's shit any longer.

"I love you, Dem, and I appreciate your concern. But I'm telling you right now, you need to stop. Either jump on board or get the hell out."

Demetri raised his hands in defeat and let them drop back down on his thighs. "Hope you know what you're doing."

"I don't know if I do, but it feels right."

"Are we going, or what?"

"Ow, ow, ow, ow," came Vin's voice from down the hall, his footsteps slapping against the floor with each step.

Niko straightened as Vin came through the door, Cat right behind him, one hand on his shoulder and the other hidden behind his back.

She sat Vin in one of the chairs facing Niko's desk. "Tell him."

Vin rubbed at his shoulder from the arm lock Cat had put him in. Demetri cleared his throat. Neither Vin nor Cat had seen him there.

"You've got company. I'll—" Vin went to stand. Cat put a hand on his shoulder and shoved him back down.

"Whatever you have to say, you can say it in front of Demetri. He's family."

Vin glanced from Niko to Demetri to Cat before his eyes landed on Niko again, an undercurrent of terror running through his eyes. What kind of trouble had he gotten himself into?

Cat thumped Vin on the back of the head, a physical encouragement to get him to speak. Whatever it was, it couldn't be that bad.

"I need a hundred and fifty thousand dollars in eleven days."

Demetri barked out a laugh. He was the only one. Niko cut him a look, the expression on Demetri's face an undeniable *I told you so*. He stood and headed for the door, as Niko's stomach stopped, dropped, and rolled as if on fire.

"Call me," Demetri said.

Cat glared after him. "What's his problem?"

"That's a lot of money." Niko kept his calm, though the inferno raging inside him made the sweat pop out on his brow. The money wasn't an issue. Not that he had that kind of cash lying around. What concerned Niko most was that maybe Demetri had been right. Had Vin been playing the long game all along?

His head agreed, but his heart... his heart refused to believe.

"What's really going on here?"

Cat put her arm around Vin's shoulder, more friend now than enforcer. "You want me to stay?"

"No," Vin said. "I'll tell him."

"Everything? Your truck, too?"

Vin nodded. "Everything."

Cat leaned in, kissing his cheek before straightening. "Call me if you need me."

Vin watched her leave the way a marooned man watches the last rescue boat vanish over the horizon.

Niko held an arm out toward the sofa. He had a feeling this discussion would take some time. They might as well get comfortable.

Vin took the sofa. Niko took the club chair across from it. "Start from the beginning."

Niko sat there, his chin in his hand. Vin's composure slipped minute by minute as the story unfolded from killing his father, to running, to ending up on the streets of LA, to bumping into Stu and the consequent blackmail."

By the time he'd finished, Vin's head lay in his hands as he stared at the fuzzy area rug beneath his feet. When he finally glanced up, his face was blotchy, and his eyes glistened. All Niko wanted to do was draw him into his arms and tell him everything would be okay, but he didn't want to lie to him.

Vin was in some deep shit.

They just needed to find the shovel big enough that could dig him out.

"Okay." Niko nodded more to himself than Vin as he absorbed everything.

"Okay? Is that all you have to say? No questions?"

Niko leaned forward, his elbows on his thighs, his hands dangling between his knees. "I've got too many questions to count, but I'm still processing what you told me. It's a lot."

Vin laughed and scrubbed his hand down his face. "No lie."

"I do have two questions, though." Vin swallowed hard but nodded for Niko to continue. "First, is this what's been eating at you?"

Again, the nod.

"Second, and more importantly, why didn't you trust me enough to tell me sooner?"

"Did you not hear me? I killed a man. My own father for fuck's sake."

"I heard you. After hearing those facts, I don't think you could assemble a jury that would convict you."

"If I had proof to back up my word. Ten years out, I've got nothing that could prove self-defense."

"You didn't answer my question. Where was the trust?"

"You've... you've done so much for me, Niko. I couldn't ask for more. You saw that look on Demetri's face. He wasn't shocked that I came to you wanting money. I didn't want to be that guy."

"You're not that guy, Vin. We wouldn't be together if I thought you were."

Vin scrubbed at his eyes with the heels of his hands and sniffed. "Fuck, I'm a mess."

Niko remained in fix-it mode. If he went to Vin now, he'd break down, and they wouldn't get anything accomplished. "The way I see it, we have three options."

Vin sat back, slouching on the sofa, completely drained. "What's that?"

"We can pay this guy. We can go to the police. Or we can get the upper hand on Stu."

Vin perked up at that. Niko pulled out his phone and ran down his contact list, found the name he'd been searching for, and pressed call.

"What are you doing?"

"I'm phoning a friend."

20

Later that night, Vin crawled into Niko's bed and collapsed, physically and emotionally spent, his hair still damp from his shower.

That Niko hadn't kicked him out of the house had been a damn miracle. That he'd actually picked up the phone and called for help, went to the kind of man Vin had known Niko to be.

He still didn't know how it would all work out. His truck remained packed just in case things went to hell fast, and he had to get out of town in a hurry.

But for the first time in a very long time, since the night his father's death had changed the course of his life forever, Vin felt a sense of peace.

Two people knew about what he'd been forced to do. And they hadn't called the police, they hadn't turned their backs. They'd asked how they could help.

Vin's chest tightened again, and he tamped down on his emotions, determined not to lose it again. It had been humiliating enough falling apart in front of Niko.

Niko came out of the bathroom without a stitch of clothing

on, flipping off the light as he went, but with Niko's bedside lamp on, there was plenty of light for Vin to watch as Niko walked around the bed.

He sat on the edge of the mattress, plugging in his phone and setting the alarm. Even with all the drama going on with Stu, they still had a production schedule to keep.

Vin moved up behind him, placing his arms around Niko's shoulders from behind and pressing a kiss at the nape of Niko's neck. "You sure you want me to stay?"

"Why wouldn't I? If you'd have let me, I would have moved you in on Sunday. When I'm in, I'm all in."

God, Vin wanted to believe that.

Why wouldn't you believe him? Everything he's said and done points to his veracity, of his intentions to take the good with all the bad.

Because no one had ever loved Vin for everything that he was and, more importantly, that he *wasn't*.

Niko reached back and palmed the back of Vin's head, holding him in place for a kiss that touched his heart and made him hard.

Niko shifted, sitting against the headboard, a stack of soft pillows behind his back, and held out an arm. "Come here."

Vin didn't hesitate. He allowed Niko to tuck him to his side, Vin's hand over Niko's heart, the steady thump, and beat like a salve on a sunburn.

"Do you really think Derek can help?" Vin asked. Derek Watts, a private investigator friend Niko had on his favorites list.

"He's the best money can buy. If he can't help, no one can."

One question nagged at Vin, afraid to hear the answer but perhaps more afraid not to. "Why are you doing all this for me?"

Niko pulled back, looking down at Vin, searching his face for what, Vin didn't know. "You really don't get it, do you?"

Vin broke eye contact and ran a finger through the trail of

hair above Niko's belly button, Niko's cock half-aroused between his legs. Vin wanted to take back the question and then take Niko into his mouth so that they both could forget. "No. I don't."

"I love you, Vin." Niko lifted Vin's face to his with a finger under his jaw. "I think I have for a long time now. I denied the truth. Looked for love everywhere but where it was. Here with you."

Vin's heart went into free fall, like those few precious seconds he had from the time he jumped out of a plane to the time he pulled the ripcord. Those exhilarating, life-affirming, game-changing seconds.

If this was what being loved felt like, he never wanted to land.

"I love you, too." The words tripped out of his mouth in a rush of air.

Niko's grin took over his face until his eyes shone, and his breath hitched. "Are we nuts?"

Vin laughed. "Maybe. But that doesn't mean it's not right. But, you know, I'm the kind of guy that needs proof. You can't just say something like that and expect me to believe it."

"Oh yeah?" Somehow Niko's grin got even wider. "How would you suggest I prove it to you?"

Vin reached down and took Niko's cock in his hand, giving him a long, delicate stroke. "You need to back up your words with action." He dropped his voice suggestively. "*A lot* of action."

Niko rolled Vin onto his back and straddled Vin's hips. He braced himself on his hands as he ground his cock against Vin's, their combined pre-cum slicking Vin's abdomen. With a hand behind Niko's neck, Vin pulled him in for a kiss, their tongues fighting for dominance, though Vin happily surrendered.

Niko reached into the bedside table for the condoms and the lube, quick to put one on. "I can't wait until we can ditch the condoms."

They'd gone into the testing center the day after they officially started their relationship to be screened for STIs. They had both been clear but had decided to wait the additional three months to be tested again before they went condom free.

"Only eighty-seven days, sixteen hours and..." Vin reached for his phone and pulled up his countdown app. "Six minutes and fifteen seconds."

Niko laughed, a joyful, pure sound that made Vin's chest hurt and his throat tight. Niko stripped the phone out of Vin's hand. "You're the fucking best."

———

"Hey," Vin called out as he came through the front door. "I'm home."

Despite what lay before Niko, he smiled, loving the way Vin already called his place home.

"You're back early," Niko hollered out.

It was Saturday night, the night before they were supposed to meet Stu with the blackmail money. He'd sent Vin out for a night with Cat, Sebastian, and Grant wanting time alone to get a few things accomplished. But there was no way he could hide what he was doing by the time Vin came into the kitchen.

Vin rounded the corner as Niko finished counting another stack of hundred-dollar bills. "What's all this about?"

"I'm getting the money ready for tomorrow."

Vin stopped at the kitchen table, picked up a banded stack of bills, and thumbed through them. "I've never seen this much money in one place in my life."

Vin tossed the stack onto the other fourteen. "I thought Derek said he was onto something."

"That was a couple days ago, and since then, he hasn't had anything new to report. I wanted to be ready in case we ran out of options and had to pay. I had to get the ball rolling early. It takes time to liquidate assets, and most banks don't carry this kind of cash on hand on a daily basis."

Vin ran his hands through his hair. "Fuck. I'll be paying you back for the rest of my life. I mean, I like to think I'm better than the average guy at giving head, but I'm not sure I'm a hundred and fifty grand good."

Niko came around the table and wrapped his arms around Vin's waist. "It's a gift. Gifts don't require paybacks."

"What if you and I don't work out?"

"This money, it's not conditional on our relationship, making it for the long haul. That's not how gifts work. I would have given you the money no matter what. That wasn't ever even a question."

Vin rested his head on Niko's chest. "I'm so sorry I dragged you into all of this."

"Don't be. This time tomorrow, this will be over with, one way or the other."

"What if we give him the money, and he comes back at us for more later?"

"We'll deal with it as it comes."

Niko kissed his forehead and patted Vin on the ass. "Come on, it's late. I want to be well-rested for tomorrow."

They tossed the stacks of money into Niko's briefcase and locked it in the safe in Niko's office. Niko took Vin's hand and flipped the light switch to head up to their room.

Niko's phone rang.

Vin laughed. "Is that the theme song for *Dragnet*?"

The heat rushed up Niko's face. "Maybe." He turned the office light back on and answered the call. "Hey, Derek. Do you have something for me?"

Vin circled around behind Niko, hugging him from behind

and resting the side of his head on Niko's back. Niko mentally crossed all his fingers and toes, hoping for good news.

"Can I come over?"

"Yeah. We'll be in the kitchen. You remember the gate and door codes?"

"Yeah. I'll be there in fifteen. Twenty tops."

"Looking forward to it." Niko ended the call and patted Vin's hands locked around his belly.

"This is bad, isn't it?"

"Derek can be pretty hard to read, especially over the phone. But I've got to think this is good."

Vin kissed the spot between Niko's shoulder blades. "I hope you're right. We could use some positive news."

They went back to the kitchen, and Niko pulled out a beer for himself and Vin—whose 'no alcohol' rule lasted about a week—and they waited for Derek's arrival.

By the time the entry keypad beeped as Derek typed in the lock code, Vin had shredded his beer label with his thumbnail until tiny confetti strips littered the kitchen table.

Niko stood to shake his friend's hand. "Thanks for coming so late."

"I'm just sorry it took me so long to get what I wanted."

Vin rose, and Niko introduced the two men. "Wow," Vin said. "You could totally be one of those undercover cops from *21 Jump Street*."

Derek chuckled. "I'm a lot older than I look, but sometimes looking like I've barely hit puberty has its advantages." Derek motioned toward the table with the file folder he held in his hand. "We should sit."

Vin sat, his hand shaking as he brought the bottle to his lips. He put the bottle down and held his hand out in front of him. "This is embarrassing."

Niko pulled his chair closer and rubbed Vin's back and

kissed the side of his head. "Nothing wrong with being nervous. What do you have for us, Derek?"

Derek opened the file and pulled an eight-by-ten photograph from the bottom of a thin stack of papers and slid it in front of Vin.

It was a telephoto picture of a man in faded jeans and a Chicago Bears T-shirt with a large hole in the left armpit coming out of a liquor store. The man had gray hair at his temples, with salt and pepper sprinkled throughout his stubble.

Vin sucked in a breath. More of a gasp really. His color drained away, and Niko almost rapped him on the back to get him breathing again. He glanced back up at Derek, his voice barely audible when he said, "Where did you get this?"

"I have a colleague in Chicago. This was taken yesterday on Halsted Street."

Vin still hadn't seemed to catch his breath. Niko didn't want to jump to any conclusions, so he waited Vin out. "We lived around the corner from that liquor store."

"Vin," Derek said, his voice full of patience and compassion. "Do you recognize this man?"

Vin swiped at the moisture on his cheeks. "It's my father."

"Holy fuck." Niko blew out a breath and sat back, his focus on Derek when he said, "Are you kidding me? The man's alive?"

"How?" Vin managed. "How is he still alive?"

"Took some time to find someone who could pull the original police file. Police answered an anonymous disturbance call. Found your father on the floor in the kitchen, unconscious in a pool of blood. Paramedics were called. He got twenty stitches to the back of the head and had a concussion. Told detectives someone broke in and knocked him out. The case was filed as unsolved after the statute of limitations ran out."

Vin ran his hands down his face, a brittle laugh escaping. "The police were never after me."

"No. Either that knock to the head gave him amnesia, or he came to his senses long enough to know he was in the wrong. Either way, the police never knew about you. There are no warrants out for your arrest. Basically, you were never on their radar."

Derek pulled out another photo. "This was from the police file."

The photo was of a kitchen with a large pool of blood all over the chipped and cracked linoleum. To Niko, it might as well have been the inside of a slaughterhouse. "But I can see why a kid might think he was dead. Head wounds can bleed profusely."

Vin buried his face in his hands, his shoulders shaking as he quietly sobbed. Niko wrapped his arm around him and held him as tight as the chair allowed. Knowing you hadn't killed your own father—even if he was a violent, homophobic asshole—that you weren't a wanted man after ten years of not knowing, had to be an enormous relief.

Niko pointed to the folder. "Mind if we keep that?"

Derek slid the rest of the file over to Niko. "All yours, buddy." He hitched a thumb over his shoulder. "I'll see myself out."

"Thanks, Derek. I owe you one."

"Happy to help."

"Come with me." Niko helped Vin to his feet. He guided him to his black leather couch and pulled Vin onto his lap and just held him tight.

After considerable time, the hitching of Vin's breaths finally eased. Vin used the hem of his T-shirt to dry his face. He sniffed, and his self-deprecating laugh came out more like a cough. "What a fucking mess."

"Good news, yeah?"

"Yeah," Vin managed, his voice still tight. "I never wanted him dead. I just wanted the bullying and the beating to stop."

"I know that, babe. I never thought any different."

"You could reach out to him if you want. I'm sure Derek could get his number, and—"

"No." The word came out soft but emphatic. "I want to put all this behind me and not look back. I would like to think he could accept me now, but he's not the type of man who easily evolves. I don't want him back in my life, even for a minute."

Vin shifted, scooting down on the sofa, curling up on his side, his head in Niko's lap. Niko absently ran his fingers through Vin's hair, as the relief and calm settled over them.

After a prolonged silence, Vin said, "I can't wait until tomorrow when we can ruin Stu's day."

Niko chuckled. "You and me both."

———

VIN WOKE MORE NERVOUS THAN THE SITUATION CALLED FOR. He barely had an appetite for breakfast, even for the omelet Niko had made for him. Hell, he'd barely been able to hold his coffee down.

Niko picked up his keys off the kitchen table and slung a fanny pack over his shoulder. "You ready to go?"

Vin stood and dumped his cold coffee in the sink. "I guess." He bobbed his chin toward the pack. "What's in there?"

Niko stepped over and pressed a kiss to Vin's forehead, but all he said was, "Insurance."

Whatever the hell that meant.

Vin was too worn out to argue. He should have slept like a baby, knowing his father was alive and that Stu had nothing on him, but he'd tossed and turned all night until Niko finally threw a heavy leg over both of his and pinned his lower body to the mattress.

They drove across town to the same dump of a coffee shop

where he'd met Stu two weeks before. It seemed fitting that it would end there.

They parked in a lot around the corner from the shop, and Vin grabbed Niko's hand in his, linking their fingers, his grip locking their hands together. He tucked the folder Derek had given him under his other arm.

Niko chuckled. "I think I'm losing circulation in my fingers."

"Sorry," Vin said, though he didn't loosen his grip. He practically pulled Niko down the street, wanting to beat Stu to the shop.

He drew up short outside the coffee shop as a cop walked toward them and sat in one of the two rickety tables on the sidewalk. Sweat beaded on Vin's upper lip, and he lost all feeling in his legs.

He stumbled, and Niko caught him. "Relax," he muttered under his breath. Niko smiled at the cop. "Morning, officer."

The man tipped his cap. "Morning."

Niko opened the door, ushering Vin inside. *Fuck*. Stu sat at the back table where they'd met before, facing the door. His stupid grin on his face fell when he realized Niko was with Vin. Stu started to get up, but Niko reached the table first and laid a firm hand on his shoulder and sat him back down.

Stu's face went red as the muscle worked at the corner of his jaw, his voice barely above a whisper when he hissed, "I told you to come alone."

"That wasn't going to happen," Niko said, setting his phone face down on the table and slinging the fanny pack over the back of his chair.

"What's that?" Stu nodded at the folder Vin set on the table in front of him.

"Just a little something I have for you," Vin said.

"Where's my money? If you don't give me my money, I'm going straight to the cops, and I'm telling them everything."

"Relax. We'll get to the money," Niko said. Vin loved Niko's calm energy. He laid a hand on Niko's thigh, drawing from his strength and composure. "First, Vin has something he wants to show you."

Vin almost couldn't contain his smile as he pulled the photos and Derek's report out of the folder.

"What the hell is this?"

"My father," Vin said. "Alive and well, according to the date and time stamp on the photograph."

"He's alive?"

Niko sat back, allowing a ghost of a grin. "It appears so."

"I don't understand." Stu deflated in front of them.

"The only thing you need to understand is that my father is alive and well. I didn't kill him. You've got nothing on me."

Niko picked up his phone and activated his screen, and showed Stu the recording app on his phone, the seconds ticking on. "But it seems that we now have something on you. Blackmail is a crime." Niko glanced over his shoulder at the officer outside drinking his coffee. "I'm sure Officer Hamilton would love a copy of this to back up the charges we could press."

Stu blew out a breath, his hands rubbing up and down on his thighs, his eyes darting around the coffee shop to the officer and back to Niko, entirely at a loss for words.

Niko took the fanny pack off the back of his chair and plopped it on the table and pushed it toward Stu.

"What's that?" he asked.

"Ten thousand dollars."

Vin squeaked. What the hell? But Niko silenced him with a squeeze on Vin's thigh.

"The way I see it, you have two choices. You can take the money and disappear and never show your face in the valley again, or I can call Officer Hamilton in, and we'll see how long it takes him to put you under arrest. Your choice. Tick-tock."

Vin coughed to hide his laugh, loving how Niko had used Stu's words against him.

Stu unzipped the bag and, sure as shit, Niko had put one of the stacks of hundred-dollar bills into the fanny pack. Stu's eyes darted around the shop again, but they were the only ones there except for the barista arguing with her boyfriend on her cell phone.

Stu stood and shouldered the pack.

"Disappear," Niko said.

Stu started backing out of the shop as if he expected Niko to run after him or steal the cash back. At the door, he turned and shoved through, the door slapping against the wall as he practically ran out.

The cop glanced into the shop. Niko nodded and waved at him then caught the barista's attention as the cop tossed his coffee cup in the trash and left. "That officer's coffee is on me," Niko said.

Vin turned in his seat to get a better look at Niko and the foolish grin he had on his face. "What just happened here?"

"That's a friend of mine with the SFV PD. He owed me a favor. I thought his presence might come in handy."

"I thought Stu would shit a brick when you told him you were taking the recording to the police. You do know California is a two-party state? It's illegal to record someone without their consent."

Niko hit delete on the recording. "I know that. Stu didn't, though."

Vin caught Niko behind the neck and kissed him, wanting to take it deeper, but managing to restrain himself in public. "You're brilliant. But I don't understand why you paid him."

"I figured it was the easiest way to make sure he left town. It was money well spent if you ask me." Niko stood and tossed some bills on the table, more than enough to cover the cop's coffee and add a generous tip for the barista.

Vin grabbed his hand. "Let's celebrate."

"I've already got that covered," Niko said.

They walked out of the shop. The sun seemed brighter, the breeze felt fresher, and somehow the street didn't look so grimy.

They turned the corner, headed back to Niko's Jag. "I can't believe it's over."

Niko pulled him up short in the shadow of the building and caught Vin's chin between his thumb and forefinger. "You're wrong, babe. I love you, and this is only the beginning."

He leaned in, pressing his lips to Vin's, taking the kiss deeper, only breaking apart with a salacious grin when someone catcalled from the open window of a car.

Niko lifted Vin, drawing Vin's legs around his waist. Vin shouted out in surprise. "What are you doing?"

Niko started walking the last fifty yards toward his Jag, unfazed by the attention they drew. "I'm taking you home. You've got a truck to unpack because you're not going anywhere for a very, very long time."

Keep reading for an excerpt from Demetri's story, *Art of Love*, Book 1 in the upcoming Valley Boys series.

ART OF LOVE (EXCERPT)

Demetri Stavros stepped into Premier, the most prestigious
art gallery in the San Fernando Valley. He didn't quite know
what he was doing at a kid's art opening, but his cousin Niko
had invited him. And as one of the art professors at Winston
College, Demetri rarely passed on a chance to see new art, even
from a kid.

From what he'd heard, his Tavi, was some kind of an art
protégé, so he'd come even if he'd had to come alone.

Demetri shoved thoughts of Marcus into the back of his
mind and effectively put him out of his life. One or two date
cancellations were no big deal, but in Demetri's book, you don't
bail on your date on multiple occasions without notice or reason
or apology and expect to remain in their lives.

"Hey, you made it," Niko said as Demetri walked through
the door.

His cousin's smile was more genuine than Demetri had seen
in a long time. It had little to do with how glad he was that
Demetri had shown up and more to do with how happy his new
boyfriend, Vin, made him.

Demetri was happy for them both. Really. And if he had to

force a smile onto his face, he'd do it. He could go home and feel sorry for the sad estate of his own love life later.

Maybe over a glass of single malt scotch.

Or two.

Demetri pulled Niko in for a hug and said, "You look good."

Niko chuckled and straightened his black tie. "Vin said I cleaned up well."

"It's not the tux, it's the grin. You look happy. I'm glad you two found each other. I really am."

"But?"

"No but."

Niko glanced behind Demetri at the door Demetri knew wouldn't open. At least not by Marcus' hand. "Where's—"

"He couldn't make it."

Niko cocked his head at the bite in Demetri's tone. "You're going to find someone. You're—"

Raising a hand, Demetri shut Niko up. "It's fine. I'm here to see some art, not talk about my crumbling love life."

Niko leaned in. "Hey, with the new semester starting up soon, I'm sure you'll have a whole crop of hot college guys to choose from."

Demetri cut him a look that would have left a lesser man abraded and bloody. "I don't date my students."

"Yeah, I had that rule about dating my employees, and we all saw what happened there."

Vin shouldered his way through the surprisingly large turnout with two flutes of champagne in his hands. "Oh, hey."

Niko took the glass Vin offered and was quick to put a hand around Vin's waist. Vin held the other flute out to Demetri. "Want one?"

When Demetri's feeling sorry for himself, a little bubbly wasn't his classic drink of choice. Only something stronger would do. Demetri bobbed his chin in the direction Vin had come. "I'm just heading to the bar. I'll catch up with you guys later."

But before Demetri could make it as far as the bar, the crowd shifted and parted. He had a direct line of sight to Tavi standing by a wall hung with his art, looking stiff in his rented tux as he plucked at his too-short cuffs again and again.

Demetri detoured. The whiskey could wait.

One of the gallery's patrons finished up their conversation with Tavi as Demetri stepped up. Tavi tugged at the collar of his shirt, a fresh razor cut on the edge of his jaw. He was a lean fifteen-year-old with a messy mop of hair who would have looked much more comfortable behind the counter at the tattoo shop he apprenticed at than gracing the halls of the gallery.

"You hanging in there?" Demetri asked.

"I think." It came out more like a question as if Tavi wasn't sure how he was doing. "When I won the art contest at the Center's fundraising event, I figured when the exhibit came, I'd be pacing an empty gallery counting the minutes until it ended. I never expected people to come *and* want to talk to me about my art." Tavi raised his hands out to his sides. "I mean, I'm a kid and—"

"And naturally gifted and talented," Demetri added. "Seriously..."

He stared at the drawing on the wall. An enlargement of Tavi's winning illustration. The emotion in each line, each stroke was something hard to teach. It had to come from within. Demetri would love to get this kid in one of his classes when he was old enough. "You've got the stuff."

Tavi's eyes dropped to the floor, and the color rose to his cheeks, looking nothing like the defensive, hard-knock kid his cousin Sebastian and his boyfriend Grant had pulled off the streets and fostered. "Thanks."

An older couple approached, and Demetri knew they would

have questions for Tavi. He took a step away. "Enjoy your night. You deserve this."

Demetri backed up and leaned against a pillar, taking in the drawing from afar. He couldn't take his eyes off of it. The contest prompt had been 'family,' and Tavi had nailed it in the scene of himself, his boyfriend, Grant, Sebastian, and his Nana in a booth at a local pizza joint.

The way Tavi had captured the love in Sebastian's eyes as he glanced over at Grant brought a lump to Demetri's throat that only the whiskey would wash down.

Demetri turned and started a determined walk toward the cash bar set up at the back of the gallery, pointedly avoiding Grant and Sebastian as they stood hand in hand beside Grant's grandmother and talked to a couple Demetri didn't know. He'd swing back through the gallery and speak to them later, but not before he had a drink.

Demetri waited in the short line, watching the twenty-something bartender work. He watched the play of the man's biceps as he poured and mixed drinks. The tight white shirt across the man's chest contrasted with his dark skin. He looked like he belonged naked under the lights on the dais in Demetri's live drawing class, not behind a bar.

The line shifted, and Demetri found himself at the front of the line, staring into the most mesmerizing green eyes he'd ever seen before.

"What can I get for you?"

An EKG, Demetri wanted to say, because, fuck, his heart had just quit on him. "Um... I..." He couldn't spit the word 'whiskey' out. Instead, he said, "Surprise me."

The man grinned, and Demetri's heart jolted, thumping against his sternum. *Guess you haven't died and gone to heaven after all.*

"Enjoying your night?" the man asked as he pulled out a

stainless-steel shaker and poured in different liquors, a mixer Demetri didn't immediately recognize, and a few cubes of ice.

"It's improving." Demetri held in the eye roll.

Cheesy ass line, Stavros. No wonder you're not getting laid.

Demetri waited for his drink, then he'd go find Sebastian. The bartender was here to work. Not flirt.

The man put a wedge of lime on the rim of the glass and set it on the narrow bar top, his grin impossibly wide. "Funny, I was going to say the same."

Demetri handed over his cash along with a healthy tip and took a sip of the mystery concoction. It had a bite and a tang, that made the alcohol slide down smooth. If he wasn't careful, he'd could quickly get drunk on it and never see it coming. "What do you call this?"

"Why don't we call it The Spice of Life."

"Never heard of it."

"That's because it's a one-off I made just for you."

The bartender probably said that to all the guys he served drinks, even if he'd said it in such a way that Demetri felt like he'd been the only one.

Demetri held up his glass and started to leave. "Thanks for this."

"Come back and see me," the man said. Was the guy interested in Demetri's generous tip or was he interested in Demetri's? Or maybe that was just dickful thinking on his part.

Demetri returned to the main gallery, nursing his drink as he circulated among his family and colleagues from the art department, his attention divided the whole time between the conversation, the drink in his hand, and the captivating man who'd made it.

As the evening wore on and the crowd thinned, Demetri wandered back to the bar and the bartender stacking dirty glassware into bins for the caterers.

The bartender glanced up and smiled as Demetri approached. "If it isn't Mr. Spice of Life. I thought you'd forgotten about me."

Forgotten about him? Not likely. And Demetri sported a semi behind the flat front of his tux pants to prove it. "What was in that drink, anyway?"

"My little secret. Everyone needs a little mystery in their lives, don't you think?"

"Maybe." Was the bartender flirting with him?

The man leaned against the bar and gave Demetri a glance up and down. "Want more?"

They weren't talking about drinks anymore.

Definitely flirting.

"Does anyone tell you no when you ask that?"

"I've never asked anyone that before." The bartender's voice dropped low, an intimate growl meant only for Demetri's ears. "At least not while I'm working."

From somewhere behind him, Demetri heard Sebastian laugh, reminding him he hadn't come to the gallery tonight looking to hook up.

But then again...

"What time do you get off?"

A LETTER TO MY READERS

Dear Reader,

I hope you loved the men of Black Stallion Studios as much as I loved writing them!

Art of Love should be out early-ish in 2020. If you want to be notified when the pre-order is available, you can join my newsletter or follow me. You can find the links in my About the Author section.

Until then, I have many more books you can enjoy!

Your next adventure starts here:

ROMANTIC SUSPENSE

Lazy S Ranch Series
Cowgirl, Unexpectedly (Book 1)
Must Love Horses (Book 2)
Hot on the Trail (Book 3)
Cowboy, Undercover (Book 4)
Cowboy, Unbridled (Book 5)
Cowgirl, Unbroken (Book 6 Coming soon!)

Wright's Island Series
Don't Look Back (Book 1)
In Her Defense (Book 2)

Steele-Wolfe Securities
Wyoming Confidential (Book 1 Coming soon)

CONTEMPORARY ROMANCE

Rockin' Rodeo Series
Luck of the Draw (Book 1)
Photo Chute (Book 2)
Reined In (Book 3)
Rockin' Rodeo Series Collection (Books 1-3)

MM ROMANCE

Black Stallion Studios Series
One Shot (Book 1)
Key Grip (Book 2)
Best Boy (Book 3)

Valley Boys
Art of Love (Book 1 Coming soon)

ABOUT THE AUTHOR

Vicki Tharp makes her home on small acreage in south Texas with her husband and an embarrassing number of pets. When she isn't writing, you can usually find her on the back of her horse—avoiding anything that remotely resembles housework—smelling like fly spray and horse sweat.

Join my newsletter at: http://eepurl.com/croJgz
Join my street team and receive free Advance Reader Copies of my upcoming books at: http://eepurl.com/cWhXbD
You can find my website at: www.VickiTharp.com
I love to hear from readers. You can email me at vwtharp@VickiTharp.com

Or you can stalk me at:

facebook.com/VickiTharpAuthor

instagram.com/author_Vicki_Tharp

bookbub.com/authors/vicki-tharp

amazon.com/author/vicki_tharp

twitter.com/vwtharp